Lights Out

By W J Stopforth

First Edition

Copyright 2015 by W J Stopforth

All rights reserved. This book may not be reproduced in any form, in whole or in part, without written permission from the author.

ISBN-10: 1519190832
ISBN-13: 978-1519190833

In the end, we only regret the things we didn't do.

CONTENTS

Chapter 1   Pg #1

Chapter 2   Pg #9

Chapter 3   Pg #14

Chapter 4   Pg #20

Chapter 5   Pg #32

Chapter 6   Pg #38

Chapter 7   Pg #41

Chapter 8   Pg #48

Chapter 9   Pg #58

Chapter 10   Pg #68

Chapter 11   Pg #76

Chapter 12   Pg #85

Chapter 13   Pg #88

Chapter 14   Pg #105

Chapter 15   Pg #118

Chapter 16   Pg #125

Chapter 17   Pg #136

Chapter 18   Pg #143

Chapter 19   Pg #149

Chapter 20   Pg #157

Chapter 21   Pg #161

LIGHTS OUT

Chapter 22　　Pg #167

Chapter 23　　Pg #170

Chapter 24　　Pg #175

Chapter 25　　Pg #200

Chapter 26　　Pg #210

Chapter 27　　Pg #225

Chapter 28　　Pg #242

Chapter 29　　Pg #244

Chapter 30　　Pg #253

Chapter 31　　Pg #270

Chapter 32　　Pg #276

Chapter 33　　Pg #289

Chapter 34　　Pg #296

Chapter 35　　Pg #303

Chapter 36　　Pg #320

Chapter 37　　Pg #325

Chapter 38　　Pg #327

Chapter 39　　Pg #331

Chapter 40　　Pg #340

Chapter 41　　Pg #345

Chapter 42　　Pg #347

Chapter 1

Ryan Harper pulled on the roller-blind cord. It was stuck again. With a resigned deep sigh he gave it a second harder tug whipping up the blind and pulling the cord promptly from between his fingers. He pressed his forehead gently on the cool glass and looked out at the heavy overcast sky that seemed to hug the shapely hills and jutting high rises of Hong Kong, expertly wearing the smog like a grey fur coat.

Ryan breathed in deeply then slowly released his warm breath onto the cold window, fogging it up until he could no longer see the view. He breathed in deeply again only to catch his breath mid-way as the first hacking cough of the day consumed his chest and burned the back of his throat.

I really must stop smoking, he chastised himself, knowing as usual that it was an empty promise.

Rubbing the back of his neck with his hand Ryan made his way to the shower. The cool slate tiles felt good against his bare feet. The sudden blast of the hot water spiked and stabbed at his skin waking him up completely.

He let out a groan as he felt the foggy effects of a hangover begin to vice grip his skull. He leaned back into the full stream of the shower in an attempt to wash the feeling away. Closing his eyes for just a moment Ryan let the water flow over his face, taking in little mouthfuls swirling it around his dry, dehydrated mouth before spitting it out like a cherub in a fountain.

Ryan Harper had worked for the Response Security Group (RSG) in Central London for several years. He'd been there since graduating from University, having worked his way up from a trainee Security Supervisor, learning the ropes, to a fully-fledged Security Consultant. His job entailed speaking daily to leading retail banks across the Country, advising them on all aspects of security. He oversaw the installment and operation of in-house security systems through to the daily delivery of cash, cards and checkbooks.

The Company paid enough to offer Ryan a comfortable lifestyle and a nice car and his salary was topped up with a generous bonus each year, but Ryan was finding it a struggle to remain motivated and excited about his career. He had reached a plateau. He was bored.

His social life was not much better. Most of his friends were now either married, getting married, or busy having families of their own. His Friday and Saturday nights were becoming non-existent, as one by one his friends disappeared, spending more of their time instead with their new wives, or new families and not in their local pub after work with him. Ryan would get the occasional token invite to a dinner party, or a weekend BBQ, but recently he felt less inclined to accept. They invited him because they felt sorry for him, or were trying to set him up with an array of unsuitable single female friends, so that he could also become part of the club. Then his friends could legitimately see him more often.

LIGHTS OUT

It had crept up on him slowly, but finally the realization had sunk in that he was thirty, single and very unhappy with his current life.

Ryan's transfer to Hong Kong was perfectly timed. RSG had brokered a groundbreaking deal with The Asia World Bank, which thrust the company into the Global arena. The Company had made the decision to tackle one of the busiest banking City's in the World, and knew that if they did this successfully, that it would open up all kinds of doors into the retail banking sector across Asia. RSG needed *'one of their own'*, so his boss had said, and they felt that Harper was perfect for the job and ready to take on the challenge. He would be given full carte blanche on the team that he would need to employ and would be responsible for building close relationships with the existing Managers and Directors of the Bank.

Ryan was reminded several times before leaving London that it was a high-pressure job, not that he needed the reminder. He was feeling the weight of responsibility as the time was drawing close to moving. He knew that his performance would be closely watched by John McIntyre, a fifty-something British expatriate, John had been with the World Asia Bank as their Security Director for over ten years. A formidable man who took his job very seriously. John carried out his duties with great pride. It had taken a lot for the Bank's Directors to convince him that it was time to outsource to a new security company to satisfy its members. Finally after months of continued pressure he had been persuaded to make the change. With a clean slate with no attempted robberies or breaches in security for his entire career, John was intent that it was to remain that way and spent a long time weighing up the pros and cons of RSG and Ryan Harper. This didn't worry Ryan. He was confident in RSG. He also knew that if he worked well with John, and continued to build confidence and continue the success rate, it would open up all kinds of opportunities with other Asian Banks.

After all, John McIntyre knew everyone there was to know in the Hong Kong banking arena.

Ryan pressed his hands against the glass and dropped his head down letting the steaming water massage his back. The vice grip on his skull loosened a little leaving behind the gentle throb of a headache. He stood there for a few moments enjoying the heat as the water gathered and flowed between his shoulder blades forming a rapid before finally hitting the shower floor and spiraling down the drain.

His thoughts wandered back to his first week in Hong Kong.

Ryan embraced his new expat life absorbing everything around him like a sponge. He spent most his spare time exploring on foot, walking the city like a tourist and taking in all of the Asian influences and what was left of a pre-handover Hong Kong.

He found the local Chinese culture loud and crass when they spoke. To him it sounded like a chatter of noisy birds. He discovered that he loved the wet markets and the haggling process, the hustle bustle of tradesmen bringing in trays of fresh fish and vegetables. At times the smells in the markets were so strong that he had to cover his nose and mouth with his sleeve to stop himself from gagging but still he found it fascinating, colourful and vibrant.

In total contrast Ryan found the city modern and cosmopolitan. He discovered traditional Chinese *di pai dongs* nestled in between modern restaurants offering every type of food imaginable. To Ryan, Hong Kong was a City that would never go hungry.

Most of all Ryan was drawn to the architecture, the mixture of the old and the new. At night the high-rise buildings were all lit up like a Christmas tree sending shafts of light hundreds of feet into the night sky for everyone to see, blotting out the stars. The buildings were a giant mass of glass and metal, and had mostly been built and designed using the rules of *feng shui*. Ryan had picked up quickly that a good number of Chinese people were superstitious. He learned that desks must be placed always facing an open door. He saw that aquariums and fish tanks were present in almost every reception area with rare and expensive breeds of fish swimming around opulently decorated tanks. Even the buildings appeared to have been erected in such a way to encourage and bring prosperity and good luck to all those who worked behind the glass walls and metal structures. It was all part of a culture rich in history and beliefs, which made it a unique melting pot.

Ryan's only task during his first week was to find himself a suitable place to live.

RSG had placed him in a fully furnished serviced apartment in a fashionable area in the heart of the city. It was close enough to the bars and restaurants favored by other foreigners. Ryan knew that it would be fine short-term, but he was keen to get settled, and to finally ship his London belongings across the Ocean to start his new Hong Kong life. He was tired of living out of a suitcase.

After viewing an assortment of apartments he finally found the perfect one.

Hugging the side of Hong Kong Island's tallest mountain, The Peak, sat Cameron Mansions. It was a spacious modern apartment building with views towards the city in one direction, and breath-taking views of the outlying islands and the Ocean in the other direction.

Part of Ryan's package included his relocation from London, a monthly housing allowance and a cash lump sum for him to use as he pleased to furnish his new home. As Ryan wrote his signature on the new lease, there was no doubt in his mind that he really had landed on his feet. RSG had never sent anyone this far afield before and they obviously wanted to make a good impression.

Six months into his new job and it was going well. Ryan had managed to employ a strong local team comprising of on-site security officers, site security supervisors, and two security managers that reported directly into him. They all worked well together as a team and so far he had found John McIntyre to be tough, but also open to suggestions for improvements. Ryan was happy with their progress, as was RSG in London.

Finally showered and dressed Ryan checked his reflection in the bathroom mirror. He was broad-shouldered and measured just over 6'ft 2" making him tall for Hong Kong standards. He often found himself peering across the top of a sea of heads whenever he stood in an elevator. He was in reasonable shape and made good use of the banks' in-house gym during his lunch hour and ran outdoors whenever he could.

Ryan held onto the bathroom sink and leaned into the mirror to get a closer look at his face. Dragging his fingers tips across his cheeks and chin, he pulled at the loose skin under his bright blue eyes. He was handsome, his skin a little worn from too much sun, reminding him of days spent on the beach. His blonde hair was still thick and it curled around the nape of his neck. He had a lazy smile, which his mother used to tease him for and women seemed to like. Ryan spoke out-loud to his reflection.

"You need to slow down, stop burning the candle at both ends." He said, and then smiled at himself. He sounded just like his Mother.

Dressed in his usual uniform of dark grey pants and a crisp white shirt, and black tie, Ryan gave the mirror one final glance. Satisfied with his overall look, he stepped out into the lift lobby closing the door behind him and pressed the lift call button. He rummaged into his back pants pocket until his fingers found the cigarette packet. He pulled it out hastily, eagerly anticipating his first smoke of the day.

He reached the bottom of the lift and stepped out into the foyer, cigarette smoke dissolving quickly behind him leaving only the unmistakable aroma of fresh nicotine.

"Good morning Mr Harper'. Ryan was greeted by the building caretaker, Mr Wu, "You know very well there is no smoking allowed in the lift Sir?" he said to Ryan as he playfully wagged his finger.

The old caretaker, now well into his sixties had worked in the building for the best part of forty years, a gentle old man, slightly hunched over now, his white hair poorly dyed jet black, leaving obvious roots, which were easy for Ryan to see in his lofty position. Mr Wu's English was impeccable with hardly a trace of a Chinese accent. He appeared always smiling and happy and ready to help.

Ryan flashed him his best smile.

"Right you are Mr Wu, I'll try to remember in future!" Ryan said as he walked towards the exit of the building.

Mr Wu gave a resigned smile and shook his head, slowly turning his old body and walking back to his small office.

As Ryan walked outside he looked up at the heavy overcast sky. He paused for a moment trying to decide whether to run back for his umbrella, but looking at his watch decided against it. He continued his usual walk down the concrete sloped driveway and on to the busy main road.

A sea of bright red taxis greeted Ryan. Hong Kong Taxis were always in abundance, driving up and down the mountain road, picking up and dropping off. There was never a shortage. Within seconds Ryan had hailed a taxi and swiftly slid into the back seat of the red Toyota entering an entirely different world. The back passenger seats were covered with clear PVC to protect against spills and stains of customers. Miniature figurines of cartoon characters with heads that bobbed and moved as the car swerved, adorned the dashboard almost obscuring the drivers view. There was a small wrapped bunch of tuber roses dangling from the rear view mirror with a tiny tinkering bell that rang as Ryan closed the passenger door. Ryan suddenly found the strong floral aroma mixed with the faint smell of cigarettes over powering. His hangover didn't help matters. It made the interior feel dark and dingy and he instantly began to feel nauseous. He wound down his side window to try and get some air, whilst he gave his directions to the driver in an attempt to get the car moving. "Queens Road Central. The World Asia Bank please".

The driver looked at Ryan in his rear view mirror and offered a faint silent nod before sniffing back phlegm, letting it swirl in his mouth, winding down the drivers side window and expertly spitting the contents on to the road below. Suppressing the urge to vomit, Ryan quickly scanned the inside of the taxi to find something to distract himself. He noticed a jar of Chinese tea precariously perched in the center compartment between the two front seats, and focusing on the tea leaves he watched as they twisted and turned in the water, following the movements and sways of the taxi as it swerved and cornered down towards the City.

Chapter 2

As Ryan's taxi neared the Asia World Bank, the traffic started to slow down. The taxi radio crackled and jumped to life, barking loud instructions in Cantonese to any available driver listening in. Ryan could see that the traffic was starting to gridlock, and he only had a short distance left to walk. Still feeling slightly nauseous, Ryan asked the driver to stop. He quickly paid, relieved to no longer be twisting and turning and stepped out onto the pavement. He took in some deep breaths and immediately started to feel the nausea ebb away. He made his way to a nearby newsstand and purchased his daily *Morning Post*, paying with loose coins from his pocket. Ryan felt a piece of paper under his fingers folded into a small neat square. He fumbled for several seconds for the correct change, paid the vendor and walked towards *Starbucks* to order his usual take out latte.

Ryan smiled to himself as he pulled out the folded piece of paper from his pocket, remembering the evening that he had finally managed to get her number. He unraveled the note and read the stylish handwriting in black ink.

Lily 9304 8621 x

Ryan placed the note back in his pocket. *I'll call later*, he thought.

Ryan had been walking for just a short distance, enjoying the effects of the coffee as it began to clear the fog in his head and thought about the day ahead. It was always so noisy in the Central Business District, but today the surrounding noise appeared even worse than usual. At seven o'clock in the morning the taxis were already starting to fill up the roads. Delivery vans were double parking. Ryan noted the rubble and building debris was already being loaded onto a pick-up truck down a narrow side street next to the Bank. People on the pavement around him were rushing to and fro in all directions. Their heads down and focused as they walking deliberately and quickly, oblivious to other people around them. It was a cacophony of taxi horns, people talking and shouting and the sound of the trams running alongside the cars. Ryan started to find the noise unbearable, when without warning, a loud *CRASH* echoed behind Ryan silencing it all.

Ryan jumped and swiftly turned to see what had caused the noise. One of the red taxi's, in a hurry to avoid the gridlock had ran into the back of another taxi, leaving the metal bumper twisted and separated from the back of the car. The two Chinese drivers were already out of their seats shouting and waving their arms in the air like two passionate Italians. The two taxis had blocked part of the main road, making the gridlock complete. The sound of the horns combined with the raised voices began to increase again in volume like a crescendo in a symphony.

Once Ryan had satisfied his curiosity along with many other onlookers, he turned and continued to walk towards the Bank entrance, happy to be leaving the chaos and noise behind him. As he drew closer he became aware of other angry raised voices, this time from inside the Bank. Through the reception glass he could see two of his security officers talking to a man with his back to Ryan.

Ryan slowed down his pace and slipped his hand into his back pocket. He could feel his mobile phone, which made him feel better somehow.

He stepped a little closer to the entrance and could see more clearly now. One of the security officers was talking into a radio; the other officer was still in debate with the man. Ryan could see that the conversation was getting heated.

He paused for a moment, catching his breath and then entered the reception area behind them hoping to be able to help. The man with his back to Ryan was shouting in rapid Cantonese, he was dressed like one of the building contractors. He was short and slightly overweight, wearing an ill-fitting pale grey overall that was clearly too big for him. In his left hand he was carrying a small black duffle bag. The old man was gripping it so tightly that Ryan could see that his knuckles had turned white. Looking down he noticed that he wore old black plimsoles on his feet.

Whatever they were discussing it was clear that the man was frustrated.

Hearing someone enter the building, the contractor spun around to face Ryan.

Ryan noticed that his hair was slicked back and thinning, but it was still dark. His face was round and smooth which made Ryan think that under other circumstances that it could have been a happy face smiling back at him not a frightened one. Ryan could see beads of sweat forming into small droplets on his forehead, his expression was one of helplessness and desperation and he had fear in his eyes.

Seeing that Ryan offered no threat, the old man swiftly turned his attention back to the security officer; his eyes now wide open with fear and determination. Shaking uncontrollably he stuffed one hand into the hold all bag and pulled out a handgun thrusting it in the direction of the security officers shouting instructions. He dropped the bag on to the floor and began to wave the gun around in the air, his words becoming more frantic and loud.

Ryan was frozen to the spot, his feet unable to move as he watched the event quickly unfold before him.

"Get down" suddenly one of the security officers yelled at Ryan jolting him out of his trance. Immediately Ryan threw himself down onto the cold hard floor, his newspaper scattered out in front of him, the pages opening up and gracefully gliding to a halt. His coffee cup hit the ground to his left and Ryan watched silently as the brown steaming liquid slowly seeped across the white marble floor. Ryan kept his eyes down toward the floor as he covered his head with his hands. He could feel his heart pounding in his chest against the cold floor. Above him, all that he could hear was the turbulent shouts of the old man and the officers in a tongue that he couldn't understand.

Less than a second later a loud noise cracked high above Ryan's head. He knew instinctively that a gun had been fired.

Ryan slowly lifted his head and stole a glance at the three men. For a moment they all stood facing each other, perfectly still and silent as though someone had pressed a pause button.

To begin with Ryan couldn't tell who had fired the shot. Then, slowly, the contractor took an unsteady step backwards. His arm dropped to his side and the gun clattered loudly to the floor, echoing around them as it spun to a standstill in front of Ryan. The old man slowly crumpled sideways, his head hitting the hard marble floor resounding with a sickening thud, followed by deafening silence.

Ryan slowly stood up. His legs felt shaky and heavy and his heart was still pumping wildly. He looked over at the man now lying on the floor just a few feet away. He could see a pool of blood forming underneath his back and a dark patch seeping through the fabric on his chest, slowly changing the colour from pale grey to a dark inky black.

The dead mans head lay to the side and his eyes looked in Ryan's direction, still open and fixed. His mouth sagged a little and a small line of blood trickled down his chin and dripped without a sound onto the floor.

Ryan looked around him. Both security officers were now on their radios, shouting loudly in Cantonese. Ryan could hear a siren in the background, but his head was pounding. All he could think about in that moment was that John McIntyre's clean slate had just been tarnished and that his hangover had abruptly turned into a nightmare.

Chapter 3

Ryan looked around him. It was such a basic, simple room. Cold.

He sat on an uncomfortable black plastic chair at a square white Formica table. Two empty chairs were positioned opposite him.

A steaming cup of Chinese tea in a plastic holder was just to his left. Ryan watched the tealeaves slowly unravel in the hot water, until they finally descended to the bottom of the cup.

He looked around. There were no windows in the room, just a single door. Above his head he could see strip lighting. One of the long glass lights was flickering slightly causing it to make a loud buzzing noise in the quiet room.

The door, directly in front of Ryan, opened and two plain clothed Police officers walked in. The male officer sat down opposite him. He looked very young, although to Ryan all Chinese people seemed to look younger than they were. Ryan guessed that he must be in his mid-twenties. He wore blue jeans, and a freshly ironed white Polo t-shirt. On his wrist was a sporty looking IWC. *Probably a fake*, Ryan thought.

The woman that accompanied him also looked young, but he thought probably closer to her mid thirties. She was dressed much smarter than her colleague. She had black slim fitting pants with a matching suit jacket and a crisp white shirt underneath. Her thick black hair was pulled into a high ponytail, tight against her head. Her complexion was smooth and even, and her skin tone olive. Ryan noticed that she had dark, almost black eyes. Ryan considered that she looked mixed race rather than completely Chinese making him wonder where she was from. Her face was angular and serious and she didn't smile.

She sat down promptly and turned her attention to Ryan.

"Mr Harper, I'm Detective Inspector Lam, and this is Detective Officer Chow", Sarah Lam motioned to the young Chinese man to her right, surprising Ryan that he could already be a DI at such a young age.

"Apologies if you have been kept waiting. I can see that you have some tea already. Is there anything else that I can get for you?" Her English was faultless. *Clearly a rich kid educated overseas*, Ryan thought, surprising himself that he felt so irritated.

"Maybe just an ashtray, I really need a cigarette." He replied whilst fishing out a crumpled packet from his jeans and placing it on the table in front of him.

"No problem", the young Detective Officer Chow eagerly stood up and left the room in search of an ashtray, whilst Ryan pulled out a cigarette and proceeded to light it.

Sarah Lam broke the silence. "I just have a few questions for you, it shouldn't take long." She said as she opened her file and arranged the papers inside. From where he was sitting Ryan could clearly see photographs of the dead Chinese man in between sheets of hand written reports.

Chow re-entered the room slightly out of breath and holding triumphantly a plastic cup, which he promptly passed to Ryan with an apologetic smile.

"It's all I could find."

"Thanks' Ryan said, balancing his cigarette on the edge of the cup.

Ryan switched his gaze to Lam and waited for the questions.

"Just explain in your own words what actually happened this morning." Detective Inspector Lam pulled her chair closer toward the table. As she leaned in Ryan noticed her jacket flap open slightly revealing the corner of a shoulder holster. He shifted in his chair. Lam, aware that Ryan was looking at her, pulled her jacket in and quickly buttoned up the front.

"At the beginning I had no idea how serious the situation was. I was a bit pre-occupied watching a road accident that had just happened. It was only as I got really close to the Bank entrance that I could see two of my security officers arguing with an old man." Ryan picked up the perched cigarette from the edge of the plastic cup and took a long drag, pulling the smoke into his lungs before gently blowing in out.

"Yet you still decided to enter the building?" Lam looked directly at Ryan. He wondered if she was trying to intimidate him. She didn't. Maybe this was her tactic when interviewing people, he thought. Everyone is a suspect.

"Detective Lam, I don't speak Cantonese, I had no idea what they were arguing about, or how serious the situation was. I held back for a few seconds, but then decided to walk through to see whether there was anything that I could do. If I'd even thought for a second that this guy might have a gun, I would have kept my distance. Believe it or not, I don't have a death wish Detective" Ryan said curtly as he flicked his ash into the cup watching it crumble into a pile of dust.

"Do you recall seeing anyone else close to the entrance, or anyone looking suspicious?" Lam asked whilst Chow sat next her scribbling notes.

Ryan took another long drag of his cigarette and thought back to the events of just a few hours ago.

"No, nothing unusual. People walk past the entrance all the time. It's a public courtyard and a short cut between the two main roads." He was less curt now, wanting to get through this quickly so that he could leave.

"Can I just ask, who was the old man? He looked so out of place there and genuinely frightened." Ryan asked Lam.

"The suspect had no identification on his person. We think that he may be from the mainland, but we have quite a bit of work to do before we can verify that." Lam responded.

"And of course there's no CCTV footage for you to look through". Ryan said, almost apologetically.

Lam shot Officer Chow a sideways glance. Then turned her attention back to Ryan.

"Yes, of course you would know about that. Due to the Banks timely security upgrade, we have no way of seeing which direction he entered and the exact time frame and sequence of events. We only have your account and the two security officers at this stage." Lam finished. Ryan could sense that Lam was annoyed. He had only been in her company for a short amount of time, but already he could feel that she didn't like him much. He didn't know why. He had just been in the wrong place at the wrong time, an innocent bystander. The way in which she had conducted the interview was making Ryan feel the same way about her.

Ryan was starting to feel dizzy, the effects of adrenaline and lack of food in his stomach and the cigarette was starting to take effect. He hadn't even had his morning caffeine fix, having left the contents of his drink on the marble floor at the bank. He looked at his watch. It was already 09:30am. He'd been there for two hours already.

Noticing Ryan check his watch Lam quickly continued not wanting her key witness to lose interest.

"One final question Mr Harper then you are free to go. Exactly what time did you enter the building this morning?" Lam asked. Chow's pen was poised over his notes.

"Oh, it was just after 7am, I've been in early this week because of the renovations and the CCTV upgrades." Ryan replied, suddenly feeling drained.

"Thank you, Mr Harper. Do you have any business trips or personal travel planned over the coming few days at all?" Lam asked.

"No, No plans, I'll be in Hong Kong if you need me." Ryan responded flatly, desperate for the questions to be finished so that he could leave. As if reading his mind, Lam leaned across the table and passed Ryan a business card.

"If you think of anything else," she said tapping the card with her finger. "Just call."

Ryan stood on the steps outside the Police Station and looked up at the sky.

LIGHTS OUT

It was still over-cast and humid, but at least the rain was holding off.

He thought about going back to the bank, but knew that he'd have more questions to answer there, so he quickly decided against it. He just wanted to go home, *it's not every day that a man get's shot in front of you*, he thought, justifying his decision.

Ryan stepped into the road and waved for a taxi. Within seconds a bright red Toyota pulled to a halt beside him and Ryan climbed in.

'The Peak please, Cameron Mansions." Ryan said as he sank deep into the back seat and closed his eyes.

The driver silently nodded, flicked on the meter and merged into the busy traffic.

Across the street a black Mercedes-Benz with dual number plates slowly pulled away from the curb.

Chapter 4

Fifteen minutes later Ryan walked into his apartment and threw his keys on the hall table.

He felt tired. He pulled his shirt out of his jeans, and kicked his shoes off making himself feel more comfortable.

Needing some background noise he reached for the TV remote and punched the green *on* button, then headed to the kitchen to make some much needed coffee.

Ryan considered everything that had happened that morning as he prepared his coffee. He felt like he'd walked onto the set of a movie, the whole event had been so unreal. It had been over in just a few minutes, but the replay in Ryan's head was now in slow motion. He kept getting flashes of the old mans face, the sound of the gun and the sight of the dark blood slowly spreading across the floor. Ryan shook away the thoughts.

John McIntyre had been surprisingly understanding with Ryan when he called, considering the enormity of what it actually meant for the Bank and it's pristine record. John ordered Ryan to take the rest of the day off. He would call him if the Police needed any more information. Meanwhile John would handle the Bank's Directors and the media. Ryan wondered if RSG would pull his contract early, but then if he thought about it rationally, the attempted breach was unsuccessful, the only problem was the dead Chinese man. No one wanted a dead man on their hands, especially if you are a security company or a bank.

Luckily for Ryan it was Friday and he had the luxury of the weekend to get his head straight and then he'd be back to work as normal on Monday, *no big deal*, he thought.

Ryan finished making his coffee and headed back to the lounge. He slumped his tired body into an armchair and picked up the remote control increasing the volume in an attempt to block out all thoughts.

A young enthusiastic female news reporter stood with a large microphone outside the front entrance of the Asia World Bank.

"Joining me live is Detective Inspector Lam to comment on this mornings attempted robbery at the World Asia Bank, which resulted in the death of an unknown gunman". The reporter turned toward Lam as the cameraman panned out to show the Detective and the reporter standing together. The yellow and black police tape was still visible behind them, blocking off the bank's main entrance whilst the general public jostled for position behind a line of police officers to get a better look.

"Detective Inspector Lam, Thank you for joining us. Hong Kong is normally a very safe City. In fact in Hong Kong's history there has never been an attempted Bank robbery before. What can you tell us about this morning's events?"

The cameraman moved the camera and focused in on Detective Inspector Sarah Lam. She looked uncomfortable, Ryan thought. She was professional looking in her dark suit with her severe tied back hair, but her body language told him that she was not a natural in front of the camera and was hating every minute of it. He watched with interest now.

'Thank you Kate". Lam offered a brief smile to the reporter. "It is a highly unusual event for Hong Kong and we are treating this case in isolation. We are still in the process of identifying the gunman. We cannot confirm at this stage whether this was in fact an attempted Bank robbery, but we have not ruled this out entirely."

Lam said and then turned to face the camera directly.

"I would urge members of the public that have any information regarding the shooting to come forward. The Bank has offered a substantial financial reward for any information that would shed light on the identity of the man in question as well as related information regarding the event this morning." Turning back to the young reporter Lam nodded signaling that she was done. "Thank you detective Lam". The cameraman zoomed back into the reporter as she continued to repeat the same story again, whilst in the background, Ryan could see Lam walking back toward the bank and away from the camera and crowds.

Ryan shook his head. "Incredible". He said out loud. Ryan lent back in his chair and sipped his coffee, *they don't have the faintest idea where to start*, he thought.

In the background the news continued, this time from inside the newsroom.

'Protests erupted in Central again this morning after an environmental bill was rejected. The controversial 'Lights Out' organization have been publically lobbying local manufacturers to pay fines on environmental waste dumped in unauthorized locations around Hong Kong and the New Territories.

This is an ongoing campaign for the improvement of air pollution in Hong Kong. Their normally high profile theatrical protests have drawn negative support from Government officials and policy makers over the last few months. However, their current 'Lights Out' campaign enlisting major Banks, Retailers and Hotels to agree to actually switch off their lights for eight minutes on the eighth of August, in support of the Campaign, has started to draw Global attention forcing officials to finally start listening.'

The TV projected still images of various dumpsites across the territory, areas that Ryan didn't recognize. In some of the shots it showed industrial waste piled up high, sitting precariously on top of unkempt landfills full to the brim with plastic, twisted metal, canisters with hazardous signs, pools of black liquid sitting in puddles. All over flowing into un-spoilt areas of the countryside.

Ryan hit the volume button to 'mute' drained his coffee and fished into his pocket for his cigarettes.

His mobile phone rang. He picked it up to check the caller ID, lit his cigarette and pressed the call button.

"Hi Rob', Ryan answered in a tired voice, lazily blowing out the cigarette smoke at the same time.

'Ryan, I've just heard the news. The office is buzzing with the story. I can't believe what happened to you. How are you feeling? Why didn't you call me?' The friendly familiar voice spoke quickly with concern and just a trace of excitement. Ryan thought.

Ryan was happy to hear his friends voice and pleased to have a distraction.

'I'm fine, really I'm fine, still dazed a bit, it's all completely surreal.' Ryan paused not knowing how else to describe how he felt.

" I know", Rob interrupted, "Oh, hang on, another call's coming through. Listen, I have to take this. I'll come over tonight at Eight. Take it easy buddy.'

'OK, but I'm not really in the.' Click. Ryan heard the sound of the phone being switched off before he could even finish his sentence. Ryan smiled to himself and sighed at the thought of Rob. He was always in a hurry, like a whirlwind, Ryan thought. He lay down on the couch and closed his tired eyes for just a moment. Within seconds he was asleep, his breathing fitful and fast, his cigarette burning slowly between the index and middle finger of his left hand. The hot ash crumbled onto the floor next to him, whilst the smoke danced and spiraled, twisting up toward the ceiling as he fell deeper into a troubled sleep.

The intercom buzzer pierced the silence waking Ryan with a start. Blinking away the sleep, he sat upright and saw that his apartment was in pitch dark with the exception of the brilliant glow from the silenced TV that flickered, making shapes and shadows across his living room walls. He turned his wristwatch toward the bright screen so that he could check the time. It was exactly 8pm. Ryan stood up and made his way over to the intercom, switching on lights as he went.

He pressed the button.

"Hello?"

'Mr Harper' I have Mr Black for you.' Mr Wu's familiar voice crackled through the speaker to Ryan.

'Send him up, thank you Mr Wu'. Ryan said.

He put his door on latch, and walked back to his living room.

A few moments later Ryan heard the tell tale creak of the wooden floorboard outside his front door, followed by the sound of the heavy Oak door opening and footsteps entering his hallway.

"Come in Rob, I'm in the living room". Ryan yelled in the direction of the door.

Still in his work attire and carrying a black gym bag, Rob Black entered looking every inch like the City banker that he was.

Sitting down heavily on the big leather armchair and dropping the bag next to him on the floor, Rob loosened his tie with one hand and popped open the top button of his shirt. He leaned back allowing his body to mold into soft cushions. Without saying a word to his friend, Rob leaned over toward Ryan and plucked his freshly lit cigarette from his fingers, and placed it straight to his mouth. He took a long slow dramatic drag. To finish the theatrics, Rob leaned his head back, and slowly released perfect smoke rings toward the ceiling. Once he had finished blowing out the remainder of the smoke, he turned his head and smiled broadly at Ryan.

'What a day'. He said.

Rob Black was about 5'9 and portly. He had dark wavy hair and smiled easily and often. No one would ever describe him as typically good looking, but Rob always surprised Ryan with his success with women. He was smart with a self-depreciating sense of humor. Most importantly, he was Ryan's closest friend in a City where friends became the only family you could have.

Rob had been at the bank for almost six years, an ex-pat from New York, he was delighted when a new single playmate joined the ranks. Their motto was always *'work hard, play hard'* and they stuck to it as though their lives depended on it.

Within Ryan's first week, he had found himself sitting next to Rob during a compulsory and tedious, training day. They became friends from the onset. Thrilled that Ryan was new to the City, Rob made it his sole duty to become Ryan's official tour guide. Before long Ryan knew all of the drinking establishments spanning across the Island as well as Rob did. They would often finish up their nights in Wan Chai, one of the darker districts of the social scene. Sitting in the heart of the City, and famed for it's strip clubs, happy hours and late night shows that once lured Sailors. Ryan and Rob could frequently be found in a small smoky club, drinking whiskey, surrounded by beautiful girls. The bars and back streets offered them a glimpse into another time, a hint of the mysterious past of the Orient. Ryan often imagined what it must have been like as a young Sailor coming in from the port, excited about being in a tropical paradise, remembering the stories told whilst at sea. Being greeted by an array of girls; all dressed in exquisite silk Cheong Sam dresses. Not the demure kind like the traditional girls wore, with just one small slit on one side, but the kind of dress that demanded attention. The sleeves short and capped to show long slender olive arms with the dress buttoned high into a mandarin collar, secured with individual fine silk knots. The body of the fabric following the shape and contours of the figure beneath, stopping demurely at the knees, but teasing the observer with high slits at the sides revealing young firm tanned thighs. It was too much to resist for some men. They would be lured easily with promises of drinks, dancing and more. Now only snippets of the past were still visible, an old silk lantern here, a secret covered doorway there, it felt a lot less glamorous and lot more seedy. Neon strip lights flickered overhead, framing small door entrances with brightly lit arrows pointing to hidden staircases. Ruby red velvet curtains, that had seen better days, now hung heavily over windows, worn and faded with the smell of old tobacco. *Mamma Sans* sitting on low stools with toothy grins offering pretty girls and massages, dancing girls and drinks to anyone as they walked by. Rob and Ryan were fascinated by the Tattoo parlors. Not brave enough to ever have one of their own, they would look at the images that showed pictures of half naked bodies covered in intricate tattoos of dragons and elaborate Chinese inscriptions that they couldn't understand. They spent many nights gracing the smoking lounges and the sleazy and dingy back street clubs. It was a common end to their evening, tumbling out of darkened nightclubs in fits of laughter over something that they would later forget, squinting into the bright daylight and heading home to sleep.

'I bought you a present, thought you might need something to calm you down a bit.' Rob leaned forwards and rummaged in his gym bag for a moment before retrieving his gift. With a big smile he planted a bottle of 12-year old Glen Fiddich Special Reserve on the glass coffee table between them.

"Perfect", Ryan said with a smile as he stood up to fetch two glasses. 'On the rocks or straight?' He asked as he walked through to his kitchen.

'Straight. Don't ruin the amber nectar with ice." Rob countered back, horrified at the suggestion.

Ryan walked back through carrying two whiskey glasses. Rob was eager to pour with the opened bottle waiting in his hand. They sat in silent appreciation as he poured the dark amber liquid into the first glass, watching it swirl in the bottom like liquid metal. He passed the glass to Ryan and then filled his own.

"Here's to nine-lives." Rob said, clinking his glass heavily against Ryan's.

"I'll drink to that." Ryan said as he took a large sip of the whiskey. He let the liquid trickle over his tongue savoring the myriad of subtle flavors that merged into one another, hints of smoke and wood mixed with fruit and liquorice, before swallowing it slowly. He felt himself relax.

'This is good.'

"Tough day at the office?" Ryan asked his friend.

"No worse than usual, but pretty boring compared to yours. Tell me everything." Rob said sipping his drink.

Ryan spent the next ten minutes without interruption telling Rob all of the days events. Rob listened intently, nodding and gasping at all the right moments. Ryan felt like he was living it all again as he explained in detail about the gunshot, the man falling, the blood seeping across the floor, the old mans distorted face. After he had concluded his story Ryan could feel that his heart was racing. He took another sip of the whiskey to calm his nerves.

Seeing that his friend needed to change the subject, Rob switched to a lighter topic of conversation.

"OK, enough about Bank robberies and dead people, let's talk about girls. Have you called Lily yet?"

"No, not yet", Ryan replied, pleased with the sudden change of topic. "I was planning to call today, but maybe I'll call over the weekend."

"Are you kidding me? That girl is hot, and it's a Friday night! You seriously could have died this morning. If I were you I'd be out there making the most of it. Call her right now." Rob pushed his mobile phone across the glass table to Ryan.

"Just see if she's out tonight?"

Ryan laughed, took another mouthful of whiskey and swallowed hard.

Without saying another word, he reached for the phone, pulled out the folded piece of paper from his pocket and punched in the number.

Beluga was a small stylish restaurant in the heart of the fashionable SOHO district, a name coined by locals referring to its location South of Hollywood Road. The restaurant boasted a curved walnut bar counter with plush grey velvet seating against the surrounding walls. It had tall pedestal tables, which stood facing the dramatic glass entrance. At the rear, a few intimate tables were pushed closely together in a small wooden decked area, full with trees and plants. The art against the red walls was striking. Large canvases of contemporary oil paintings hung from the ceiling creating the feeling of a gallery. The lighting was warm and subtle and candles shimmered behind glass holders on each tabletop softening the skin tone of anyone sitting close by.

The music was a perfect mix of Jazz and R&B. Not too loud that that you couldn't talk and not too quiet that you couldn't hear it. Already Beluga was filled with people laughing and chatting. All of the seating had been taken early on and the floor space leading to the bar was heavy with people jostling to get the attention of the bar tender.

Ryan found himself blocked in as he tried to maneuver his way through the crowds to the back of the restaurant without treading on toes or knocking people with his elbows. He finally reached his destination and turned to see if he could locate Rob in the throng of people behind him. Sure that his friend would find him eventually, he turned to face the beautiful woman that sat quietly at the corner back table, drinking Champagne.

"Sorry we're late." Ryan said apologetically and nodded toward the heaving crowd of people behind him.

"It took a while to get here."

"Well, you're here now". The woman said smiling broadly, as she stood to greet Ryan.

She was taller than Ryan remembered. He noticed that she was wearing tight black jeans showing off her long lean legs. She wore a simple black cashmere sweater cut to a deep v at the back. Her hair was pulled back from her face into a loose ponytail that swung to the side, falling across her shoulder as she moved. She didn't need make-up, but was wearing eyeliner and lip-gloss, which made her eyes look smoky and her lips smooth.

'Where's our boy?' Lily said softly as she leaned in to kiss Ryan's cheek. He could smell her perfume and he found himself inhaling her scent for a brief moment.

'Oh, he's here somewhere," Ryan said totally distracted by her, wondering if he should have come on his own to meet her.

Ryan felt a firm hand rest on his shoulder and he turned to face a beaming Rob, slightly out of breath from pushing through the crowd, and armed with a new bottle of Cristal Champagne tucked under one arm, and three glasses in his hand.

"*HELLO* Champagne!" Rob shouted happily above the noise, before placing the glasses and bottle on the table. Lily and Rob exchanged amused glances before laughing fondly at their friend. Ryan shook his head, rolled his eyes at Rob and smiled. Finally, the thoughts of the day were drifting out of his mind and were replaced with thoughts of the fun night ahead.

Chapter 5

Sarah Lam sat in her office pouring over the details in the police report. Her coffee mug sat untouched on her desk, the milky brown liquid now cold to the touch.

So far she had not been able to identify the dead Chinese man. The circumstances surrounding the shooting at the Bank that morning were still ambiguous. She had a lot of people still to interview and seemingly a lot of information missing. She had sent her partner home a few hours ago already. Chow had a young family and she often felt bad keeping him at work late, away from his wife and child.

Now her office was quiet, and only a few lights were on in the building.

She sighed and put down the report for a moment. She rubbed her temples with her long fingers, trying to massage away the headache that was threatening to present itself. She straightened her back and sat upright in an effort to refresh her mind and picked up the report again.

LIGHTS OUT

Lam scanned the paperwork familiarizing herself with the details. The dead Chinese man, she suspected, was probably from the mainland. He appeared to be some kind of manual worker based on the calluses found on his hands and sunspots visible across his face, neck and arms. She guessed that he was from simple means, and definitely not the mastermind behind the attempted breach of security.

Her mind began to shift into gear as she ploughed through the file. If a bank robbery was the intention, she thought to herself, then it would have been a fruitless attempt. The Bank was impossible to rob, especially single-handed. Security was extremely tight, too complicated for an old man on his own. Even if he had managed to get past the entrance undetected, where was he planning to go? What was the purpose of his break in? Sarah mulled over this for a moment.

Clearly there was more than one person involved in this, she concluded. But this is where her investigation fell short.

After interviewing the two security officers on duty, Lam felt sure that they were telling the truth and this collaborated with Ryan Harpers account of the events.

She imagined the scene in her head.

The old man had walked into the Bank and attempted to enter the main door using a swipe card. Having interviewed the two security officers independently, and verifying the procedures with the Bank's Security Director, Lam now knew that all contractors must report to the duty security officer at the desk in the lobby before entering the building. This was their standard procedure. All work contractors knew that they had to pick up their new security tag as well as their daily swipe cards. The tags would be permanently clipped onto their overalls for the duration of their time on the premises and the swipe cards would allow them limited access to the fourth floor.

The swipe card that the old man attempted to use had immediately flagged up an error message, and raised the alarm to the security officer on duty.

When the officer approached the old man and asked him to sign in at the desk and follow the procedure, he told the officer that he was late for work, if he could just be swiped through by the officer, then he would be on his way.

The officer asked again and this time requested another form of ID from the old man. The old man refused, but was insistent upon getting through the door. He continued to push his card through the scanner in the futile hope that the door might eventually open.

The officer radioed through to his colleague, who promptly joined the two men at the door. After which they their argument began.

From her notes, Lam knew that it was at this point that Ryan Harper had entered the Bank. She wondered for a moment about Harper. There was something that she couldn't put her finger on. Perhaps she just didn't like these self-assured Westerners. She often found them too confident for their own good. She shook the negative thought from her mind and carried on. Harper was apparently oblivious to the breach of security and only seconds later had found himself lying on the floor and a single shot was fired.

With no CCTV footage on hand, Lam had no choice but to believe each witness account at this stage.

Lam read through the interview notes that Chow had written up on the on-site project manager, Lai Wong. He had worked for Wing Land Holdings for several years and was managing the fourth floor renovations at the bank.

There were twenty building contractors employed by Wing Land to carry out the work. They had been hired to renovate the entire fourth floor of the building. This was to become the new private banking section for exclusive use of the banks elite customers. There was a lot of demolition work, most of which was completed outside of normal banking hours. Every day, between 06:30am and 07:30am, all of the previous days rubbish and rubble would be removed from the building, and loaded onto a truck before the roads became too congested with traffic and before the bank opened to the public.

Lai Wong advised Chow that completion was due in three weeks time and they were on track, with no issues to speak of.

Lam had also spoken to the Bank Security Director, John McIntyre who collaborated everything that Lai Wong had said in the report. He also wanted to add that the authorization and restricted security access that had been introduced for independent contractors, had, until that moment been working well, and the fact that the old man had not been able to successfully penetrate the security, in his mind, meant that the system worked.

Lam referred back to the forensics file.

The old mans clothing had been removed and sent to the lab for testing. They used one of the Wing Land standard overalls as a comparison.

Even though the overalls were similar in style and colour, the conclusive tests confirmed that it was not from the same manufacturer. The fabric weight and construction was different, and an alternative dyestuff had been used to attain a similar grey colour. The twist on the sewing thread was tighter than the original making it absolutely impossible for it to have been made in the same place or on the same machine. It looked as thought the overalls had been either custom-made or purchased for the sole purpose to make the old man look like one of the contract workers.

After lengthy discussions with both the construction company and the bank, both sets of records showed that all workers were accounted for that day, and all security swipe cards and tags had been handed back in to the Bank security desk. Not a single thing was unaccounted for. At this stage none of the bank personnel or the employees of Wing Land were under suspicion.

She had nothing.

Sarah closed the file, slipping it back into the pile of papers on her desk. She sat back for a moment to think. The Chief was giving her a hard time over this one. The Asia World Bank's CEO had personally called his good friend the Police Commissioner to apply a little pressure. "*A man shot dead at a major bank is not good PR, no matter which way the press handle it.*" The Commissioner had said. The Chief relayed the message to Lam and Chow. If there was something more sinister behind this botched attempt, the Chief wanted them to find out what it was, and quickly.

Lam checked her watch, it was long after midnight and the last few hours had slipped by surprisingly quickly. Lam could feel that she was losing the battle against her headache and would be of no use to anyone here.

She roughly straightened her files, not wanting to leave her desk in a mess, and gulped down the remainder of the cold coffee. Then giving the room one final glance, she flicked off the light and headed home.

Chapter 6

Ryan lay on his bed with his right hand pressed firmly against his eyelids in an attempt to keep his eyes from moving under the lids.

His head was pounding so hard that he was convinced that he could feel his brain move underneath his skull. He tried to swallow, but the saliva simply sat underneath his tongue useless against the dehydration. He had no idea what time it was – he didn't want to know. He just wanted to stay completely still and quiet and let the hangover pass.

Ryan heard a movement, his hearing now acute in the quiet room. He listened again, this time holding his breath with his eyes shut tight against his sweaty palm. There was a rustle of the bed sheet next to him, a deep contented sigh and then even steady breathing.

Suddenly the previous nights events came rushing back. With great effort he moved his head slightly to the left and lifting his fingers opened one eye, immediately regretting the action as his head threatened to explode.

Lily was lying on her back and was looking up at the ceiling with a sleepy smile on her face. She turned in his direction and looked at him.

"Good morning' she purred, "How are you feeling?"

"Like death warmed up", Ryan's hoarse voice croaked the reply. He pressed his temples with his fingertips and watched her for a moment.

Feeling his eyes on her, Lily sat up in bed, pulling the white sheet with her. Her long thick black hair fell onto her shoulders. Her eyes were bright and awake now and she still had her eye make-up on. It had smudged slightly during the night giving her a Bridget Bardot look. Ryan thought that she couldn't be more beautiful.

Lily twisted her body to face Ryan and planted a playful kiss on his forehead. She then swung her long legs over the edge of the bed and leaving the white sheet behind her stood up gracefully and padded naked into the bathroom.

Ryan lay for a few moments and listened to the mesmerizing sound of the shower, his eyes started to feel heavy and without effort he fell back into a deep sleep.

When Ryan woke up again, the apartment was silent. He stretched his arms and legs slowly, then propped himself up on one arm and checked his bedside clock.

12.03pm

With a groan and a cough, Ryan moved his body like an old man to the edge of the bed. He turned back to look at the ruffled sheets where Lily had been sleeping. Perched on top of one of the pillows was a piece of white paper folded neatly in half. With some effort Ryan stretched across the bed and grabbed the paper with his fingertips. He unfolded it quickly and read the now familiar handwriting.

Dinner tonight? Say 8pm at Cru?

I'll call you later

LX

Ryan smiled to himself. He had the whole afternoon to get over his hangover. He lay back on the bed and pulled the sheets around him, quickly falling back to sleep.

Chapter 7

Fifteen miles away, a car pulled up outside of the Water Margin Chinese Restaurant on the Kowloon side of Hong Kong. At first glance the passenger that stepped out of the black Mercedes-Benz looked unremarkable, his black hair was slicked back neatly against his head. He was dressed in a black suit with a black tie, and looked like so many other Chinese businessmen from the City. The only thing that stood him apart from everyone else was his unusually white skin. If it wasn't for his dark hair and black eyes, he could easily have been mistaken for an Albino.

In his right hand he held a newspaper. As he approached the entrance of the restaurant he tucked the newspaper under his arm and opened the door.

Once inside, a pretty Chinese hostess was waiting to greet him. She was dressed in a full length pale yellow silk Cheong Sam covered with delicate embroideries of plum blossoms and oriental birds. Her thick black hair was plaited and sat over her right shoulder almost reaching her waist. She gave him a gentle nod of recognition before averting her eyes and motioned for him to follow her.

They walked in silence to the back of the bustling, noisy restaurant and down a narrow corridor with a large fish tank situated against the wall. The décor was dark and ostentatious with red and gold patterned walls. Traditional Chinese artworks, vases and dragon sculptures sat on pedestals lining both sides of the corridor.

The air smelt both perfumed and smoky. The Chinese man could detect the aroma of incense burning in a room somewhere. It's distinct smell giving the restaurant an air of tradition and mystery.

As they reached the end of the corridor there was a dark wooden door to the left. Here the hostess stopped and knocked once, then swiftly turned and left the Chinese man waiting. The door promptly opened from the inside releasing cigarette smoke into the corridor. The pale Chinese man stepped inside and the door closed behind him, leaving the smoke hanging mid- air momentarily before it rose up to the ceiling and dissolved.

Upon entering the room, the Chinese man observed the large, centrally placed circular table covered with a heavily embroidered red silk cloth, typical in private dining rooms. On top of the cloth was a round piece of glass protecting the fabric from spills and stains. Each chair around the table was upholstered in extravagant jacquard silk fabrics set into intricate wooden carved frames. Along the back wall hung heavy deep red velvet curtains, draped from floor to ceiling and closed, shutting out any daylight. A chandelier was set high above the centre of the table directing the main pool of light into the middle of the room whilst casting ominous shadows into the corners.

Only two people sat at the table facing the Chinese man.

A slim elderly Chinese woman, slightly hunched with age, sat gracefully at the table. Her white hair was pinned up in an extravagant oversized bun, held into place with a single gold pin. She was wearing a dark gold silk jacket with a high mandarin collar and matching long straight silk skirt that touched the floor. She sat on a chair that had been placed parallel to the table making it easier for her to sit. Her walking stick was propped up against the side of her leg. She had light transparent skin, delicately folded with age. Pale blue veins and brown sunspots scattered her features, poorly hidden by her thick make-up. Her left hand was calmly resting in her lap, whilst she leaned with her right arm on the table. She was smoking a cigarette through a long black cigarette holder reminiscent of another time. She had a distinct yellow gold and jade ring on her right index finger and wore a long jade pendant in the shape of a dragon around her neck and dainty jade drop earrings.

A young Chinese woman sat next to her. She was good looking, with long straight black hair that tumbled down her back. She wore very little make-up with just a hint of mascara around her large almond shaped eyes. She wore a simple black dress with a round neck and no sleeves, showing off her lean tanned arms. She wore the same yellow gold and jade ring on her index finger as the elderly woman. Both women exuded an air of confidence and impatience, indicating to the late arrival, that it was time for their meeting to start.

"You're late ", the young Chinese woman broke the silence. Her voice was clipped and sharp.

"I had a unavoidable stop to make on the way" the Chinese man spoke softly, promptly pulling out a chair and sitting down across from the two women. He threw his newspaper onto the table allowing it to slide across the glass towards them.

"It didn't go as planned" he said now motioning to the front page. A large picture of the Asia World Bank dominated the newspaper followed by the headline;

Bank security prevents robbery bid.

"But of course you know that already", he said with a trace of sarcasm toward the young woman. "We hadn't anticipated that the security guards would be armed with live rounds, and we've since learned that the swipe card that we had been given was void." He flashed an accusing look toward the young woman. "We can afford to lose one man." He continued, "He was not important, a simple fool. We can use someone else, a real worker from the construction company, but this time we'll ensure that he's discreet, fast and successful."

The old woman slowly positioned her long cigarette holder against the ashtray allowing the smoke to twist and spiral upwards instead of putting it out.

"It does not matter if the cat is black or white, Ghost Face, as long as it catches mice." Her voice was hoarse with age and smoke. She continued, looking directly at him.

"But there is no time to repeat any mistakes. This was an unnecessary error, which has cost us valuable time. If there are strong Generals, Ghost Face, there should be no weak soldiers. A poor selection on your part I believe." Her crooked gnarled fingers moved across the table to a slim wooden box. Drawing the box closer to her body, she proceeded to gently drum her fingers across it.

Ghost Face, nodded respectfully in the direction of the old woman.

"Understood" he said, his voice now calm. "I will not fail you a second time".

She turned towards the young Chinese woman sitting next to her.

"Lillian," she allowed herself a small smile, bearing browned old teeth as she spoke her name, "your news?"

"The man that we plan to use for the security access for the main bank entrance and the vault is almost on board", she replied with confidence. "I don't see that it is going to be a problem".

Ghost Face interrupted her thread.

"In case there is a problem" he interjected, "We have something that will ensure that he'll become a willing participant."

"And security?" The elderly woman asked. "Are you going to be ready this time?"

"There's no doubt that security will be a focus for the bank for the next few days. It's nothing that we can't handle. All of the new cameras will be in place and operational by next Monday. I have the five men that I need for the job, all experienced, and all trusted members." Lillian said.

Ghost Face spoke to both women.

"My police contact tells me that they have nothing on the old man, it's a cold case for them. They have nothing to link him to us and so I feel that we can still proceed with confidence." He finished.

The old woman continued to drum her fingers on the slim wooden box.

"There can be no more mistakes." Her voice was calm but firm. "I will not accept failure on any level. Any mishap could be very damaging to our business."

The old woman stopped drumming her fingers and spoke to them both;

"We don't need to meet again now until after the event."

"You can take one of these phones", She said, as she opened the lid on the wooden box and took out two brand new white mobile phones. She pushed the white phones toward the centre of the table. Continuing, she said, "It is now the only phone from which you can contact me and each other, these, I am told, cannot easily be traced." "There is one for each of you."

Lillian reached forwards to take her phone and slipped it immediately into her bag.

"You can now leave", the elderly woman said to Ghost Face and Lillian as she drew again on her cigarette, and exhaled blue smoke into the air between them, confirming that the meeting had indeed finished.

They looked at each other in silence and nodded. They swiftly collected their belongings and exited the room, leaving the Chinese woman sitting alone at the table.

When she was sure that they had gone, she leaned forward and placed her cigarette against the ashtray.

"You can come out now", she said.

There was a rustle behind her and from behind the heavy red curtain stepped a Chinese man. He was tanned and sinewy with shoulder length greasy black hair, slicked back and tied into a ponytail at the nape of his neck. He wore a plain black t-shirt, denim jeans and black trainers. His forearms were covered in tattoos depicting a tiger on one side and a dragon on the other, both animals wrapping themselves up the full length of his forearms and disappearing into his sleeve. His face was pot marked and scarred and his features motionless. He stood before the elderly woman as silent as he had behind the curtain.

"I don't trust Ghost Face. I want you to follow him and report back to me. I want to know everything that he does, every move that he makes and every person that he sees. Now go".

Without saying a single word the man bowed and slipped silently out of the room.

Outside the restaurant Ghost Face lit up a cigarette. The air around him felt humid and sticky. He was distracted. He didn't like it when things didn't go to plan and he found working with Lillian insufferable.

He put his hand into his inside pocket and pulled out the new white mobile phone.

He punched in a number and waited.

"Yes" a male voice replied.

"We need to talk"

"OK, tomorrow morning at ten, the usual place."

Without responding Ghost Face tapped the off button on the screen and slipped it back into his pocket.

Chapter 8

Ryan sat in the restaurant waiting for Lily to arrive. She was late, more than fashionably late. He pushed back the cuff of his shirt and checked his watch again.

He had opted to sit facing the entrance so that he would be aware when Lily arrived, as well as offering him a good view of the other diners.

He shifted in his chair to try to get more comfortable.

To Ryan's immediate right sat two women in their mid-thirties, very well dressed and clearly close friends. They were leaning towards each other across the small round table in deep conversation, broken only by the occasional raucous laughter and a pause to take a sip from their wine glasses, oblivious to anyone else around them.

Ryan passed his gaze across the rest of the large room. She'd chosen well. The restaurant was a well-known hot spot in Hong Kong popular among Thirty-Somethings. A combination of rich dark wooden floors and off white walls with high ceilings gave it an air of sophistication without being too formal. The seating and couches dotted around the restaurant were filled with squashy velvet cushions making it a comfortable and relaxed setting. Black and white framed photographs of old Hong Kong filled the walls with hardly space to spare in between each one, which gave Ryan something to look at whilst he waited. Individual candles on each table glowed softly. In the background a mixture of jazz and lounge music played. He approved, it was all very well chosen.

The waiters all wore the same black Mandarin collar shirts with large black wrap around aprons with the restaurant name embroidered in white into the corner. All were local Chinese with the exception of one convivial red haired woman, who appeared to be keeping 'front of house' and greeting everyone upon their arrival with air kisses, hand shakes, and lots of 'good to see you again" as people entered. Ryan wondered fleetingly if she was the owner.

Just past the entrance, Ryan could see out onto the busy road and into the restaurants on the opposite side of the street. People were walking past quickly and determined, heads down, unaware to the social world surrounding them. Perhaps they were heading home after a long day in the office, or maybe just starting their work. Clusters of people were standing outside on the pavement holding their drinks and smoking. Post-work drinks, he thought. If he looked hard enough he'd probably recognize some people from the bank.

Ryan returned his observations back to the inside of the restaurant. He noticed two men on his left having dinner. The man closest to Ryan was western, with thick blond hair and wore a well-cut suit; he was fixated on what the man sitting opposite him was saying. The man that he was listening to looked Indian. Ryan thought. His complexion was a rich dark olive, his hair thick and black. He was leaning back casually in his chair with one leg crossed over the other at the ankles. He was wearing a black full-length wool coat over a pinstripe suit, which Ryan supposed was more for a look that he must have been trying to achieve rather than for the current temperature. Unable to hear their conversation, Ryan quickly lost interest and looked around again. Other tables held larger groups of friends and colleagues, people were laughing, talking over one another and having a great time.

One table caught Ryan's attention. Situated close to the entrance was a table with just one occupant. Ryan continued to study the man sitting there quietly. He was smartly dressed and sat looking out of the window with an open book in his hand. He wasn't reading. He looked distracted, or in deep thought. He had smooth porcelain-like skin, with the ethereal light of the restaurant highlighting his high cheekbones and sinking almond shaped eyes. His demeanor was one of a man on edge, waiting for someone or something to happen. With the single place setting, it was easy for Ryan to assume that he was alone. After watching him for a few minutes Ryan noticed that his attention was suddenly drawn to the entrance.

Ryan followed his gaze to see Lily walk in. He watched her scan the restaurant, and then finally rest her eyes on him. She smiled and waved and rolled her eyes mouthing 'sorry'.

Ryan grinned back. Suddenly everything else in the restaurant evaporated. As usual Lily looked stunning. Effortlessly chic in a simple ivory silk tunic shirt and black slim fitting pants and heels. Her long, black glossy hair tumbled onto her shoulders.

As she worked her way between the tables Ryan couldn't help but noticed that she was receiving admiring glances from every table that she walked past. It made him feel very proud that she was with him and not at all troubled that she was late.

She slid into the chair opposite Ryan, slightly breathless her mouth pouting naturally.

'Would you like a drink Miss'? A stealth waiter was already standing next to their table armed with a wine list.

"Thank you", she nodded to Ryan's almost empty glass, "I'll have the same, I'm sure it's very good."

Ryan smiled, and turned to the waiter, "I'll also have one more glass. Thanks."

The waiter thanked them and noiselessly withdrew from the table leaving them alone.

Taking Lily by surprise, Ryan unexpectedly stood up, his chair scraping the wooden floor loudly as he did so, causing a few diners close by to look up to find the source of the noise. He leaned over the table and roughly planted a kiss straight onto Lily's lips. Ryan promptly sat back down in his chair, grinning at Lily's stunned expression and felt suddenly very pleased with himself.

"Sorry", he said in a whisper. 'You just looked perfect and your lips…well, I didn't want to miss the opportunity'.

Lily shuffled uncomfortably in her seat for a moment, glancing around her at the other tables, her eyes darting back and forth for a moment to see if anyone had seen the display of affection. She pulled a loose strand of hair from her forehead sweeping it deftly behind her ear.

Composing herself, she finally flashed Ryan one of her best smiles.

"Hopefully there will be more opportunity for that later', she whispered back.

Ryan smiled to himself, he loved that she was a little sassy. But he also loved that he had caught her off-guard and was sure that she had blushed slightly.

The waiter promptly returned with their wine, and they took a silent sip, watching each other across the top of their glasses.

Finally Ryan spoke.

'So, this is date number two, officially." He said, his mouth curling up into a smile.

"And I still don't know that much about you yet"

"OK" Lily countered, "ask me anything, whatever burning questions you have, now's your chance." She sat back with an amused look on her face and crossed her arms in anticipation.

"OK, fine, let's do the boring stuff first"

"Where did you grow up?" he asked.

"That's easy… Hong Kong",

"OK, can you expand on that, did you go to school here, overseas…you know."

"OK, I was born here and completed my primary & secondary education in Hong Kong, then my parents decided that I needed to get a more rounded life-education, and as I'd done well, I was shipped off to the States for my University career. I'm a bit of a tech nerd so managed to get a place at

MIT."

"Wow, impressive," Ryan said, genuinely impressed. "So you are both beautiful AND smart." He teased her, exaggerating the 'and'.

"What captured your attention at M.I.T, what was your major, or whatever they call it in the States."

"Well I decided to do Electrical Engineering and Computer Science, and I loved it. I ended up doing quite well, so my family backed me and I set up my own Company in the US and earlier this year set up a small Hong Kong company, just to test the water. That's why I'm back here, but I travel back and forth quite a bit." Lily took a break to take a sip of her wine.

"Umm, this is nice," she said referring to the wine and taking another sip.

"What does your company do?" Ryan continued with his stream of questions.

"This is where I may lose you", she said with a rueful smile.

"Try me," Ryan countered, "I can be a bit of a tech nerd myself sometimes."

"I set up an IP Video Technology Company. We saw a need for something to replace CCTV cameras and had the know-how to develop digital versions, which incorporate features that analog cameras are unable compete with. Things like enabling the camera to pan and zoom, audio surveillance that can be used later for voice recognition, motion detectors, alarm integration…I could go on, but I think you'd fall into a deep sleep."

"No, no, this is actually bizarre. You know what I do right? " Ryan asked a little excited.

Lily shook her head, "well I know you work at the bank, but just assumed that you did the same as Rob". She said shrugging her shoulders innocently.

"No, no, I'm a security consultant, I work for a company called RSG in the UK, and they transferred be out here six months ago to work for the Asia World Bank."

"What's the name of your company, I probably know it." Ryan laughed at the coincidence of it all.

"You will know it, we won the contract for upgrading your CCTV camera's, this is totally weird," Lily exclaimed.

"IP Holdings?" Ryan interjected, and Lily nodded "Oh my god, that is weird. I work with some of your colleagues and I've been managing and advising on the new camera installation."

"How come I've never had the opportunity to deal with *you*?" Ryan said, pulling his face into a frown with mock disappointment.

"Luckily, I don't have to do the day to day. I help negotiate some of the contracts, but I generally let my right hand man handle all of the accounts, it frees me up to work on other projects."

"Wow, OK. Let me think, what else can I ask you?" Ryan said playfully.

"I know," he continued, "Tell me how you met Rob."

Lily smiled a big smile at the question.

'I've known Rob for a long time now. We met in Boston whilst I was studying. He was on a weekend away from New York with some of his friends, and I was out with my University friends." Then, laughing to herself Lily said, "Gosh it's funny now. He tried to hit on one of my girlfriends and failed dismally, but I found him so entertaining that we just got chatting and became firm friends". Lily's face then turned dark. "We lost touch for quite a while, around the time when my parents died'. Lily trailed off, suddenly losing the moment. She smiled ruefully at Ryan. 'Sorry, not a happy time in my life."

Ryan reached across the table and touched Lily's hand. She'd pulled her fingers into a tight fist, and now Ryan was gently smoothing them out one by one.

"It's OK," Ryan said. "I didn't mean to bring up any bad memories".

"They were killed in Hong Kong while I was away studying. A car accident, my Grandmother told me. It was quick, so they didn't suffer. I came back for the funeral, and spent about a month here. Then went back to finish my studies. That was my focus. That's really when Rob and I lost touch." Lily was silent for a moment, trying to shake the sad feelings that were welling up inside her. She hadn't expected it. It still rolled over her like a wave, crashing against her and pulling her under until she almost couldn't breathe.

Lily leaned forward and picked up her wine glass. She took a full slug of wine, and as she swallowed, she forced the lump in her throat down along with the liquid.

Feeling as though the worst was over, Lily tried to get the conversation back on track.

"Rob isn't one for taking no for an answer, so he managed to track me down. Then shortly afterwards he transferred to Hong Kong. We lost touch again until I came back a few months ago, and then he introduced me to you…and….', she trailed off seductively, slowly removing her hand from his and sliding it back onto her lap.

'And?' Ryan responded with amusement, relieved that the sadness appeared to be gone now.

"Well, let's just say, the rest is history", she finished.

The man that Ryan had earlier observed sat at the restaurant entrance watching the couple intently. He was feeling irritated and impatient. He had better things to do than sit here.

He had been monitoring Harper for three days now. Studying his routine, his friends and his habits.

He watched Harper and Lillian together at the table. Their body language was obvious. Harper had fallen more quickly than he had anticipated. Or maybe it was just how Western men were with Chinese girls. No respect, only thinking of one thing.

He looked at Lillian with contempt. She was the end result of good Chinese breeding mixed with a filthy American upbringing. He hated everything about her and what she represented. He still hoped that soon there would be an opportunity to remove her from the society. It had been so easy to get rid of her parents, he mused. It would be as easy to get rid of her, when the time came. Having Lillian in between him and Guan Yin made him uncomfortable. He was ready to take the lead as soon as Guan Yin could no longer continue, or until she was no longer around, not Lillian. She was not ready to take the lead. She would never be ready. When he looked at her, all he saw was a young, impulsive woman, not a leader. The only thing that she had was the same blood as Guan Yin, nothing else. A Master only by descent, that was all.

He had a vision. He would embrace the triad society and its entire heritage. He would be a good leader. He would make it his sole duty to re-instill the rules to everyone and they would respect him for it. Guan Yin was slipping. She was old and weak and let the members run themselves. They didn't respect her anymore. They respected *him*. They listened to *him* and followed *his* orders. He would never allow it to happen.

Two hours later he had left without eating, leaving just his empty tea cup and scrunched up napkin on the table.

Lily and Ryan were still so engrossed in their conversation that it was only when the waiter presented them with the bill that they realized that they were the only diners left in the restaurant.

Without looking at the waiter or taking his eyes off Lily, Ryan pushed his hand into his back trouser pocket and pulled out his wallet to pay.

Chapter 9

Ghost Face sat in the corner of a dingy Dai Pai Dong café nestled down a narrow side street, calmly drinking Chinese tea and waiting for his guest to arrive. He was wearing the same black suit as the previous day. The only difference to his attire was his black tie. It was missing. He'd forgotten to put it on in his haste to get out of his apartment on time. It was unusual for him and he reprimanded himself for it.

He felt tired today. He hadn't slept much, and had spent many hours the night before pacing up and down his apartment until he couldn't stand it any longer. The pent up excitement of what lay ahead was almost bursting out of his body. Images flashed and danced in front of his eyes as he remembered the previous encounter. He wondered if the chill that he suddenly felt running through the entirety of his body was from the cool air conditioning in his apartment or from the adrenaline that was starting to course through his veins.

Thumbing through the local newspaper he'd quickly found the Sex101 ad that he was searching for. There were hundreds of women offering their services, that he was almost spoilt for choice. Ghost Face hurried down the page, scanning the brief descriptions and paused over one particular ad. There was a tiny thumbnail image in grainy print of a young looking woman. Her name was Ling Ling. She had a tiny figure quoting 34B-23-34 and a height of 5'4". She offered full services and described herself as a *smooth skinned phoenix, ready to fly*. Her working hours were listed as 12:00 noon until 02:00am. Ghost Face dialed the number and waited impatiently for it to be answered. Finally Ling Ling picked up the call and spoke in a soft seductive voice. "Ling Ling, how may I help you?"

It was one step closer for Ghost Face and he allowed a thin smile to escape across his mouth as he spoke. "I need to see you now." He stated.

Well practiced in the art of closing a deal and used to all kinds of callers, Ling Ling immediately fell into her normal sales patter that she used on all first time clients. "The full service is $1'600 Hong Kong Dollars, which you pay in cash before we begin. I can offer other services later, like massage and reflexology if you like. Is the price OK with you?"

Ghost Face breathed deeply into the receiver trying to control the eagerness that was filling his body. "The price is fine, I'm sure you will be worth every cent." He prolonged the 'every' making Ling Ling shiver on her end of the phone.

"Where do you live?" He almost whispered the last question.

Ling Ling read out the address to Ghost Face as he mentally stored it in his head. Without saying another word, he switched off his phone picked up his wallet, and walked out of his apartment.

Across the City in a run down area of Sham Shui Po district, Ling Ling started to prepare her room. She'd been doing this now for two years on and off and was used to strange and weird men calling her for appointments throughout her day. This call had been no different. She'd had a quiet day and was glad for the last minute appointment. It was late now, so she suspected that he would be her last one for the night.

Ling Ling walked through the basic one bedroom apartment plumping cushions and straightening curtains. She lit another incense stick in her bathroom, and topped up the water in the t-lite burner that she had placed in her kitchenette stove. She loved the smell of frangipanis' and had been delighted when her sister had given her the tiny jar of oil. Now the smell was working it's way through to the bedroom and Ling Ling breathed it in deeply. She lowered the lighting, switching off all the main lights and just keeping her side lamp on. She'd thrown a red silk scarf over the white plastic lampshade to give the room an exotic feel. She'd seen this in a magazine and thought that it improved the atmosphere. She gave the room one last glance, and satisfied with how it looked she went to the bathroom to prepare herself. Ling Ling's working attire consisted of black lacy lingerie, normally a bra and tiny panties and she always wore a silk patterned kimono over the top when greeting her client. She had her hair twisted and secured with a single long pin, so that she could shake her thick long mane of hair out in a hurry if she needed to. She checked her face in the mirror and noted that still had enough mascara on. She expertly touched up her base and lips and added a tiny drop of the frangipani oil to her wrists and the nape of her neck. She was ready. The smell of the fragrance always reminded her of her sister. Only the day before she had dropped by to chat. She had sat Ling Ling down and warned her about the recent one-women brothel slayings, telling her that she was worried about her. She'd begged Ling Ling to re-think her career and had so many suggestions of what she could do, all of which Ling Ling dismissed. She was street smart. She knew how to handle herself, and had told her sister as much. She didn't need to be taken care of. They hugged, and then her sister left, promising to drop by in a few days.

Twenty minutes had gone by since Ghost Face had called the girl. Now he found himself in a run down area of Sham Shui Po, bordering the old fabric markets and wet markets. It was deserted with the just the occasional taxi or pedestrian passing by. The address that he had memorized was leading him to a small low-rise apartment block. He walked passed shuttered entrances scanning the numbers until he found the one that he wanted. 78. He looked around and slipped unnoticed into the building entrance and walked down a narrow hallway before finding the stairs. The narrow winding staircase was dimly lit, but he took the steps two at a time and quickly made his way up to the 5th floor. The landing was dark and poorly lit except for a single yellow light bulb above the doorway. To the right of the door was the number; 5B etched into a metal plate and an intricate scroll design of what Ghost Face could only assume was a phoenix. He straightened out his clothes smoothing down his jacket and trousers, and ran his fingers through his hair smoothing it back into place, then he stepped forwards into the yellow light and gently knocked on the door.

Ling Ling answered at the first knock and inspected her visitor through the gap in the door leaving the security chain across. Ghost Face forced one of his thin-lipped smiles showing his yellowing teeth. Ling Ling nodded politely and quickly closed the door to release the security chain then she opened it wide enough for him to enter. He stepped over the threshold in one stride and Ling Ling silently closed the door behind him, slipping the chain across as she did so, so that they wouldn't have any surprise disturbances by her neighbours or the Police.

Ghost Face immediately slipped off his shoes at the door and turned to face her.

Ling Ling gave Ghost Face her well practiced respectful look and gently reminded him of the $1'600 dollars up front in her most apologetic voice. She didn't like the business side of things and was always relieved when a client handed over the money so that she could concentrate on the job at hand.

Ghost Face looked around the shabby dimly lit room. It was a tiny apartment, maybe only 300 square feet he estimated. She had a double bed situated under the only window in the room with an oriental silk printed quilt draped over the top piled up with cushions. A dark wooden Chinese-style side table with a small lamp in the centre sat next to the bed, covered with a red silk cloth, which he thought looked cheap. Heavy old grey curtains hung precariously above the tiny window. He noticed that the bathroom was to the left and a small kitchenette to the right. Ghost Face focused his attention back to his prize. He looked at her more closely. She couldn't be a day over eighteen. Her hair was long and piled up high onto her head in an attempt to make her look older. She had make-up on, probably freshly applied, knowing that he was coming. She wore a cheap silky kimono style dressing gown with wide sleeves, depicting oriental cranes and flowers covering her small frame. She had tried far too hard, but she was pretty. He couldn't tell what her body was like yet, but it didn't matter to him now, she would do perfectly.

Ghost Face didn't speak. He put his hand into his pocket and pulled out the $1'600 dollars in bills and pushed them into her outstretched hand. He sensed her relax a little as she turned and quickly went over to her bedside table, opened up the front drawer and slid the money safely inside. She then turned back to Ghost Face and with a nervous smile, undid the waist tie holding her kimono together revealing her lacy underwear, hoping that her client would approve.

Ling Ling felt a little unnerved at his silence. He wasn't a good-looking man, she thought. So pale and there was something about his demeanor that was unsettling to her. She hoped upon hope that he wouldn't be too rough and that it would be over quickly. She'd had her fair share of assholes to deal with and didn't feel like a fight tonight.

Taking her by surprise Ghost Face took a sudden step towards her and gently pushed her backwards toward the bed, she stumbled slightly, but obliged him and straightening herself up she took another step back herself. He leaned forward and tugged on the kimono's wide sleeve causing it slip off her shoulders altogether and watched with satisfaction as it fell into a silky pile at her feet. He pulled the pin out of her hair and let it fall onto her shoulders and down her back. Ling Ling suddenly felt exposed and a little awkward, she hadn't experienced this silence before. She pushed her sister's warnings to the back of her mind, shaking them off as ridiculous, and tried to give him her best smile. She dropped her hands modestly to the side and waited for him to take the lead. It was clear to her that this client wanted to feel in control.

After a few moments of just standing, Ling Ling broke the silence. "What do you want me to call you?" She asked.

Ghost Face was serious now. His breathing had increased as he took in the view of her body. Her ad had stated that she was smooth skinned, and she certainly was.

Ignoring Ling Ling's question, Ghost Face hungrily pulled her closely to him forcing her small body against his strong frame. With one hand he held her wrist tight behind her back squeezing hard so that she couldn't move, and with the other grabbed clumsily at her bra strap pulling it down as far as he could until her firm left breast bobbed out of the lace.

"That…that hurts a little", Ling Ling managed to say, trying to keep the anxiety out of her voice.

Ghost Face leaned in close to her face squashing his cheek up against hers. He whispered close to her ear, gripping her wrist even more tightly.

"Good."

Fear seized Ling Ling as she wriggled her wrist to try and free herself from his tight grip. With her other hand she pushed against his upper body as hard as she could, but the attempt was futile, he was so much stronger than her.

"Stupid, stupid girl", he snarled, starting to enjoy himself. He could feel his erection grow as he pushed his body towards hers until they reached the side of the bed.

Still with his face against her cheek, Ling Ling could hear his breathing quicken. She could feel her own heart was beating faster, and a cold panic began to take hold as she realized that she was in mortal danger. Survival kicked in as she forced herself to focus. *Maybe*, she thought, trying to calm herself, *if I just let him do what he wants to me without fighting, then he'll leave*, she reasoned with herself. She'd had enough rough clients before and had always managed to survive the night.

Any glimmer of hope that she had at that moment diminished immediately.

"You should always double check who you let into your home." Ghost Face rasped the last sentence. Unable to hold back any longer he pushed her down onto the bed with his one free hand as he quickly fumbled with the belt and zip of his pants with the other.

Before Ling Ling could say another word, he had covered her mouth with his hand, and pushed her legs open. Her eyes were wide with horror now as she could feel the pressure of his hand across her nose stopping the flow of air. He pushed down against her, and yanked the delicate lace underwear, ripping the elastic to one side grazing her hip in the process, and pushed himself inside her. He could feel that she was tight. He looked down at his prize. She was gripping onto his wrist with both hands trying to lift his arm away from her nose and mouth desperate for air, but his whole body weight was now against her small frame. He took pleasure from the look of sheer terror on her face; he always did like this part the most. The more she struggled to release herself, the more he pressed down and the harder his erection became. He could feel her gasping and struggling to breathe, her muffled sounds worked well as background noise, complimenting the lighting and shadows. Her grasp became less urgent now and he moved his hand away from her nose and mouth and settled his grip firmly across her throat moving the pressure to her windpipe. Ling Ling could only manage a small gasp. Her mind was in turmoil now as she could feel her lungs screaming for air. She fought unconsciousness as the black spots danced and flickered in front of her eyes, the crushing pain across her neck spiked through her whole body. Now she didn't have the energy to fight. Her body began to submit as the black closed in around her. Her eyes became glassy as she looked up again for the last time at her killer, his face now out of focus and slipping further away. She lay still as he moved in an out of her body. Her knees flopped open wide on either side of her, whilst he continued to move back and forth forcing down on her with as much strength as he could muster. Now he had forgotten her completely, lost in his own fantasy, his eyes closed enjoying himself to the end. He could feel the odd twitch and movement beneath him, but this just heightened his pleasure.

Finally Ghost Face finished, his eyes were closed tightly, his head back. Sweat was dripping off his pale forehead falling onto her semi naked body. His hair flopped across his eyes, no longer the neat, slick back style that he had arrived with. He looked down at the girl beneath him. Her face now softened in death, her long black hair framing her head and shoulders, only her wide eyes gave away the terror that she had endured. He removed his hand from her crushed neck, leaving behind the indents of his fingers and the first signs of the familiar bluish purple bruising. Her arms dropped down to the side of her body.

He calmly made his way to her small bathroom, and turned on the single naked bulb using the pull cord, careful to wipe away any fingerprints from the small plastic end piece. There was just a plain, unframed mirror on the wall over the sink, a toilet and a basic shower. He carefully removed his clothes, folding them one by one, resting them on the toilet seat lid before stepping into the shower. He scrubbed his body in the hot water, ensuring that every last bit of her was cleaned away. Stepping out, he dried himself down with one of her towels and wiped down the shower cubicle behind him. Next he dressed himself, and meticulously wiped down every last surface. He walked out of the bathroom and over to the bed, and looked at Ling Ling. In that short time, deep bruises had formed across her neck, appearing like a scarf. He had enjoyed her very much. He gazed at her for a moment longer, losing himself in his thoughts, then reluctantly continued his clean up. He reached into her bedside drawer to retrieve his $1'600 dollars, careful to wipe down the handle and anything that he touched and put the money back into his pocket. Taking one last look at her body, he switched off the side lamp taking with him the red silk cloth, a small trophy. He walked over to his shoes and slipped them on, using the towel to wipe any footprints that they may have been left behind. He undid the chain and silently let himself out of the apartment taking the towel with him. He swiftly re-traced his steps down the winding staircase and back again onto the main street. Satisfied that no one had seen him exit, Ghost Face crossed the road, and made his way back towards the now silent harbour and to the refuge of his apartment.

Exhausted, Ghost Face had arrived back to his apartment at 4am and managed to sleep fitfully for five hours. At 9am daylight finally stole his sleep. His mind was immediately engaged before he climbed out of bed. The previous evening was now a distant memory, stored away until he needed to draw upon it. Now he had more pressing things to focus on.

The sound of his phone ringing quickly brought Ghost Face back to the present moment. He reached across to his bedside, swiftly scooping up the phone and pressed the answer button. Holding the handset against his ear he simultaneously looked at his wristwatch whilst he listened to the caller. A few moments later, without emotion or acknowledgement, he simply ended the call, stood up and quickly started to dress.

Chapter 10

AUGUST 8: LIGHTS OUT

Ryan sat at his desk unable to concentrate. He had read and re read the same email several times, but he couldn't stand the noise. The renovations at the Bank had been going on for weeks now. Early every morning the contractors would clear out the rubble and rubbish from the previous days work. Then throughout the morning, he would have to endure the scraping and banging. It felt to Ryan like it was his head being pounded, not the walls. It was pulling his concentration far away from his work.

Ryan looked at his calendar and sighed with despair. They had at least another 10 days to go before all of the demolition work would be complete.

Coupled with the distraction of the building work, Ryan's morning had been continually interrupted by his colleagues dropping by to see how he was doing and to find out more details of Friday's shooting incident. Finally, and thankfully John called him into his office rescuing him from the constant flow of people at his desk.

As Ryan entered John's office he was pleased to see him sitting back in his chair relaxed and smiling.

"Ryan, you seem to have a gained a bit of notoriety in this office', he spoke with a broad smile on his face. Ryan simply smiled back, not sure whether it was meant as a jibe against his apparent lack of work or just a friendly comment. He decided to lean towards friendly comment, preferring that to any negativity generated from the event.

"I do have a bit more information for you with regards to Friday, but didn't want to bother you over the weekend, so I thought I'd wait until now. Obviously there's no question that there was a major mess-up with the security cameras that morning. I'm not blaming you Ryan, but of course it's Sod's Law that the only morning that the camera's are not rolling, is the very same morning that someone tries to get in. It is a smudge on our faultless record. But, arguably, he didn't get in, and that's primarily because your guys did what they were supposed to do." He paused.

"So all in all it's a bit of a back handed compliment." He finished, taking a look at Ryan to see his response. Ryan looked subdued and guilt ridden.

"Are you OK? Are you up for being back at work so soon?" John's face suddenly looked concerned, it reminded Ryan of a look his Father gave to him from time to time.

'John, really I'm fine. Really. In fact Rob's been baby-sitting me pretty much all weekend. I'm actually fine. I was a little shaken up on Friday, but OK now." Ryan still wasn't sure if that was true. However, he didn't want John to think that he wasn't man enough to deal with it.

"OK, good. On Friday the Police were all over the Bank. They think the old man could be from the mainland. Working for someone else, but they don't know who yet and definitely not an inside job. Which is always a relief." He smiled a half smile, taking small consolation in that fact.

"The Police think that it was just a bad attempt at a bank robbery." John said, his smile shifting into something more serious.

"You do know it's impossible to break into this bank. With the new camera's and our security measures. Anyone would be a fool to try." He said to himself more than to Ryan.

"Busy day with this Lights Out thing tonight, Bloody protesters got their way." John sighed and looked at his watch, notifying Ryan that he had more important things to be getting on with.

"Thanks John. I have to do a report for RSG in London by end of day, so I'll send you a copy once it's complete." Ryan said.

"Thanks Ryan, I'd be interested to read it".

Ryan stood up and made his way back down the corridor and to his own cluttered and busy desk. As he arrived, his next visitor was already waiting for him.

"Hey buddy" Rob was sitting in Ryan's office chair pushing it around in a circle.

"Just thought I'd check in and see how you are?"

"I'm good. I've just had John asking me the exact same question." Ryan perched himself on the edge of his own desk. Ignoring Ryan, Rob continued his own line of questioning.

"So tell me lover-boy, how's it going with the lovely Lily?" Rob teased.

"You know I don't kiss and tell." Ryan replied. "Suffice to say, she's a biscuit." He gave Rob a wink and a broad smile.

"C'mon man, don't leave me in the dark." Rob said pouting. "I need to know."

Ryan laughed, "don't you have some stocks to trade or something?" Ryan checked his watch.

"I'll leave you to your sordid thoughts whilst I go for a run."

Ryan stood up from the desk and lent down to grab his sports bag next to Rob's feet, as he stood up he pulled on the back of the chair that Rob was sitting in and gave it a hard shove. Leaving Rob spinning in the chair.

'I'll have to prime you with a drink, if I'm going to get any gossip out of you." Rob responded with a laugh. 'I don't give up that easily.' He leaned back with his arms across his chest as the chair slowed to a stop.

"Well, you are persistent, I'll give you that", Ryan said gripping his sports bag and giving Rob one last smile as he headed off down the corridor.

It was 12.30pm. The hottest time of the day for running, but the only chance that Ryan had would have that day. The air felt humid, which made it hard for it to reach Ryan's lungs. He breathed in again, sucking the sticky air through his nose and expanding his chest. It was sweltering, around, 32 degrees. There was no breeze, just the wet heavy atmosphere making the sky appear lower than normal. Ryan breathed in one last time, stretched his arms above his head and slowly stepped into a gentle jog.

Increasing his pace Ryan tried to focus his mind elsewhere. His feet were pounding hard on the pavement; his breathing was loud and heavy. He could immediately feel the heat on the back of his neck, reminding him that he had no sun protection.

Ryan always ran on the same road. Hidden away half way up the mountainside it was a running and walking path. It spanned a total of eight kilometers weaving and snaking around the mountain. Trees hung over sections of the path offering some shade, but the majority of the run was open to the elements. Along the road there were just two exit paths forking off down the left side of the mountain, offering those less fit or willing to take an early exit.

When Ryan ran this path in the mornings he would often see old Chinese men and women doing their early morning exercise. Stretching their bodies as best they could trying to remember old Tai Chi moves that they could no longer do effectively.

Running always made Ryan feel relaxed. He was in his own world here. The running path was close enough to the City to still feel the hustle and bustle. Over-looking the high-rises and the skyline, but far enough up the side of the mountain to block out the drilling, shouting, honking and chattering. It allowed him to lose himself for a short while. Today there was no view. The clouds hung low and sat like hats on top of all the high-rise buildings. Ryan just focused on the path and his breathing.

Lost in his own reverie, Ryan jumped when Detective Lam unexpectedly paced herself next to him.

"Hey, sorry if I startled you", Sarah said, slightly breathless.

Ryan looked at Detective Lam. He was surprised to see her running here, and impressed that she could keep pace with him.

"Hi, no problem, I was in a world of my own" he said embarrassed by his sudden reaction to her arrival.

"It helps me to get out of the office for a while. The renovations are really distracting."

"Oh", Sarah replied simply. "Me too. Running helps me to clear my head and arrange my thoughts. It's a good working process." She glanced sideways at Ryan. He looked uneasy with her running there beside him.

They ran alongside each other for some time in silence, each concentrating on their own thoughts.

Ryan spoke first.

"Any closer to finding out who the dead guy is?"

Sarah knew that they weren't, but didn't necessarily want him to know that they had no new leads yet.

"Yes, we are making headway, it may be a while before we can announce or confirm anything." She said slightly breathless using her professional police response rather than the truth.

'Oh" Ryan replied, not knowing what else to say.

He started to feel a bit awkward running alongside a Police Detective. Had she followed him here? He started to wonder if this was just a coincidence.

"So, I guess you'll just let me know if you need me for anything else?"

Sarah picked up the hint from Ryan. This wasn't her usual style, bumping into a witness on a social level, however incidental.

"Yes of course." She said. "Enjoy your run, I need to start heading back."

Sarah swiftly turned around and stepped up her running pace, leaving Ryan running in the opposite direction bemused by their encounter.

Before Ryan had a chance to respond she had disappeared around the side of the mountain.

Sarah felt irritated as she ran back toward her apartment. She was frustrated that she couldn't close the bank case. The Chief was still getting pressure from the top, so likewise he was re-directing his frustration down to her and her team. As for Harper, there was something about his involvement that made her feel unsettled; she couldn't put her finger on it. She just had a feeling that things were not as they seemed with him. Or maybe she was just imagining it. She chided herself for letting her thoughts run wild. Facts. That's what she needed, facts and leads, of which she had precious little of either.

Ryan finished his run, but didn't feel any better for it. Hoping that the run would free up his mind from the noise at the Bank, all he had managed to achieve was to fill his head with thoughts of the dead Chinese man. Flash backs of his pale waxy skin, the soaked overalls, wet with blood, the coffee cup slowly rolling across the floor, spilling the brown liquid content onto the white marble. He couldn't shake it. He wondered if it was like this for everyone who had ever seen a dead body. Constantly appearing at inappropriate and unwelcome moments.

Ryan stood under the hot shower in the staff changing rooms for a few minutes. Finally thoughts of the old man began to wash away and were replaced by thoughts of his afternoon ahead. Suddenly his head was filled with deadlines and reports pleased that he had something that would keep him busy for the rest of the day.

He grabbed his towel and dried himself down, then pulled out his clothes and sports bag from the locker.

Once dressed, Ryan made his way back to his desk and listened to the scraping and banging of the renovations.

Chapter 11

AUGUST 8: 1:00pm

Officer Chow was sitting at his desk carefully going over the case files that Lam had placed on his desk before lunch. He was supposed to go through every one in fine detail to see whether they had missed anything, any detail, no matter how small. He had read and re read the files, but there was nothing. He could sense that she was under pressure. She was generally very non-communicative at the best of times, but when she was under pressure from the Chief, she became snappy and irritable and it was normally down to him to bear the full brunt of it. Finally, to his relief, she had gone for a run to clear her head and would only come back to the station later in the day.

So far he didn't feel that he had been much help to Lam. He was desperate to be given a meaty case, and to be the one to solve it. He wanted to get the pat on the back from the Chief and earn respect from Lam. If he had that chance to prove himself and he did a good job, then Lam would at least ease up on him a bit.

He liked her and respected her, but she was so tough on him. Always barking instructions, or freezing him out whilst she went off to investigate something herself, leaving him deskbound with a list of things to do. It wasn't quite how he had imagined it to be when he'd been assigned to her.

His wife couldn't understand why he put up with it all. She asked him time and again to ask to be moved. But he found himself always defending her, telling his wife that he would learn from the best and then he would gain respect among his colleagues. If he gave in and transferred to another department, then he would lose face. That would be a worse fate for him than to stick it out with Lam.

Before accepting his new post, he had listened to all of the stories about her past, but thought that his colleagues were prone to exaggeration, just trying to make him feel nervous. But now that he had worked with her for six months, he could see that they were all right about her. No one volunteered to be placed with Lam.

A Police Office interrupted Chow's reverie. "Chow, I've got a man at reception asking for Lam. Apparently it's to do with the Bank case, but refusing to talk to anyone but her. Any chance you could try and talk to him? I think he's planning on waiting here indefinitely."

Chow was on his feet and heading to the door before the Officer could even finish his sentence. This was the break that he needed.

When he got to reception a young slim Chinese man, in an ill-fitting suit and tie, sat uncomfortably on a chair. Hunched over with his head in his hands, he looked as though he'd been crying.

Chow walked over the chair and gentled placed his hand on the man's shoulder.

'Excuse me Sir?' he said quietly. 'I believe you are here in reference to the Bank incident?"

The young man looked up at Chow. He looked tired with dark circles under his eyes. Chow estimated that he was around nineteen or twenty years old.

"Where's Inspector Lam', his voice cracked. "I thought I was going to see her?'

'Inspector Lam is out for the rest of the day, but I'm her partner, I'm working on this case with Inspector Lam. I can help you." Chow stated

The young man started to shake his head, 'No, no, it's OK, I – I can wait." He said and placed his hands gently on his knees.

'It's OK' Chow tried again. "I am here to help you."

They both remained silent for a few seconds, the young man considered his options, torn between waiting and getting something off his chest.

Eventually he looked at Chow with a resigned face.

'OK" he said simply. 'But only you, I'll only talk to you."

Chow nodded and spoke to the reception Officer. A few moments later he had ushered the young man through the side door and into the nearest interview room.

Chow left him sitting on a chair in the interview room with his hands resting on the table. He stepped outside the room and went next door to gather himself, trying to retain his excitement.

He observed him through the two-way mirror for a moment. The young man sat very still, his hands resting calmly on the tabletop, but it didn't mask the frightened look in his face. *He is upset about something*, Chow thought, *or someone*. Once Chow had composed himself and mentally prepared his questions, he went back into the room.

The young man shifted uncomfortably in his seat when Chow sat down opposite him.

'You don't have to be nervous here', Chow smiled kindly, trying to put the young man at ease.

Without looking at Chow, the young man started to talk. His voice was quiet, like a whisper and Chow had to lean in to hear what he was saying.

"My name is Stephen Lau." He spoke in a whisper. "I saw Inspector Lam on the news after the Bank shooting." He kept his eyes focused on his hands. He had interlocked his fingers and was twisting and untwisting them as he spoke. Chow prompted him further.

"Yes, that's right. Is there something that you know about the case that you would like to tell me", Chow urged, hoping that his gentle nurturing would give the young man confidence.

'Yes…I" he stuttered, "I think the dead man is my Father." Stephen Lau spoke with his eyes cast down towards the table. Chow thought he could be silently crying, so he lent across the table and reached for a packet of tissues, pushing them across the table towards Lau, Chow pressed on with his questions.

"Why do you think it's your Father? We haven't released a photo or description", Chow stated.

Lau rubbed his forehead with both hands and rubbing his eyes sat up straight to face Chow.

"My Mother had been worried. My father left home just over a week ago, telling her that he was coming to visit me in Hong Kong. I moved here from China to study just over six months ago. My parents had saved up enough for me to attend the Hong Kong University, but I knew that it cost them a lot of money. Then my father lost his job, and my Mother is not well and needs a lot of medical treatment, so I think their money ran out." He sighed sadly before continuing.

"I speak to my Mother every week. When my Mother called me to ask if my Father had arrived safely, it was the first I'd heard of his visit. He never came to see me. So then we became worried. My mother started to ask around some of his friends, and finally one of them admitted that he knew where he had gone." Stephen Lau tugged one of the white tissues from the packet and blew his nose. He screwed the tissue up and pushed it deep into his trouser pocket before continuing.

" My mother found out that when one of his ex-work colleagues heard that my Father was having money trouble, he put him in touch with an acquaintance in Hong Kong who was looking for someone to do some odd jobs. Apparently the pay was OK. So my Father accepted without really asking too many questions. He was so foolish." Stephen Lau, sat silently, not wanting to go on.

"Carry on." Chow said. "In your own time".

"He knew what he was doing was high risk, but he agreed anyway. He told his friend it was simple. All that he had to do was to walk into a bank to test their security system. To see how far into the bank he could get before being stopped by the security guards. It was supposed to be that simple. If he managed his task successfully, they were going to give him RMB50'000.00 for that one easy job." Stephen Lau's shoulders sank. "There's no such thing as easy money." He said to himself.

"He'd told all of this to his friend and asked his opinion. His friend said that he should find something else to do, another way to raise the money. But the offer was too great. He really thought he could just do it and walk away. It's more money than he could earn in half a year." Stephen was crying now. He grabbed another tissue to dab the tears, sniffing them back.

"Of course he never made it out of the bank, and he was never paid the money." Stephen looked up at Chow, his eyes red now from the tears, his nose swollen.

"My mother told me all of this and I didn't believe her. I couldn't believe it. Then I saw it on the news here in Hong Kong, now I know that it's true."

Chow leaned forwards and rested his hand on Stephen's shoulder. It seemed to sag under the weight of his hand.

"I'm sorry Stephen."

"He was not a bad man, just trying to help his family." Stephen said as he slumped back in the hard wooden chair.

Chow sat back considering the young man before him. It was such a sad common theme, one, even in his short career, that he had heard many times over. Struggling mainland families trying to keep things together, lured down a slippery slope hoping for a quick fix, with promises of money, work and opportunity in return for nothing but trouble. *There is always a price to pay*, Chow thought sadly, and he had paid the highest price of all to keep his family afloat and his son at University.

"Your fathers friend, the one that he confided in, does he know any more about the man that asked him to do the job?" Chow asked, hopeful that this would give him the lead that they needed.

"All my Mother told me is that he's from Hong Kong. A gangster. No one knows his real name, but they call him 'Ghost Face'. " Suddenly Stephen looked uncomfortable, as though he had given away too much.

"I shouldn't even be here telling you this." His eyes looked anxious.

"It's just that my Mother wants me to bury my Father. That's why I'm here. My Father is not to be disgraced, he needs a proper burial." Stephen finished.

'It's OK, Stephen, I understand." Chow said, his mind now racing with the lead that he had just been given.

"We will need to hold your Father's body here for a while longer. No one else knows anything about you or your Mother. Just me, you need to trust me that everything will be OK."

"We will need to speak to you again, so for the moment you should remain in Hong Kong and we will need to speak to your Mother and your Father's friend, but we will be discreet. We will make sure that you are safe." Chow looked at Stephen and hoped that he had given the boy some security.

"I'm sorry that your Father became involved in something like this and that it ended this way for you and your family." Chow said sympathetically.

LIGHTS OUT

"I will do my best to find the man responsible".

Stephen nodded silently.

"If you think of anything else, any detail, then just contact me directly. Here's my number." Chow reached into his trouser pocket and pulled out a card with his direct number on it and passed it to Stephen. Then pulled out a pen and a second card.

"I'll need your number and contact details, and I will call you once your Fathers body is ready to be released."

Chow watched Stephen concentrate as he scribbled his name and number on the back of the card and pass it back to Chow.

"Thank you Stephen, you have been a great help. I'll walk you out."

After walking Stephen Lau out of the station Chow sat back down at his desk. He couldn't believe his luck. He had a lead and a name. Chow was sure that he had heard this name before.

He thought that it was triad related, convinced of it. He would have to call in a favour with his friend at the Organised Crime and Triad Bureau. Seconds later Chow was on the phone.

Chow sat tapping the wooden desk impatient for the return call. He'd spoken to his contact and he had agreed to do some digging. Within minutes the phone rang. Chow grabbed the receiver so fast he almost lost his grip. Fumbling with the phone he finally got it to his ear. "Yes, hi, what do you have?" Chow vigorously wrote down everything that he was being told on a scrap of paper.

"Yes, I understand, no direct contact." He listened intently.

"OK, yes. This is huge I owe you one.'

Chow replaced the receiver. This was it. He could feel it. A satisfied grin slowly stretched across his face as he grabbed his bags and made his way out of his office.

Chapter 12

AUGUST 8: 4:00pm

Officer Chow stood at the corner of Tai Lam Street in front of a small alleyway. He was close enough to the café and made sure that he was shielded by the 7 Eleven signage so that he could keep himself tucked far enough away and out of sight. He had a good view through the main café window and also the main doorway. He had been there for over an hour having followed Ghost Face. The Triad Bureau tip-off made it easier than Chow thought possible. He was under strict instructions to observe and not approach Ghost Face under any circumstances.

What he didn't expect to see through the café window was Ryan Harper, the eye witness from the bank with a very good looking young Chinese woman. *This*, he thought excitedly, *was all a bonus*. The three of them were in deep discussion with their heads bent forwards making it impossible for

Chow to take a clear photograph. His mind was racing. He had genuinely believed Harper to be an innocent bystander, but certainly not now. Now Harper was very clearly involved in whatever this was. Minutes later Ghost Face stepped out of the café and looked across the street directly towards where Chow was standing. Chow quickly flattened his body hard against the wall to try and hide himself. *Shit, shit,* he said to himself. *I don't think he saw me.* Chow waited for a few seconds longer and then carefully moved himself forwards to look back toward the Café. Relieved, he saw that Ghost Face had gone. He could still see Harper and the woman inside talking, so now Chow decided to wait and see where they went next. Five minutes after Ghost Face left the café, Harper also left, leaving just the woman still sitting inside. He managed to get a few full face shots of Harper with his camera as he walked down the street on the opposite side, totally oblivious to Chow's presence.

Chow felt the exhilaration bite in his stomach. He knew he was onto something major. He just needed to hang on and wait for the woman now, and then he'd follow her. Once he had a bit more information he'd call it in to Lam. He didn't want her all over it before he had a chance to get something concrete. If his gut feeling was right, and if he managed to pull this off, it would absolutely give him the recognition that he deserved, but he first needed to be clear with his facts.

Lost in his own reverie, Chow almost missed the woman leaving the café. She walked with intention. Her large black leather bag slung over her shoulder. He watched as she slipped on her dark glasses and made her way down the street. Chow bent down and hastily grabbed the handle of his backpack. He was about to follow the woman when he heard a scraping noise in the alleyway behind him. He swiftly turned his head to give a cursory glance. As he did so he saw a flash of silver metal and felt the cool pressure across his neck. He didn't have time to make a noise or respond. The razor-sharp knife moved silently and swiftly in front of him, doing its job effortlessly. Chow slowly slid down the wall sideways until he was squatting on the floor, his forehead gently resting against his knees and his arms loose by his side. His last breath exited his body along with his life's blood as it trickled and weaved down the alleyway following his killer, his camera and his backpack.

Chapter 13

AUGUST 8: 7:30pm

The second hand on the metal analogue wall clock ticked loudly. It was 7:30pm and Ryan had already been sitting in his apartment staring at the clock for thirty minutes. He found the waiting almost unbearable. It was as though time itself had suddenly decided to slow down, teasing him as each second ticked by. He was sure that the sound of the clock was becoming louder and louder with each tiny movement of the hand. It was the only sound that he could now hear.

He shifted his gaze to the palm of his hands. They felt clammy, so he rubbed them on his trousers, all the while listening to the deafening noise of the clock. *Tick tick tick*. His apartment felt eerily quiet. He stood up and started to pace across the floor, stopping in front of the hall mirror. He considered his clothes. Everything was black tonight. From his black rubber soled shoes to his trousers and long sleeved t-shirt. He even wore black socks. *Just like she said*, he thought to himself.

He continued down the hallway to his bathroom and turned on the cold water tap, cupping his hands underneath, he let the water slowly fill them up, then he splashed the cold water across his face. The unexpected coolness of the water forced him to take in a sudden short breath, which immediately sharpened his mind. He was grateful for the change in temperature and welcomed the feeling as his skin prickled. He lifted his head and looked into the mirror considering the reflection before him.

The lighting was bright and harsh, highlighting the purple rings that were visibly forming under his eyes. Ryan could feel his empty stomach churning and swirling, partly from nerves, and partly from hunger. If he ate something now, for sure he would be bringing it up again in no time, so he tried to put the thought to the back of his mind.

Turning off the tap, Ryan straightened up and dried his hands slowly and thoroughly, taking time over each finger and palm until he was sure there was no moisture left. He careful replaced the towel on its hook and looked again at his wristwatch. It was 7:35pm. Ryan's stomach somersaulted again, lurching every time his thoughts drifted back to earlier that day. He replayed the scene once again in his head.

AUGUST 8: 3:30pm

'So what do you think we should do?' Ryan asked, his voice low.

Lily sighed heavily and shook her head. She cast her eyes down to her cold coffee and played absentmindedly with the teaspoon, stirring the brown liquid around and around in the cup as though she would find an answer inside if she stirred for long enough.

They had been sitting in the café for over an hour now talking.

Ryan had told her what he knew so far. Rob had just seemed to disappear from work, followed by the terrifying phone call. He'd tried calling Rob's cell phone several times. It just went straight to voice mail. Ryan's gut instinct was screaming at him, but at that point he just didn't know which way to turn and whom he should go to. Lily had been his obvious choice to call.

It had been made very clear to him by the caller that he was not to discuss anything with the Police. But Lily knew Rob better than anyone. She was his safe option, and she was willing to be there with him.

Lily suddenly tapped Ryan's arm causing him to look at her. Her face had stiffened a little and she was staring straight ahead at the café entrance.

A pale faced Chinese man walked slowly towards them. He was wearing a black suit, and black tie. Ryan looked at the man with vague recollection. He wracked his brains trying to place him. Where had he seen him before?

He had almost reached their table, when Ryan suddenly remembered. He had been sitting at the restaurant window when he and Lily had been on their dinner date. He now recalled the pale face, sitting alone with just one table setting. A stab of fear gripped Ryan as he realized that it was not a coincidence that he had been there that night. He looked across at Lily, his face now filled with concern as he tried to work everything out in his head.

Lily gave the man a silent nod of recognition, and Ryan watched as he took a chair from the next table and positioned himself facing them both across the small wooden coffee table.

Ryan kept his eyes on Lily, the knots in his stomach twisting uncontrollably, telling him that something was terribly wrong. No one spoke. Ryan looked between Lily and the new arrival and finally broke the awkward silence between them.

"Lily, what's going on?" Ryan murmured.

The Chinese man spoke before Lily could respond.

"We have spoken before Mr Harper. I'm sure my voice is familiar to you?"

Ryan heard again the same cool tone that he had listened to earlier that day. It was still as threatening and it chilled Ryan to his core, causing him to shiver involuntarily.

Ryan remained silent, not sure of himself any longer, not sure of anything.

"I'm very pleased that we have finally been able to meet." The Chinese man continued to speak to Ryan as though this was just a social meeting.

Ryan's mind was racing. None of the past few hours had made any sense to him. He couldn't fathom why this was all happening. Why he found himself sitting in a café, with a woman that he thought he was having a relationship with, his closest friend disappearing without trace and sitting opposite a total stranger who was successfully intimidating him. Finally Ryan spoke again, he needed to understand. He needed it all to be explained to him.

"Where is Rob, is he OK?" Ryan was trying to remain calm, but the strain in his voice was audible.

"Your friend is quite well. But it's time that we explained to you why I'm here and why you are here." He said to Ryan. "You have something that I need, and you are going to help to me to get it."

Ryan sat quietly waiting for him to continue.

"Just in case you had any stray thoughts of contacting the Police or the Bank, I've brought this along to show you."

Ryan watched as he slipped his hand into the inside pocket of his jacket and produced a Polaroid picture. He slid it across the table to Ryan.

Ryan looked at the image before him. It took only a second for the reality of what he was looking at sink in. His mouth dried up immediately and his heart began to pump adrenaline through his body.

The grainy Polaroid featured Rob sitting on a metal chair in the middle of an empty well-lit white room. He was wearing his work shirt, no longer white and crisp. It was now crumpled and covered with a mixture of dirt, and what Ryan assumed could only be blood. His trousers and shoes had been removed, leaving him in just his boxer shorts and socks with his legs bare. His feet and ankles were taped with silver duct tape to the chair legs. His hands had been taped to his thighs rendering him helpless. Rob's nose was bleeding heavily and Ryan guessed that it was probably also broken. His lip was swollen to the point of splitting and his left eye was black around the socket, with a cut above the brow. His hair was messy and hung down across his other eye. He was reluctantly looking toward the camera, clear that he had been told to do so under duress.

Ryan's hand shook slightly as he passed the Polaroid back across the table. Alarmed now, he looked at Lily for help.

"Did-did you know about this?" Ryan muttered quietly. He looked into Lily's eyes, hoping that she would be as horrified as he was at the sight of their friend, severely beaten and clearly distressed, that he would see the same fear that now gripped him.

Almost before he had finished saying the words, the truth of what he had hoped he wouldn't have to face collapsed completely when he saw the affirmation in her eyes. She knew. The realization made him feel sick and for the first time, since the pale Chinese man had entered the café, Lily's tight grip on Ryan's arm slackened. For a fleeting moment Ryan thought that she looked almost sad, then she straightened her back and slowly removed her hand altogether from Ryan and answered his question.

"Ryan" she spoke softly and slowly now as she tried to choose her words carefully.

"I knew about Rob. But I didn't know that he would be treated so badly, this was not part of the plan." This comment she flung across the table accusingly, before returning her attention back to Ryan.

"You need to do everything that he tells you to do, and I guarantee that Rob will be released, unharmed, as soon as it's all over. I'm sorry Ryan, but you have no choice at this stage".

For a brief moment Lily's eyes began to moisten and she quickly blinked back the hot angry tears that threatened to spill. She was angry and emotional. Angry that Ghost Face had put her in this position, and that she had allowed her friend to be hurt unnecessarily.

"Save the dramatics", Ryan said harshly. He turned his head toward to café counter. He couldn't bear to look at her. He suddenly felt like such a fool. He took a few deeps breaths and when he spoke again, he was calmer.

"What do you want from me? What do you need me to do?" He managed to get the words out this time without his voice cracking.

Ghost Face's mouth formed a thin smile.

"Good" he almost whispered to Ryan. "You may have just saved your friends life."

"You, Mr Harper, are going to help us to break in to the World Asia Bank".

Ryan blinked once. His mind now trying to process what had just been said.

"W-what", he stumbled quietly over his own words. "What?" incredulous, he repeated himself again a little louder this time. "What!" Then taking them by surprise, he laughed out loud.

His laugh echoed across the café, making people turn and look at the three of them sitting around the table, perhaps enjoying a good story or a joke. But it was no joke. Ryan could see the seriousness in their faces.

"How am I supposed to do that?" He looked first at Lily and then Ghost Face, whose thin-lipped smile had quickly disappeared leaving behind a deadpan glare.

"It's very simple Mr Harper, you have two things that I need". He said, his voice steady and calm with his customary trace of coldness.

"Firstly your hands, or, more precisely, your fingertips, and secondly your security access. "

"Oh" Ryan muttered weakly.

"I'm sure you've heard of the Lights Out Campaign. It's been busy gaining popularity over the last few months. We've been following it closely and helping it along where we can. They have successfully managed to enroll all major buildings and businesses across the City to join their campaign. Your Bank is one of them. And tonight, when the lights of Hong Kong go out at

LIGHTS OUT

8pm and we are all plunged into a City of absolute darkness, we will enter the bank, and we will break into the vault using your security access."

Ghost Face continued, almost breathless now. "If you do everything that we say and we are successful, then we will release your friend alive."

"And if I refuse? Or-or if we fail?" Ryan already knew the answer, but he needed to hear it out loud.

Ghost Face leaned in so close to Ryan that he could smell his warm stale breath, making Ryan recoil slightly in his chair.

"If you refuse Mr Harper, we will first torture you until you give us the access codes, cut off the hand that we require, and then kill your friend. If you prefer it that way."

Ryan was unable to mask his own feelings of despair as he reluctantly agreed to do what he needed to do, to save Rob. His heart was now pumping so hard that he feared that they could hear it beating outside of his body. He knew in that very moment that he had been stripped of any choice. The responsibility of what he was going to have to do, and the thought that he held his friends life in his hands, started to descend heavily upon his shoulders.

He refused to allow himself to wallow too deeply in self-pity and started to consider what lay ahead. Questions now started to pour into his already busy head with a multitude of potential obstacles and concerns.

"Since the attempted breach last week we have tightened security everywhere. Even I can't simply switch everything off whilst you do your thing." He looked at Lily now, trying to fathom her involvement in this.

"Lily, you know this. You installed everything, but now that it's all in, we manage it all ourselves. If I try to mess with the security cameras, sensors and alarms, everything will be recorded. The date, the time, who changed the settings. It's impossible to change without one of the alarms being raised."

Ghost Face spoke now, his face shining with excitement.

"Ah, all good questions Mr Harper." He said. "Your good friend here, Lily, has taken care of everything." Ghost Face moved his gaze to Lily then back to Ryan, enjoying the moment.

Ryan had been well and truly played. He thought back to his first meeting with Lily and tried to dissect it. He remembered that she had shown mild interest in him, but had still been reserved, even a little demure. She certainly hadn't thrown herself at him. It had been Rob that had massaged their relationship, pushed him to call her, thought it was all a great idea. Ryan couldn't believe his luck that she had even been interested in him. Now he knew why. He had been such a fool, so easily deceived. *Poor Rob*. Ryan suddenly thought. This was so much worse for him.

"How could you do this to Rob?" He asked almost in a whisper, all of his energy was now ebbing away.

Lily moved her body so that she was fully facing Ryan. She tried to ignore Ghost Face observing her now.

She rested her left hand gently on Ryan's arm, testing the reaction. He didn't move. He was frozen to his seat.

"I had no choice, it was the only way to convince you to be involved. Rob doesn't know about my connection. He doesn't even know who has taken him and why. It's for the best." She paused. "Ryan, it was always going to be you. You are a faithful friend and you have something that we need. I knew you would help us. I knew you wouldn't let your friend get hurt."

"Don't patronize me", Ryan said, suddenly angry. " This is not a game Lily, you can't play with people like this. This is serious stuff. Stuff that gets you thrown into jail or killed."

"It never was a game Ryan. I am, by choice, involved in this, from start to finish, something that I would never expect you to understand, even if I explained it to you. I'm sorry, but I need you to do this one thing".

Ryan was struggling to stay calm. He wanted to grab her shoulders and shake her, make her see that she was making a huge mistake, that she was putting them all at risk. He wanted to just get up and leave, to go straight to the Police and tell them everything. But he knew that he couldn't do it. He knew that he could never live with himself if Rob was killed at his expense. He suddenly imagined his old life. His boring job, and his boring friends and what he would pay to be back in boring England now. He would never complain again.

Ryan felt a cool distance between them now. No longer the warmth that had been there earlier, or days before when they had been wrapped around each other in his bed. All of that had now dissolved, evaporated the second her true colours had been exposed. He didn't recognise this Woman before him. The calm exterior, the serious face. She was all business now. He heard her talking again as she pulled him away from his troubled thoughts.

"Ryan, the rules are quite simple. Do as we tell you, and when it's over, you can go back to your life as though this never even happened."

Ryan looked from Lily to Ghost Face and back again, incredulous that she actually believed what she was saying.

"And you really, really think that you can get away with this?" He looked at them both eyes wide waiting for their response.

"Yes, we do." Lily said simply.

Ryan slumped back in his chair. He was silent for a moment, trying to reconcile himself. He was about to agree to something so against everything that he believed in, so that he in turn could save his friend.

"OK", he said, now resigned. " What do I need to do?"

"Lily will run through the plan with you now, it won't take long, then you will go back to your apartment and wait there until I come to collect you in a few hours. Your phone, keep it close at hand, if I need to contact you, I will call you." Ghost Face gave Ryan a twisted smile. Ryan wanted to throw up there and then and it took all of his concentration for him to keep the bile down.

"Lily, the details." Ghost Face motioned with his pale hand for Lily to get started. She leaned down to her black Hermes bag sitting on the floor next to her chair and pulled out a brown dossier.

"Now, you need to listen carefully", Lily began as she leaned over the coffee table and closer to Ryan. "We will guide you tonight, but you need to understand exactly what is going to happen." She folded out the file onto the coffee table in front of them.

She sifted through the papers until she found the drawing that she was looking for. Looking down at the paper Ryan scanned the image before him and immediately recognized the plans of the bank's ground floor and vault.

"OK, we only have eight minutes tonight, so we have no time to hang back or pause, every member of this team has a job to do, including you, and every second counts." She looked at him seriously and he nodded back silently, trying to focus on what she was saying.

"As soon as the lights go out across the City, the stopwatch starts which Ghost Face is going to monitor throughout. We will all slip into the entrance and the first hurdle is the door leading towards the vault entrance. Here we will need you to swipe your card to get us all through." Lily traced her finger across the plans indicating to Ryan their direction.

Ryan stopped her before she could continue.

"What about the cameras and sensors? He said that you had everything covered? How can we proceed undetected? He asked Lily.

Lily nodded expecting the question.

"As you know this is my field of expertise. Alongside developing the new IP technology that replaced your CCTV cameras, we also developed software that allows us to manipulate the images seen from a remote location. It's already built in to your system. It's just that you are not aware of it. We cloaked it. The video signal is digitalized, using a special decoder that also contains an onboard web server. This acts as a network device, which allows the images to be viewed through a routed network, but also through a web browser. All this can be done in another location, and it's all completely wireless. We already have all of the footage that we need to send back through the system, which will replace the real footage for exactly eight minutes. As soon as we are done, all of the cameras will be switched back to real time as though nothing ever happened. We can also remotely disable the motion detectors area by area. The security officer on duty will be none the wiser, and it will appear that we were never even there."

Ryan sat motionless for a moment whilst he arranged his thoughts.

"So when the cameras were down a few weeks ago during the attempted break-in, that was on purpose?" Ryan asked looking directly at Lily.

"Yes, it was a trial run that didn't quite go as planned." Lily said dryly, shooting a fleeting glance across the table at Ghost Face.

"So your company is actually a total front? Incredible!" Ryan blinked in disbelief. They had all been fooled. The bank. John McIntyre. Rob and of course himself. All of them had been sucked in by her charms and her clever lies.

"So what is it exactly that you plan to do?" Ryan asked, now curious.

"We plan to steal $20 million USD in $100 dollar bills." Lily stated simply. She looked across at Ghost Face. He was amused, enjoying himself at Ryan's expense.

"Is-is that all?" Ryan asked, surprising them both. "I mean, if you are in the vault and you can pull this off, is that all you think you can get out? Why not more?"

"It's a very good question". Lily said.

"We have a lot of factors against us for this one. We have an absolute eight-minute time frame in which to carry this out. We have four men, people that we have used before that we know and trust. They are professional, discreet and strong, and we are not going to be greedy. Greed is often the thing that catches a person out, or causes a plan to fail. If you get lost in the moment, take just that little bit more than you intended, then you stop following the rules, and you open yourself up to problems."

"Are they just going to carry the money out in bags? Ryan asked. "Casually walk out of the bank's entrance with $20 million dollars. How's that even possible?" he asked.

"How much do you think $1 million USD weighs?" she said, looking at Ryan.

"I have no idea?" He said truthfully.

"It weighs just 10kgs, in $100 dollar bills. It's easy to carry. We know that the bank stacks the notes two ways in the vault. We expect to find them either in stacks of four, measuring just over 1ft high, or they will be sitting in stacks of six, measuring just over 20cm high. The stacks are wrapped in plastic and bound. All of these factors have been included in the total weight calculation. Of course whichever way that we find the stacks, it will still come to a total of 10kgs in weight." Lily paused allowing Ryan to take everything in.

"So we have calculated that we have our four men, and you, to carry the money." She gave Ryan a brief smile.

"Me?" Ryan spluttered, "I thought I was your code and palm guy".

"Well, yes you are, and the extra muscle. It has to be five guys in total to get the value that we need out. You will all carry 40kgs each in duffle bags that have special weight bearing back straps on them." She said.

"We've worked out all the ratio's. The average Chinese or Asian man is around 5ft, 6" tall with an average weight of 70-80 kilos. So based on their weight to height ratio and the theory that everyone can in fact carry 50% of their total body weight, means that if the four Chinese men that we have selected can do it, then so can you. You are taller, and weigh heavier than 80 kilo's, so for sure you can manage it."

Lily continued. "Stealing the money and getting the money out is not a problem. It's getting past all of the security and into the vault, and that's where you come in."

"We have the first door which requires a swipe card, then the second door to the vault entrance, requiring the same key card access but with additional key code, then there's the main vault entrance. This is where we'll need your palm imprint and key code. Once we are inside, then we only require your key code to gain entrance to the gate to the holding room, and once we have that, then our men will do all of the loading." Lily finished.

"You still haven't told me how you plan to get the money out once you have it?" Ryan asked.

"You're right. I haven't." Lily said. "You don't need to know everything at this stage."

"Once we get out, we will be long gone before the bank even realizes that they have been robbed."

"And you think you can achieve this all in eight minutes?" Ryan said, not sure if he could even believe this himself.

"Yes, I know we can." She said, confident in her reply, "We're ready".

Lily took the dossier from the table and closed it, then slipped it back inside her bag.

Ryan was impressed with her confidence and knowledge. She had thought of everything it seemed, but he still doubted that they could pull it off in that timeframe, even if they did manage to get through all of the security, there were still so many things that could go wrong.

Ryan looked across at Ghost Face. He had stopped watching them a while ago, allowing Lily to explain the plan to Ryan without interruption from him. He now sat sideways with his legs crossed, casually looking out of the main window towards the 7 Eleven store across the street.

"So what now?" Ryan said to Lily.

Ghost Face turned himself back towards them.

" You leave after me, in five minutes. When you get back to your apartment go through your wardrobe and pull out anything black. You need to be covered from head to toe. Your shoes need to be soft soled, nothing too noisy on the marble floor. We'll provide the headwear. We will come and collect you when it's time, then you will simply do as we tell you." He said.

Without another word, Ghost Face stood up and walked out of the café without looking back.

Ryan turned to face Lily. Ignoring Ryan, she raised her hand and waved towards one of the waiters. Once she grabbed his attention she made the 'bill' signal with her hand and dug her hand into her bag to find her purse.

"So that's it?" Ryan said, feeling deflated and out of control.

"That's it Ryan." Lily replied simply.

"What do you want me to say Ryan? At the end of the day there are some things that you just have to do. For me, this is one of them." She then threw two crumpled hundred-dollar bills onto the coffee table to cover the drinks.

"You'd better go now", Lily said looking at her watch.

Ryan stood up from his chair, and started towards the door, then turned again to look at Lily.

Before he could say anything, Lily said; "I know you'll do the right thing, that's why I chose you."

With nothing left to say, Ryan turned towards the door. As he stepped into the street, the entire hustle bustle surrounding him disappeared. All that he could think about was the night ahead. He didn't know how he was going to get through this. But he knew he had to. Rob was relying on him, and he had to save his friend. Ryan made the short journey back to his apartment to prepare himself.

Chapter 14

AUGUST 8: 7:40pm

Ryan looked impatiently at his wristwatch. It was 7:40pm. *They had to be here soon*, Ryan thought.

Not able to stay still in one place, he finally switched on his TV and a live news feed promptly came up on the screen.

Ryan watched as the bubbly local female news reporter stood in the central business district surrounded by thousands of people waiting to witness the lights of the city go out. She was commentating on the event, talking to the camera, giving out facts about the Lights Out campaign and the history of some of the buildings that now acted as a dramatic backdrop. The camera panned out so that Ryan had a clear view of the masses. The sheer number of people was astonishing. People stood shoulder-to-shoulder, adults and children squashed together. He could make out the odd Police Officer in the crowd, but it would be impossible for them to monitor everyone tonight.

The camera zoomed in again to the reporter who now had her hand on her earpiece and was pressing it hard against the side of her head, struggling to hear herself think as the sound of thousands of voices and jostling crowds began to get the better of her.

Suddenly the image flicked back live to the news studio and Ryan switched off the TV.

No sooner had the TV been silenced, then Ryan felt the faint buzz of his phone vibrating in his pocket, followed immediately by his familiar ring tone. It suddenly sounded so inappropriate, the happy little tune. He quickly pressed the call button to silence the sound and placed the phone to his ear. Finally Ryan listened to the voice that he had been dreading all evening.

"I'm at your front door and we need to leave now."

Ryan clicked off his phone and made his way to the front door.

This is it, he thought to himself. *I can do this.* He told himself as he shook his limbs, from his hands to his feet like a boxer might do before a fight, in an attempt to give himself some much needed confidence.

Ryan took in a deep breath and opened the door to be confronted with the pale cold face of his fate. His skin looked even more ethereal than it had that afternoon and almost glowed under the hallway light. Ghost Face looked Harper up and down.

"Do you have everything you need?" he asked. Ryan nodded and patted his pants pocket indicating the security pass and raised his hands to show his fingertips in an attempt to lighten the mood. Saying nothing more, Ghost

LIGHTS OUT

Face motioned for Ryan to follow him.

They quickly descended the back stairs to the ground floor and stepped into the quiet car park. It was completely empty, unusually so, with the exception of the black Mercedes with it's engine quietly running. At first Ryan thought that perhaps everyone had gone down to see the lights go out in person, but as Ryan sat back in the leather upholstered seat, and tried to make himself comfortable, he realized what was wrong. As the car pulled away, leaving the building lit up behind them, he looked back to where Mr Wu, the caretaker, normally sat and for the first time since he had lived there, his seat was empty. Fearing the worst, Ryan sat immobile, with only the turmoil in his head to keep him company, as the true realization of what he was involved with finally dawned upon him.

Less than ten minutes later the car stopped two blocks from the World Asia Bank. It was as close as they could get. The streets were packed with thousands of people, all waiting to see Hong Kong plummet into darkness for the first time in history. People were laughing and chatting, children perched high up on their parents' shoulders squealing and pointing, couples arm in arm, waving at the hosts of TV cameras now set up.

Ghost Face walked quickly and with purpose, pushing Ryan slightly ahead of him so that he could keep him close. When they got within twenty meters of the bank entrance, Ghost Face guided Ryan off to one side as they slid unnoticed behind a pillar and waited. People were pushing past them, Ryan felt elbows and shoulders brush past him as they jostled and shoved to find a better place to observe. Ryan started scanning the crowd. He suddenly became aware of several other people wearing dark clothes around him and wondered if they were part of the team. He couldn't see Lily yet, but he knew she'd be here soon. He noticed several uniformed police officers slowly moving around groups of people, occasionally talking on their radios to each other. His thoughts quickly wondered what his chances would be if he now made a run for it. But then as soon as the thought entered his mind, he dismissed it immediately. Images of Rob's beaten face vividly pushed their way into Ryan's head. He wouldn't let him down. *What if it had been him?* Ryan mused. Rob would have done the same for him, of that he was certain.

Appearing out of nowhere Lily gracefully arrived wearing the same head to toe black as he and Ghost Face. She tiptoed in her flat black shoes and lightly kissed Ryan on the cheek, as though in some other life they were still a normal couple. Ryan flinched slightly and Lily looked at him apologetically. "How are you holding up?" She asked.

"I've been better." Ryan stated truthfully.

"Are you sure about this?" He asked one last time, in case by some slim chance they could simply walk away.

She smiled her dazzling smile at Ryan, but this time it was lost on him. Her magic no longer worked. He had been so blinded by her in the beginning, but now it was plain and clear to him. Here he was, standing at the entrance of the Asia World Bank, waiting for the city lights to go out so that he could help these people, whoever they really were, steal $20 million US dollars, so that he could save his friend. His normal life as he knew it was well and truly over.

Ryan leaned in to Lily.

"I need to ask you something." He said.

"Anything." Lily responded.

LIGHTS OUT

"Are you involved with the Triads?"

Lily smiled a crooked half smile to Ryan.

"Sort of." She replied. "One day I'll explain it all to you. For now, let's just get this done."

Ghost Face moved in closer to Ryan and Lily and tapped the glass face of his watch with his finger. "It's almost time", he said. The three of them, led by Ghost Face began to weave themselves between the throngs of excited people toward the banks entrance.

Lily paused to speak to Ryan. "As soon as the lights go out, I'm giving you a mask to wear. Put it on straight away and follow me, stay close". She said turning back and working her way through the last few onlookers.

They arrived at the entrance, still surrounded by people. Ryan looked around him, his eyes still scanning the crowds for policemen or security guards to make sure that they hadn't been noticed. It was unlikely, he concluded. There were too many people for them to watch. Ryan looked at Lily's all-black attire and noticed that she was wearing black cotton gloves. He leaned in and tapped her on the shoulder. "Where are my gloves?" he whispered into her ear.

"Oh", Lily smiled nervously. "You noticed that. Look I'm sorry Ryan; it's part of the plan. We can't afford to leave any fingerprints behind. But for you, well, we need your fingerprints to get us through to the vault. It's unavoidable. Which means that you can't wear gloves." Lily said, her tone quite matter-of fact.

Ryan's pulse was now racing. He could feel the thud of his heart and thought that at that moment it may actually burst out of his chest. He hissed in to Lily's ear; "This was NOT part of the plan. I'm already doing everything you have asked. When this is over everything will point directly toward me!" Before Ryan could wait for an answer from Lily, he suddenly felt a hand push him in the small of his back. He turned to see Ghost Face behind him, pushing him gently, but with enough force to direct him closer to the bank entrance.

"Enough talking" Ghost Face told them both, "We are counting down, fifty seconds", He spoke into an ear-piece that Ryan had only just noticed. "Everyone get into position. Harper, you stay with me." Ghost Face said.

Ryan shook his head to try to remain focused on the job at hand, he tried to push all other thoughts and questions to the back of his mind, but the panic still managed to seep in, as the realization of what they were about to attempt finally dawned on him. A cold shiver ran through him as he looked at the main door of the bank. *This is it*, he thought.

Everyone else surrounding Ryan was now a blur, he just looked at Lily and waited.

"Thirty seconds" Ghost Face said quietly so that no one next to him could hear him talking.

"Twenty seconds", he spoke again to the invisible team.

Lily spoke into her mobile phone to another invisible person. "Ready to switch the camera's in ten, nine, eight….", she continued the count down, all the time looking for a signal from Ghost Face.

"Five, four, three, two, now." She flicked off her phone immediately and zipped it securely in her top pocket.

People around them started to become noisier and more excited, slight pushing and movement started around them as people strained to see the big screens around them, or to get a better view of the buildings. In the distance Ryan could still just make out the bubbly Chinese news presenter getting ready for the big count-down, the cameraman was poised waiting to film the event. Everyone now gazed up at Hong Kong's famous city lights.

Then suddenly the countdown began. People all around Ryan were chanting as loud as they could, the noise was deafening; "Ten, nine, eight, seven ". Ryan felt Ghost Face push him once again in the small of the back and guided him swiftly through the remainder of the crowds until they were almost at the door. He could see the security guard at the entrance, also transfixed and chanting like everyone else.

"Four, three, two, one. "

Ryan blocked out the sounds around him and counted the final few seconds in his head. He was as ready as he would ever be.

Suddenly Hong Kong sank into total darkness, every single light was off, every street light, ceiling light, wall light, signage, building light, all gone.

Pulling on the balaclava that Lily had given him, it took Ryan a few seconds for his eyes to adjust to the pitch dark. To his left he noticed four other people slip in silently behind him. The invisible team that Ghost Face had been talking to, Ryan assumed.

Leaving behind the roar of the cheering crowds, seven people dressed from head to toe in black, walked inside the Bank's public entrance moving past the guard unnoticed. Everyone blended into the black background. Only the green fluorescent emergency exit signs could be seen flickering above doorways, letting off a dull green glow around them.

Quickly everyone moved towards the first locked entrance. Ghost Face guided Ryan to the door. Ryan had his card already at hand and he quickly swiped his card through in silence. Immediately the door swung opened, giving them access to the next area. The door closed behind with a small click as the door locked itself again.

With Ryan now at the front, they made their way to the next door, which would lead them to the main vault entrance. Ryan could hear his breathing inside the balaclava, it sounded loud to him. He began to feel trapped inside the fabric and was desperate to pull it off. It was making his face hot with his own rapid breathing. He was sure that everyone else could hear him. He took a few slow breaths and gathered himself. They'd got this far.

They arrived at the second door. This time it required both the card and a code. Ryan punched in the familiar code on to the keypad and swiped his card through again. A tiny green light flashed and the door sounded with a click, telling them that it was open. All seven people filtered through and the door closed silently behind them.

Ghost Face tapped his watch and motioned with his hand that they had only seven minutes left. They all nodded in unison, no one making a sound. Now they were in a much larger space with a modern vaulted ceiling that rose impressively high above their heads. The dull green glow from the exit signs, mixed with the blackness made it feel eerie to Ryan, like visiting a church in the middle of the night.

Directly ahead of them was the entrance to the actual vault. Ryan had been here so many times. He knew that once this door was open that his job was almost done, and then the invisible team would start their work. Ryan quickly walked to the security pad next to the vault entrance. This time the access was more complicated. It involved Ryan punching in a code onto the

LIGHTS OUT

unlit flat pad that bore no numbers, the sequence and position was all from memory, followed by the final hand scan, all on the same blank pad. This, Ryan knew, would all be logged into the main security network. There would be no doubt, when John McIntyre would later investigate the security breech, that he would find that it was Ryan Harper that had entered the Bank's secure vault on this night. Ryan tried not to think about it as he quickly and quietly did his part. Once the access was confirmed he simply stood back a waited. A second later they all heard the giant steel reinforced vault door clunk and click as it slowly opened before them. Once the vault door was fully open, they were greeted by a narrow escalator that dropped down deep into the main belly of the bank. As soon as Ryan placed his foot on the first metal step, the escalator started to move. Soon all seven of them had stepped onto the escalator and following Ryan's lead, walked swiftly to the bottom.

At the foot of the escalator they were greeted by two, closed, metal gates. The right gate led them into a safety deposit room, and the left, straight into where the money, bonds and gold bullion lay.

For the last time that night, Ryan punched in a six-digit number on the left hand gate keypad, and the gate swung open effortlessly, welcoming them in.

Ghost Face nodded at the four men and held up 1 finger, indicating that they had one minute. They nodded and set to work. Lily pulled Ryan back out of the way, and they watched in silence as the men set to work.

Ryan watched in amazement at the speed of which the men were moving around. It was clear that they had trained for this. Each man had a duty and they worked together as a team, quickly, silently and without falter. One man swiftly removed a black backpack and pulled out five oversize duffle bags, the zips were already open and he lay them carefully out on the floor, opening the mouth of the bags whilst the other three men were lifting and carrying the plastic wrapped stacks of notes to and from the bags. As each bag became full, the zip was closed and each bag was swiftly carried out of the vault and to the bottom of the escalator.

In less than one minute all five duffle bags were full and ready. Ghost Face nodded again and motioned with his fingers that they had just four minutes remaining. Each man helped the other to load the duffle bags onto their backs. The final bag went onto Ryan's back. The sudden weight of the bag took Ryan by surprise and he had to steady himself to keep his balance forwards. One of the men made an "OK" sign with his hand, and Ryan nodded and replied with another 'OK'. Lily guided Ryan towards the escalator and they started to ascend. They were slower this time. They had to rely on the escalators speed to get them to the top. Behind them Ghost Face closed the vault gate and quickly caught them up, taking two steps at a time until he was directly behind his men.

Once they reached the top, Ryan turned and closed the vault entrance, every time relieved that an alarm didn't sound as he heard the click of the door.

Ryan began to relax. He knew that they only had two more doors and they would be outside, and it would be over. He reminded himself why he was doing this, and kept the image of Rob's bloodied face clear in his mind.

But instead of retracing their steps to the next door, Ghost Face and the invisible team suddenly turned left towards the service lift. Confused, Ryan followed, the dead weight on his back was beginning to pull down hard on his shoulders and dig in to his skin. He could feel sweat trickling down his back and beading across his forehead. He looked across at Lily, hoping that she could read the confusion in his eyes. She stood calmly like the others as they waited for the lift to arrive.

Finally the lift door opened and they all stepped inside. One of the men pressed the button for the fourth floor and the elevator doors closed. The lift heaved and whined as it ascended through the bank, sending echoes throughout the empty building. Eventually the lift creaked to a stop and the doors opened. They all stepped out onto the floor and quickly walked towards some double doors to the right. It took Ryan just seconds to realise where they were heading. Everyone who worked in the building knew that this is where the renovations were being carried out, but this now confused Ryan even further. *Why were they coming here?* Ryan thought. *Surely they needed to get the money out, and fast?*

Ryan blindly followed Ghost Face, Lily and the men into the room. Unsurprisingly the door wasn't locked and there was clearly nothing of value inside. Upon entering the men swiftly dropped the duffle bags and helped Ryan to take his bag off, dropping it to the floor next to theirs. Ryan rubbed his shoulders with relief to be rid of his heavy load. He watched in silence as the men swiftly opened up five white and blue woven rubble sacks and in pairs deposited a duffle bag inside each one, quickly tying off the top securely with black cable ties. They placed the bags in among the other identical rubble sacks that had been filled that day. At a glance, nothing looked amiss. It was just a pile of rubble and sacks. Only the seven people in the room knew that there was a huge amount of money sitting unprotected waiting to be collected. As soon as they had finished tying off the last sack, Ghost Face tapped his watch and motioned forty seconds. When they exited the room, Lily was already at the lift holding the doors open. They descended the four floors quickly and silently. As soon as the doors opened on to the ground floor, all seven of them poured out and ran as fast as they could to the final door. Ryan was at the back, fear now superseding the panic that he had felt earlier. Pressing the red exit button, the last door swung open and they all walked through, no one waited this time to check if it closed behind them. As they drew closer to the main doors, they could hear the noise and excitement outside. Ghost Face pulled off his balaclava and stuffed it into his trouser pocket and everyone else followed suit. Ryan was relieved to take his off and momentarily enjoyed the coolness as the air hit his hot and sweaty face. Lily looked across at Ryan and winked as they casually walked through the door. The sheer clamor of the crowds hit them as they once again slipped past the security guard and exited the building.

Ryan looked around him. He was immediately swept up by the hundreds of people surrounding the bank. Everyone was getting ready for the second count down. Ryan was being ushered by Ghost Face in the direction of where the car had dropped them off. They found it harder this time, pushing through the crowds against the natural flow of people. He turned to see where Lily was, so that he could talk to her, but she was already on her mobile phone and working her way through the crowds in the opposite direction to them. It was too loud for him to shout her name, she would never hear him over the deafening noise of people. The remaining four men had simply disappeared out of sight. *Truly invisible.* Ryan thought.

People around them were chanting the countdown. "Ten, nine, eight." Ryan turned once more to look back towards the bank, no one was following them, there was no sign of an alarm going off, and there were no distant sirens. He was truly amazed that they had pulled this off, impressed even.

Ghost Face pushed Ryan forwards towards the car. As soon as they were in sight, the driver stepped out of the Mercedes and opened up the back door.

Ryan looked at Ghost Face, and he motioned for Ryan to climb in. Ryan bent forwards and began to climb in to the back of the car. Suddenly he felt a searing pain across the back of his neck, he reached his hands up to clutch his head, but the pain was too much to bear. He slumped forward, a dead weight himself now, and the driver quickly slipped his black baton back inside the belt of his pants and shoved Ryan's limp body into the back seat. Silently the Mercedes pulled away from the curb and began to slowly weave its way through the busy streets.

"Two, one." The whole of Hong Kong erupted at once as the City lights lit-up the sky again, erasing the stars and the darkness. The bubbly news reporter was beside herself with excitement as she eagerly talked into the camera, telling everyone watching what a success the Lights Out campaign had been, and now, Hong Kong had truly made it's mark and was well on the way to wiping out pollution altogether.

Chapter 15

AUGUST 9

Ryan lay heavily on his front, his breathing ragged and laboured. His right leg had slipped completely off the couch at some point during the night, and his right arm hung down low, the back of his hand gently touching the floor.

The sunlight was bursting through the window and now rested on his face, burning fiercely under his eyelids.

Ryan slowly started to wake up, but the throbbing on the back of his head coupled with a sudden wave of nausea rendered him motionless. He lay still for a few seconds and waited for the feeling to subside. In his unconscious state he had dribbled saliva out of his mouth and now Ryan was aware of the cool wet patch under his left cheek. His mouth felt dry, and he tried to wet his lips with his tongue, which used all of his remaining energy. He had a strange metallic taste in his mouth, which he couldn't place and he held himself still again as the second wave hit him, disabling him once more. Once the nausea had ebbed away, he slowly moved himself into a sitting position and carefully rested his fragile head in his trembling hands. Taking a few deep breaths Ryan pushed himself upright into a sitting position and tried to open his eyes. The sudden shift of position made him dizzy for a moment and he kept his eyes closed tightly whilst he breathed his way through the black spots and the head rush.

He opened his eyes to the glare of the sunlight and immediately the pain came searing up the back of his head once more and he shut them tight again. Ryan pressed his hands against his head to try and alleviate some of the pain.

He tried to remain as still as possible whilst he attempted to arrange his thoughts. Everything was replaying at full speed in his head; colours, pictures and faces were darting in front of his eyes too fast for him to see what they were. Everything appeared jumbled and disjointed. It was like the worst migraine that he had ever suffered coupled with a hangover. Abruptly and painfully everything came rushing back into focus. Rob's bloodied face, the city lights going out, the bank robbery, the black Mercedes, the pain on the back of his head. Ryan slowly opened his eyes and started to familiarize himself with his surroundings. He was a relieved to see that he was at least back in his own apartment, he was on his own couch and it was daytime. That much he knew for certain. Ryan carefully moved his hand around to the back of his head and he could feel a huge bump where he had obviously been hit. His hair felt matted, and he guessed that his head had been bleeding at some point. He gently prodded around until he located the wound. The cut didn't appear to be too deep and the bleeding had stopped.

Something small and white on his coffee table caught his attention. A pill bottle. Ryan reached for the bottle and read the label. Temazepam. He recognized the name immediately. A well known sleeping pill, *a strong one*, he remembered reading that somewhere. He shook the bottle, and popped open the round plastic lid, a few remaining small white pills sat at the bottom.

I've been drugged, Ryan thought, suddenly aghast. *That explains the metallic taste*, he thought.

But why drug me? Ryan didn't want to think whilst his head hurt so much. He was sure that he would find out sooner or later. For now, he was happy to be in his apartment, and happy to be alive.

Ryan stood up slowly and resting his hand on the arm of his couch, he started to work his was around his apartment to check if he was alone. He was. His front door was locked and all of his windows were closed.

Ryan walked to the kitchen and poured himself a glass of cold water from his fridge, which he drank in just a few thirsty gulps. The water helped to sharpen his senses and numb some of the dull pain in his head. He opened his kitchen draw and fished around blindly for some Panadol, hoping that it may just take the edge off the headache that threatened to remain. He located the foil packet, and popped out two pills, washing it down with the remainder of the water in the fridge.

Ryan looked at his watch. It was just after 11am. He walked through to his lounge and switched on the TV.

The same bubbly new reporter that Ryan recognized from the day before was talking into the camera. Ryan turned up the volume.

"After the great success of the Lights Out Campaign last night, we have woken up this morning to the news that the World Asia Bank was robbed during the eight-minute black out. At this stage the police are unclear of the details. The bank is closed this morning whilst investigators interview staff and members of the public. What we do know is that a large unconfirmed amount of money has been taken. Police are urging members of the public, or anyone in vicinity of the Bank during last nights event, that saw anything to please come forward. This comes just days after an armed man, suspected to be from the Mainland, walk into the same Bank and attempt to bypass security, which ended in a fatal shoot out."

Ryan switched the TV to mute, leaving the news reporter on the screen talking silently to the camera.

Ryan sat for a moment weighing up his options. He probably needed to go to the Police, but first he needed to make sure that Rob was OK. He fumbled around for his phone and finally found it stuffed down the side of his couch. Punching in Rob's number he sat patiently listening to the ringing tone. Eventually after several rings, the phone beeped and the answer phone clicked in. He listened to Rob's familiar voice, asking the caller to leave a message after the tone. Ryan left a short garbled message asking Rob to call him back and clicked off the phone.

Ryan considered calling Lily, then decided against it. He wasn't ready to speak to her yet. What would he say if he did call? He mused. *Hi Lily, I've just woken up, and by the way, why did you drug me last night and is Rob still alive? No*, he thought to himself. They needed him to be asleep for a reason and until he knew why, he needed to tread very carefully.

Next Ryan thought about the police. If he called them now would it still put

Rob's life in danger? His gut feeling was to call Detective Lam and tell her everything, but if anything happened to Rob because of his phone call. It would have been all for nothing. He first needed to find his friend.

A scraping noise pulled Ryan away from his thoughts.

He listened again. He was sure that he had heard something. He waited a few seconds. There it was again, definitely a scraping sound, possibly footsteps. Ryan walked silently towards his front door. He pressed his ear against the door. He could hear muffled whispers.

Slowly sliding his body higher up the door, Ryan leaned in and leveled his eye with the security spy hole. It took only a second for his eye to adjust to the dark passageway on the other side of the door. Ryan could see what he thought was two uniformed police officers outside his front door. Ryan quickly snapped his head away from the small hole before they saw him and pressed his back against the wall.

What to do? His mind was racing now, all thoughts of his throbbing head replaced with thoughts of escape. They had probably already found his fingerprints all over the Bank. He wasn't ready for this. Knowing that he only had a few moments to make a decision, he tried to rationalize everything that was happening. He heard another noise and decided that there was no time to get caught up with the robbery until he knew that Rob was safe.

In three strides Ryan was across the room and grabbed whatever he could get his hands on. His wallet, his keys and his phone and pushed them deep into his trouser pocket. He ran to his balcony door and fumbling with the lock for just a moment he let himself out through the full length, glass sliding doors and onto his small balcony. Now he could hear knocking on his door and one of the men shouting through the thick wood. "Mr Harper, it's the police, we'd like to talk with you, please open up."

Ryan moved to the edge of the balcony and looked down over the railing. He had three floors to go. He estimated that if he slid over the balcony he should be able to balance his feet on the handrail on the floor below and slide onto the terrace. Left with no other choice Ryan slid his body over the side of the balcony holding tightly to the metal railing above him. Taking a big breath for courage he dangled his feet below until he could feel the metal beneath his shoes. He then swung himself forwards and dropped down onto the next level.

Only two more to go, he thought.

Ryan heard more shouting, this time it sounded more urgent forcing him to speed up.

"Mr Harper, we need you to open up. Otherwise we will have to force an entry". The Policeman sounded more convincing now.

Ryan didn't need to be told twice. He followed the same procedure again and lowered himself down to the second floor balcony. The muscles in his arms were starting to ache as he swung his own body weight between floors. He balanced for a final time and then dropped down, this time landing on the grass with a thud. Just as he straightened himself up and dusted down his knees, Ryan heard the unmistakable sound of wood splitting, as his solid wooden door was finally forced open. He could hear the loud footsteps as the Officers ran between each room searching for Ryan. Ryan glued himself to the outside of the outer building wall, moving as fast as he could around the side of the building to the front. He hoped that if they looked over the balcony that they wouldn't be able to see past the other balconies, which would hide him from view. As he edged his way around to the front entrance he could see a police car parked in the car park. He looked more closely to check if there was anyone else inside the vehicle, and was relieved to find it empty. Ryan scanned the rest of the car park and his eyes rested on the small security office with the yellow and white crime scene police tape wrapped around it. He felt a sudden sadness as the sight of the tape confirmed to him what he already suspected, that Mr Wu, the caretaker had been collateral in this whole affair.

Focusing on the task at hand, Ryan needed to get to the main road and in to a taxi before the police officers could stop him. Catching a taxi on the road would be easy enough and then he could disappear into the city, which would give him enough time to decide what he should do next.

Hearing footsteps and shouts behind him, Ryan was suddenly in motion, running for his life down the steep sloped driveway, resisting the urge to look behind him. He ran into the road slamming his hands on to the bonnet of the first available taxi that he saw, bringing it to an immediate screeching halt. He swiftly moved around the side and climbed into the back passenger seat. Still not daring to look back Ryan sat in silence as the taxi driver shouted expletives at Ryan in the rear view mirror. Ryan didn't care, he slumped down as low as he could and accepted the barrage of insults willingly, pleased to be out of sight.

The two police officers ran out on to the busy road and skidded to a halt. A sea of red taxi's greeted them, snaking up and down the steep hairpin road. In vain they scanned and searched each cab as it drove past them.

Defeated, one of the officers picked up his radio to report the bad news.

'Detective Lam, he got away.

Chapter 16

2 hours earlier.

Sarah Lam arrived at the Bank shortly after 9am after being notified of the robbery. She'd tried calling Chow a few times, but his phone was switched off which immediately irritated her. She'd deal with him later, she thought, wondering where he may be.

She was taken inside the bank by one of the banks security officers to the entrance of the secure vault. The forensics team were already busy dusting for fingerprints and she could see that the bank had their own in-house security team on site, the area was full of people. She wondered for a moment if she would bump into Ryan Harper. As she scanned her the people around her, a familiar tall, grey-haired man walked across the marble floor towards Lam.

Extending his hand and giving Lam a firm, but friendly handshake he smiled, which made his eyes crinkle in the corners, when he spoke to her.

"Detective Lam, it's good to see you again." John McIntyre said in his deep gruff voice. "It's a shame that it always seems to be under these circumstances. If you would follow me I'll talk you through what we know so far."

"Thank you", Lam replied.

Lam was relieved to be dealing with John directly and not some other lower ranked bank official. She had met him briefly during her previous visit to the bank and had found him both amiable and helpful. She liked his calming manner and the way in which he made her feel respected. He appeared very laid back, Lam observed. Surprising considering the current situation. Lam followed John back to the main entrance.

"We know that the robbery took place during the eight minute black out. It was all very well thought out and actually very clever." He said with an awkward half smile. He pointed at the main entrance.

Lam listened and followed with interest.

"We did have a security officer on duty, we have interviewed him ourselves, but I'm afraid he was rather caught up in the moment, and spent most of his time watching the countdown outside. They must have hoped that would be the case, as they were able to simply walk past him unnoticed and enter through the first security door." John walked Lam to the first access door.

"They would have needed a security card to access this door." Lam asked this as a statement rather than a question, remembering the procedure from the fumbled attempt a few weeks before.

"Someone had a card." John replied flatly. "We have the door access time at 20:00:09. Follow me and I'll take you through to the next access door."

Lam followed John silently down the short dull grey corridor stopping at the door entrance. This door was standing open while forensics dusted for fingerprints from around the doorframe, the main door and the keypad.

"This is the second door which then leads through to the main vault. This time they used a swipe card and a key code, of which they had both. The access time was recorded at 20:00:25." John was about to walk through the door, when Lam stopped him.

"John, may I ask, should an alarm have been triggered at this point?" Lam said, motioning to the second door.

"That's a good question, but so far they haven't truly breeched security. Many of our staff members have access to restricted areas and have authority to come and go outside of normal banking hours. It's normally limited to Managers and Directors and some of senior security staff members. Also considering that the swipe card and key code was valid, nothing would have raised an alarm at this point."

"And camera's? Can you see them enter on camera?" Lam asked.

John's face stiffened slightly at the mention of the cameras. He thought for a moment before responding. It was the first time that Lam noticed that his normal calm exterior had a small crack in it.

"I'll come back to that question shortly." John replied stiffly, making it clear to Lam that she must wait for the answer. She told herself that she wouldn't ask again until he was ready.

They stepped through the access door and continued towards the main vault. Lam looked up at the vaulted ceiling above them, she followed the lines of the stainless steel beams that framed the concrete up to its highest point. The simplistic architecture impressed her. Lam felt as though she was standing under the ceiling of a modern church for a moment, rather than a bank.

"It's very impressive." Lam said hearing her voice echo. "It's a shame that it's so hidden away."

"Yes, it's one of the bank nicest features. Only a few of the staff and our V.I.P clients get to come to this point." John replied, glancing up at the ceiling.

They walked on until they were at the vault entrance. Lam noticed that the deeper into the bank they went to cooler it became, she wished she had worn something warmer.

They reached the huge steel vault door, which stood closed. Lam could see the silver dust from the forensics team that they had used to check for prints, still fresh on the door.

"This is our most sophisticated security access point." John said. "We spent a lot of time and money developing this with a company in the Netherlands." John proudly pointed to the small square screen positioned to the left of the large metal vault entrance.

"Once they arrived at this point, they would have needed two things. Firstly, a palm scan, followed by an access code." John bent forwards and leaned in closer to the small screen. Lam leaned in until her shoulder was almost rubbing John's. She looked at the screen.

"But it's blank?" Lam said, feeling a little stupid at the obvious question.

"How can you punch in your code if you can't see the numbers?" She asked.

"It's very clever." John stated. "This is the latest in biometric recognition. Every person has a unique palm print, similar to fingertips. The user presses their hand on the screen, and the ultrasonic technology scans and recognizes the print. Once the print is authenticated, which takes just seconds, then a back screen lights up revealing a touch screen keypad. It's set up similar to your run of the mill touch screen, so it's very easy for the user. Each user has a private access code, which we change frequently, however the palm remains the same, so the user always has to first pass the palm scan. It's supposed to be fail safe, and ironically, I believed that was, except…" John trailed off and straightened himself up.

"Let me guess. They had both the code and the palm?" Lam stood upright facing John, she knew the answer already before asking the question.

"Correct. We have their access time as 20:00:56. They knew that they had a limited timeframe to get this done. They were very slick, under a minute so far." John said, motioning to Lam that she must keep following him. They stepped through the giant metal vault entrance and straight onto the top of the tall metal escalator.

Lam stepped on behind John and they began their slow descent.

"You keep saying 'they'?" Lam asked.

"Yes, you will see why when we get inside the holding room at the bottom." John replied as he began to walk down the steps, too impatient to wait for the escalator to take them down to the bottom.

The forensics team were still hard at work when Lam and John arrived at the holding room. They had to stay close the wall to allow people to walk past them through the entrance, carrying boxes, lights and equipment, trying their best not to get in their way.

"We'll keep this quick." John said quietly. "I don't want to tamper with their crime scene."

"This is where things get interesting." John pointed to an area just inside the holding room where Lam could still see piles of plastic wrapped notes, bonds and gold bullion piled neatly in various sections of the brightly lit room. It looked exactly as she imagined it would.

"We know that they have taken something in the region of 150 million Hong Kong Dollars, that's about twenty million US dollars in $100 dollar bills. It would be impossible for one person to carry. That's how we know that there must have been a few people to help carry the money out, we estimate at least five, for that amount, and it's likely that they would have all been men, it's a heavy load."

John continued. "What amazes me is how fast they were. They would have used the escalator to carry the money up. That makes sense. Then they would have to open the vault door by going through the palm scan and access code procedure again. From here I've hit a wall. I'm almost one hundred percent sure that members of the public would have noticed people with large bags leaving the Bank. The bags would have been big and cumbersome and it would have been high risk for them. They would have been very exposed at that moment, especially as they pushed through the crowd." John paused for a moment.

Lam picked up the thread. "You mentioned earlier that a palm scan was used for the entrance into the vault. We should be able to pull prints relatively quickly through our system." Lam said.

John fell silent for a moment. Lam watched as the mask that John had been wearing so well up until this point, showed more cracks. His face fell and he sighed heavily as he realized that he couldn't avoid the subject any longer.

"Detective Lam, I've been skirting the topic. But I'm sure you've realized by now that to get this far into any bank in the World, it would have to be an inside job. I believe your men have sent the prints from all of the keypads as well as the palm scan back to your lab for processing. The Police have already requested a full staff list and everyone has been briefed and they are waiting upstairs to be interviewed. Well almost everyone." John said somberly.

"Is someone missing?" Lam shot back, curiosity was now starting to get the better of her.

"Actually we appear to have two staff members unaccounted for, and I'm starting to get a little concerned." John said.

"Who is it?" Lam demanded, her tone polite, but firm. "We need to find whoever it is to rule them out of the investigation."

John nodded.

"It's Ryan Harper from RSG and another staff member from the retail sector of the bank, Robert Black. Harper didn't show this morning, which is highly unusual for him. He's very prompt and would normally call me if he were running late. We know that Harper and Robert Black are good friends, so we tried to contact Robert to see if he knew where Harper might be, but we've been unable to contact him also. Everyone else is accounted for."

Lam could sense the disappointment in John's voice. It was bad enough to have a robbery on your own turf, but to have an inside job was even worse, especially if you liked the person responsible.

"OK", Lam said, processing the information quickly. It was time to ask about the cameras.

"Even though it was dark, we must be able to see security camera footage?" Lam spoke quickly now; questions were popping up in her head faster than she could ask them.

"This is another problem, it seems that whoever did this, new exactly what they were doing. It's incredibly sophisticated. All of our cameras show…" John paused not sure how to explain. "Well, they show absolutely nothing." John shrugged his shoulders, still unable to believe it himself.

"They were upgraded recently, and have been working perfectly, we test them every day." John said, making sure that Lam knew that they followed procedure. "We have looked at the footage from all of our camera's and in particular the camera's that show the route that we have just taken, no-one comes in, and no-one leaves. It looks like business as usual; we don't know how they managed to do it. It's as though the money just got up and walked out on it's own."

An uneasiness crossed Lam's face. She thought back to the day when the Chinese man was shot and killed after his poor break-in attempt. Then the simple realization hit her. The camera's that day were not being fixed, they were being rigged.

She'd been so fixed on finding out who the old man was that she hadn't even seen what was right in front of her.

"Oh, they're clever." Lam said, shaking her head in disbelief. "So clever." She said, her voice almost a whisper. Then she looked up at John and gave him a broad smile.

"Which company did you use to upgrade your camera's?" She asked John, who was deep in thought.

He looked at Lam for a moment, and tried to follow her train of thought. Then slowly the reality flooded over him in a sickening wave.

"Oh my God, we've just spent hundreds of thousands on this system." His words almost stuck in his throat as he spoke. He imagined having to stand in front of the board of Directors to tell them the news. He had been right to fight the change in security Companies, but of course they had known better. They had brow beaten him until he finally agreed, and so the contract went to RSG. But Ryan had surprised him, tricked him into liking him. He'd taken him in, wanted him to be his protégé.

Now he felt like such a fool. He thought he was a good judge of character, but he had been played all along. John felt nauseous as he silently worked through everything that Ryan would know about the bank. He oversaw every camera placement. He knew every code, and every sequence; he had access to every part of the building. Ryan Harper was a bank robbers dream accomplice.

Lam watched the emotions on John's face change as the truth sank in.

"This has been a well planned robbery." Lam said gently. "Had it not been for the fact that they had a small hiccup during their practice run, we may never have known about it. Now we know that they had access to camera's and inside help." Lam continued, beginning to feel more hopeful.

"We need the name of the company that you hired for the camera's. We will find them, and then we will find who did this." Lam stated confidently.

John glanced at his watch. "I need to prepare everything to address the board." He said to Lam. "Will you keep me updated? I'll make sure that you get the name of the company and everything that you need. I hope we can put this to bed quickly." He gave Lam the same half smile, but this time it looked a little more hopeful, Lam thought.

John shook her hand. It wasn't the same firm handshake as before. This one was more gentle and felt rushed.

"No problem. I can walk myself out. You go ahead." Lam motioned toward the exit, and stood and watched as the security Director walked quickly up the moving escalator taking two steps at a time with his long legs, until he reached the top, and then he was gone.

Lam started to walk back toward the exit leaving the forensics team behind her. Her mind was now at full speed as she started to arrange her thoughts and plan her strategy. She really needed to speak to Chow. Lam pulled out her cell phone and checked the bars. There was no signal in the vault.

When she reached the top, she had to weave between the throng of police officers and bank officials to get to the exit.

She checked the signal strength again when she reached the main doors, and it showed all six bars. She quickly dialed Chow's number and held the phone to her ear. She let it ring a few times, switching it off when it clicked to his answer phone.

Where is he? Lam thought, irritation starting to creep in. Just as she was about to try it again, one of the Police Officers came over to her.

"Detective Lam, the Chief is looking for you, says it's urgent, can you go back to the station immediately."

"Great!" she said under her breath. "That's all I need".

She thanked the Officer and walked out of the bank entrance and straight into a wall of TV camera's and journalists.

Chapter 17

10:00am

It took Lam longer than she thought to get through the throngs of reporters all wanting the latest on the robbery. Eventually after so many '*no comment's*' they had started to trail away to wait for the next poor victim to exit the bank.

As Lam walked back to her desk, she heard a familiar voice from the end of the corridor.

'Laaaam" the voice roared behind her. Lam didn't need to turn to know that it was the voice of her boss. She immediately turned on her heel, and gave him her best smile as he walked towards her.

"Chief" she said brightly.

"Lam, you're a hard woman to track down. Come into my office for a minute." He walked ahead of her, striding at a fast pace, making it hard for

Lam to keep up without breaking into a slow jog.

Chief Inspector William Lau was a larger than life character, both physically and famous for his booming voice. He'd been in the Police Force since he was a young man, and worked his way through the ranks to Chief Constable and finally Chief Inspector. He knew everyone in Hong Kong, from the top politicians, lawyers and fellow senior officers to all of the top Doctors and Bankers.

Lam respected him greatly, and liked him. But he was well known for giving his Detectives a hard time. Lam sensed that she was about to get one of his infamous lectures.

Settling himself into his large black leather office chair he leant forwards onto the desk with his elbows and waited for Lam to sit down before starting.

Lam pulled up a wooden chair and sat across the desk from the Chief. She had always liked coming into his office. It was a basic room, not perhaps what an inspector should have. She looked around at the nondescript grey carpet, the big solid dark wooden desk with turned legs that faced the door, and across at the window with the partial view of a tree and the car park below. In the corner of the room on top of his grey filing cabinet sat a plant that looked as though it needed a good watering, and a red silk wall hanging with Chinese script. What she actually liked was the fact that he always had the most up to date pictures of his family in frames sitting on his desk. No matter how tough he was, she would always sneak a look at the pictures and reconcile herself that his bark was far worse than his bite.

"Lam, I have some bad news." The Chief said somberly.

Lam was surprised by the catch in the Chief's voice. She shifted uncomfortably in her chair, a dark dread starting to rise up in her stomach, she let the feeling flow over her and then she waited for him to continue.

The Chief fought with his emotions for a moment catching Lam off guard.

"What is it Chief?" Lam prompted gently, suddenly afraid that one of his beloved family members had died.

When the Chief eventually spoke, his voice was grave and serious.

"It's Chow". The Chief lifted his eyes and looked straight at Lam.

Lam felt the shiver run down her spine. She hadn't expected this. The Chief continued.

"His body was discovered early this morning in an alleyway, next to a 7eleven store over in Tsim Sha Tsui district. One of the early morning staff went to take the rubbish bags out and found Chow's body slumped next to the dumpster. He didn't have any ID on him when they brought him in, so it took a while to identify his body."

Lam sat back stunned. She'd been so cross that Chow hadn't answered his phone, and now she knew why. He couldn't.

"How did he die?" Lam croaked the question, blinking back tears that were threatening to tumble out onto her cheeks.

"His throat was cut. He would have died instantly." The Chief leaned across the table and touched Lam's hand.

"I'm sorry.' He said sadly. "He was a good kid."

Lam stiffened at the Chiefs touch and hardened her face as she suppressed the tears. She wouldn't allow herself to cry in front of the Chief. Taking in a few slow breaths she managed to contain the pressure in her chest and the lump in her throat. She straightened herself in the chair.

"Why Chow?" she said almost in a whisper.

"We don't know yet", the Chief responded, now back to his normal self.

"We've done a bit of digging around. All that we know so far is that a young Chinese man came into the station yesterday asking for you, Chow met with him instead. An hour later he left the station and didn't tell anyone where he was going."

"Do we know who this Chinese man is?" Lam asked. " Someone must have seen him come in, his name should be on the visitors list?"

"No, he wouldn't leave a name, and Chow didn't write up a report. No one at the Station knows who this man is, or what he came in to say. We can only guess at this stage that whatever it was relating to led Chow to his death."

Lam sat back heavily into her chair. *Stupid, stupid boy*, she thought angrily.

Chow was so innocent, so keen to do well and be liked by her. *It's my fault*, she chastised herself. *I should have let him get more involved, so that he didn't have to go sneaking off behind my back to prove himself.*

The Chief's voice brought Lam back to the present.

"It's not your fault Lam", he said simply, as though he could read her thoughts.

"But I do need to know that you can deal with this. I can take you off the case if you need a few days? "

"No!" Lam interrupted a little too quickly, cutting off the Chief before he could say anything else. "That's not necessary. I'm in the middle of the Bank case, and I think it could be related. I need to find out who did this to Chow." Lam said with steely determination in her voice.

"I can do this." She said, her voice calmer now.

"Lam, it hasn't been that long since your last partner. I would understand if..."

"I'm fine Chief." Lam cut him off again, but she was less aggressive now. "I can manage this".

Lam knew that if she wavered even slightly, gave the Chief a single doubt then he would have her off the case in a heartbeat.

The Chief nodded silently, and hesitated for a moment.

"OK, keep me informed. I have the task of speaking with Chow's family this morning and I'd like to be able to tell that we are onto this, and that we can catch the bastard that killed their son."

The Chief nodded once at Lam indicating that their meeting was now over.

Lam pushed back her chair and stood up. She walked out of the Chief's office in silence. The main office was quiet. Many of the police officers were still down at the bank taking statements. Only a handful remained at their desks, much to Lam's relief. Of the few that were left, she felt their sympathetic eyes on her as she walked past their desks and down the corridor. It was as though a heavy blanket had fallen over everyone as she walked past.

She knew what they were thinking. No one expects to lose a partner, but it's inevitable in this line of work that on rare occasions it will happen. They just couldn't believe that in the short space of two years it had happened to Lam, twice.

11:40am

Lam sat at her desk flicking through a report that had landed on her desk ten minutes before. Her team had started to pull together the finer details regarding the robbery. She now had interview notes, photos and layouts of the bank and personal information about the two missing staff members; Ryan Harper and Robert Black. Lam scanned the first page of the report, she read and re-read the same page twice as she tried to absorb the words, but all she could think about now was Chow. Resigned and consumed, she closed the report and pushed it away from her.

She was under pressure for answers. She had the Chief bearing down on her from one side and the Media on the other. The media had jumped on the case, and the Police were now taking calls from every major network. It seemed that everyone wanted a statement.

The one thing that Lam didn't have yet was a positive match on the palm print and fingerprints. She had worked hard to get the lab to process the prints ahead of anything else that they were working on, and when her charms didn't work, she threw in the Chief's name to get things rolling. Finally they promised her that they would push it through as quickly as possible and would call her if a match came up.

As if reading her thoughts, Lam's phone suddenly rang, making her jump, she quickly regained her composure and grabbed at the receiver.

"Lam. Yes" Lam listened intently, a frown forming on her face. "Are you one hundred percent sure? OK, can you send it through to me. Thanks for rushing it through." Lam replaced the receiver then immediately picked up the phone and dialed a number.

"It's Detective Lam, I need you to send someone round to Ryan Harpers apartment now, you'll need a warrant. We need to have a good look inside his apartment. He may actually be there if we're very lucky. If he is at home, bring him in for questioning. Call me if you find him." Lam finished the call. Her mind was racing ahead of her now.

Lam pressed the dial button and punched in another number.

"Mr McIntyre, it's Detective Lam. Yes, I'm well thank you. We've just had the results back from the lab and we have a name. I'm sure that you won't be surprised to hear that the prints belong to Ryan Harper. I'm afraid it seems that he is a lot more involved in this than we had hoped. We are still trying to locate Ryan Harper and Mr Black." Lam said, then paused as she listened to John's reply.

"I'll keep you up to date and please just call if you have anything that you would like to discuss." Lam finished the call and sat back heavily in her chair. She was hardly going to have time to worry about Chow right now. She would put this case to bed first and then hunt down Chow's killer.

Chapter 18

11:50am

Ryan had had a lucky escape. He had slumped into the back of the taxi, and kept his head down until they reached the city. He'd asked the taxi driver to take him to Tsim Sha Tsui, via the Cross Harbour Tunnel and into one of the busiest places in Hong Kong; Nathan Road. He stepped out of the taxi and scanned the area. It would be a perfect place to hide in plain sight. Here tourists and locals filled the streets from the early hours of the morning until mid-night. There was a constant chatter in the air, people were talking on their mobile phones, every few paces Ryan was accosted by an Indian tailor offering him a made to measure suit for under four hundred dollars. He weaved between people as he walked, avoiding elbows, women with small children in pushchairs, old men with walking canes and tourists with huge camera's strapped across their bodies. There was hardly enough space to walk on the pavement without bumping shoulders with someone, or treading on toes. People here walked with a purpose. They had places to go and things to see. No one would take notice of a blonde-haired westerner in this part of the city. To anyone looking, he was just another tourist. He would be able to blend in easily whilst he decided what he should do next. Ryan stood back from the moving sea of people and stepped into a shops doorway for a moment. He still needed to find out about Rob, and the only way that he knew how, was to call Lily. He had put it off for long enough, and now he had no choice.

Ryan pulled out his phone and dialed Lily's number, letting it ring until it reached her voice mail.

"This is Lily", her familiar sultry voice purred into Ryan's ear, making him feel sick. "I'm not able to take your call, please leave a message after the tone." There was a pause and then a click.

"It's Ryan, the Police came and I had to leave the apartment. I need to know that Rob is OK. Call me." Ryan pressed the red off button and pushed the mobile deep into his trouser pocket.

He reached into his wallet and went through the back note section to see how much money he still had. He counted out one thousand dollar note and four one hundred dollar notes. It wasn't much. *I'll have to draw more*, he thought, then dismissed the idea. *What if they trace me using an ATM?*

Ryan was about to close his wallet when he caught sight of a name card. He pulled the card out of the wallet and folded out the dog-eared corners.

Detective Inspector Sarah Lam, Direct line: 2305 3886. Ryan rubbed his thumb across the name card trying to decide what to do. *Not yet*, he thought, *not yet*.

LIGHTS OUT

And pushed it deep back into wallet for safekeeping.

Ryan's mobile started to ring. His heart immediately started to pound as he clumsily fumbled for his phone. Looking down at the small screen, he could see that it was an unknown number.

Ryan took a deep breath and pressed the green call button. "Hello". He said almost breathlessly, he tried to calm himself, pacing up and down on the pavement.

"Ryan." Lily spoke calmly and gently, immediately putting Ryan on guard. "I've just listened to your message. Where are you now?" She asked with a little concern.

"It doesn't matter where I am." Ryan replied bluntly. "I just need to know that Rob's OK. I have done everything that you have asked of me. The deal was that once it was all over, that you would release Rob and I can go back to normal." Ryan paused and waited for Lily's response.

"Ryan, just tell me where you are and then we can meet and talk." Lily tone was gentle soothed him momentarily. Then he remembered.

"Do you really think that I would tell you anything? You've sent the police after me once. You could do it again. I'm not prepared to stand here and wait to be arrested." Ryan tried to keep his voice calm, but his anger was starting to work its way through.

"Look Ryan, I need to know where you are so that I can come and meet you. Rob's fine, he's alive, you kept him alive. But things have changed and we need to talk. I need to see you."

Ryan sounded skeptical. "Why Lily, so that you can kill me, get rid of any remaining witnesses. I don't think so. I want to speak to Rob." Ryan asked, this time his voice was stronger.

"You have to trust me that he's OK." Lily said.

"Trust? That ship has sailed Lily. There is clearly no trust left between you and I. I don't know what you're involved in and I don't care, but you need to keep to your side of the deal and let Rob go." Ryan said, feeling his confidence grow with each word.

"Look I think I can arrange for you to speak to Rob, but I can't get him released yet. Ghost Face wants to keep him for a bit longer, he's not happy that you have disappeared. Now he sees you as a potential risk. I can try and arrange for you to see Rob tomorrow. You'll have to wait for my call." Lily clicked off her mobile leaving Ryan standing with the receiver in his hand.

Lily punched in another number on her phone and waited patiently whilst it rang.

Eventually the call was picked up and a male voice answered.

"Yes." Was the abrupt greeting that she always received from Ghost Face.

"We need to discuss Harper. I've just spoken to him. He sounds frightened and I don't expect him to go to the Police. He won't come to me. He just wants Rob to be released as he was promised."

"No. Mr Black stays where he is." Ghost Face replied firmly.

"I don't understand why you need him still. The job is done. He has played his part." Lily said.

"Let me explain something to you. We may have been successful in taking the money from the Bank, but your friend Ryan slipping away from the Police has changed our plan and puts us at risk. So keeping your dear friend Robert will just help us to ensure that Harper doesn't do or say anything stupid. I'm sure you can appreciate the delicate position that we are in at the moment?" Ghost Face said.

Lily remained thoughtful before she replied carefully. "I understand the situation, it won't take long to launder the money, I've set everything in place. But it's better for us if he gets taken into Police custody. It buys us the time we need and that way we know exactly where he is. Once he's been arrested, you said yourself that your friend can make arrangements and tie up the investigation for a long time. It puts us in the clear. Having him out in the open and keeping Rob locked up for longer than we agreed changes things significantly. It's not part of the plan." Lily finished.

"Your plan doesn't work. I was a fool to listen to you. Now we have a loose end, which I will have to tie up myself. Keeping Ryan alive was a mistake. I should have disposed of him as soon as we finished the job."

"You're wrong." Lily responded. "I know him better than you. I think he'll go straight to the police after he's seen Rob, after he's sure that his friend is still alive, but until then, we don't know what he'll do. That's what's worrying me."

"And Rob, is he likely to become a loose end too?" Ghost Faced said, criticism lacing his words.

"Rob will be interviewed by the police. He'll think that Ryan and I have betrayed him, and had planned it all along. Eventually, Ryan will be cleared and the two of them will become friends again. Other than myself, no one else needs to be implicated. I knew that my relationship with Rob would be lost once we decided to do this. I just don't want to see him hurt or be held longer than necessary." Lily said, a trace of sadness in her voice.

Ghost Face remained silent and allowed Lily to finish her speech. A small smile tugged at the corner of his mouth.

"Interesting. I'm not sure that I really believed that you would be willing to forfeit your friendship for something far more important. It pleases me to hear that you will first protect The Family." He said darkly.

Immediately Lily could feel the colour coming to her cheeks. She had let her guard down, and shown a softer side to Ghost Face. She was angry with herself for allowing her emotions to come in the way of business.

"Until Harper is in Police custody, or dead, whichever happens first, Rob will not be released. Do what you need to do to get him into custody, but I warn you. The first sniff of deceit and he will be disposed of. Until then, there is no need for you to call me again." Lily was left with a dead ring tone in her ear. She switched off her phone and thought about what she was doing.

It was inevitable that at some point she would have to remove herself from normal life. She thought back to the night before and realized that things changed the second that she stepped across the Bank's threshold. Up until then, she still had a choice. *And now?* She thought. *Now The Family comes first.*

Chapter 19

Six Months Earlier

Lily had everything ready for her Grandmother. She'd been working night and day over the last month to get everything in place and now it was time. Now Lily sat in the drawing room of her family home, the midday sun pouring through the framed windows. Lily looked around her and allowed herself to relax a little. She loved this room. Everything was so familiar and comfortable, and relatively unchanged over the years.

She had chosen to sit on one of the comfortable mink coloured shot velvet couches that faced the centre of the room. Behind her on the vast back wall hung panels of painted silk with dramatic mountain scenes, and sunsets all hand painted. They had started to yellow slightly with age around the edges, but the paint was as vibrant as the day the brush touched the ink. Under her feet was an elegant carved carpet. It had been in the house for as long as Lily could remember. Rich with red, gold and yellow exotic birds and bordered with ornate oriental flowers that climbed and twisted across the floor.

She had placed her laptop on the low Elm wood Kang table in front of her. The exact place where years before she had knelt on the floor to do her homework. To her left, toward the main entrance of the room, stood a large wooden tea chest that held a pale grey stone sculpture. Lily knew this piece so well. It was the Goddess of Mercy. Her Grandmother had been named after this Goddess and her Grandfather had bought the ancient sculpture for his wife as a birthday gift one year. Towards the French windows that led onto the terrace was a large antique lacquered screen in black and ornate gold. She remembered hiding behind this as a child and being scolded by her Grandmother when the Amah and cook had searched the house from top to bottom, only to eventually discover her there.

The door opened and one of the maids came in carrying a bamboo tea tray. She placed it on the low table and smiled at Lily. "Your Grandmother is just coming." The young girl said and smiled.

Lily nodded and replied with a 'thank you' and busied herself with preparing the tea. Her Grandmother was very traditional and insisted on tea ceremonies during every family visit. Lily had been taught from a young age and it was expected that each time she came, a ceremony would take place.

Today they had Jasmine tea, one of Lily's favourites. Not too strong, unlike some of the other bitter black teas that her Grandmother liked, but a gentle fragrant tea, pale yellow in colour and easy to drink.

Lily slid down onto her knees in front of the low wooden table and picking up a small clay teapot, scooped in the dried tealeaves, until it was three quarters full. The fragrant smell was already potent in its dried form and Lily took in a full breath of its aroma. She took a larger clay teapot that contained the hot water and poured it into the smaller pot, raising the pot up at a full arm's length so that water poured out like a narrow waterfall filling the pot below until all the leaves were covered.

The door of the room opened a second time and instead of the maid, her Grandmother walked in.

"Just in time", Lily said as she continued with her pouring being careful not to lose her focus.

Her Grandmother sat heavily on the couch just to the right of Lily. Her old body was slow these days, but she still held herself as upright as she possibly could, always elegant and graceful despite her age. Dressed in her usual Mandarin attire, with her silver hair perfectly coiffed, she rested her hand on Lily's right shoulder for a moment before placing her hands demurely in her lap.

"Continue". She said to Lily.

Lily emptied out the first of the tea into small teacups resting on a bamboo tray and filled them until the water overflowed. She re-filled the teapot again, this time emptying the teacups over the small teapot. She did this three times, each time allowing the tea to brew for slightly longer causing the flavour to infuse even further.

Finally she poured the tea into the two teacups, and placed them onto a small bamboo holder. Holding one with two hands she passed the first teacup and holder to her Grandmother bowing her head slightly as she did so. Her Grandmother took the tea with two hands and took a small noisy sip. Lily sat back up on the couch and picked up her own tea, enjoying the warmth of the cup in her hands.

Lily finished her tea first and she placed the teacup back on to the tray.

She moved the tray towards the back of the table and made space for her laptop in front of them. Then she waited.

Soon her Grandmother had finished her tea. Lily helped her to place the teacup back onto the tray.

"Your challenge as a new member of The Family was to bring us fresh new business opportunities. I remember that I told you that you must first attain the skill, and the creativity comes later. You have studied hard, you have been privy to every aspect of the society and understand us well. All of the Masters have been impressed with you, most of all myself. Now I am interested to see what creativity you can provide for us." She smiled at Lily.

Lily started to feel a little nervous presenting to her Grandmother, but this was no trial run. This was her one shot to show her what she could bring to the table.

Lily opened up her laptop and pressed the on button. Whilst she waited for it to boot up, she began her presentation.

"I started out by looking at our strengths and what we are good at, and also looked at the Society like you would do any major company. The two big income areas for us are money laundering and security, but we've faced some difficulties with both of these over the last few years. We know that our rivals in Hong Kong are starting to compete with us, and they have managed to lure some of our less loyal members and are encroaching on some of our territory. We are lucky that we are cash rich, but we need new ways to move our money, so that we can clean it quickly and get it re-invested elsewhere. I also believe that we must step up our security offer, and I think I've found a way to do both." Lily said, and positioned the laptop screen so that it faced her Grandmother.

"What I can offer, and what the Society is lacking, is technology." She stated. "I did some work on digital video technology as part of my studies and managed to build a unit that can be manipulated by me, or people that I train, remotely." Lily tapped on her keyboard and pulled up a black and white image that filled the screen entirely.

Lily's Grandmother leaned in and squinted at the image for a few seconds, and then sat back in her chair.

"Where is this?" She asked Lily, observing the moving image of people going back and forth into a building.

"It's the entrance to one of our busiest strip clubs in Wan Chai. We've had trouble with some of our rivals threatening the staff, getting past the security on the door and as you know, last week, we had a small fire breakout. Our CCTV camera's can only record, but can't help us to stop what is happening, we can only watch it unfold after the event." Lily could see her Grandmother lose interest, so she quickly continued.

"Keep watching. I installed this camera system last week after we received the first round of threats."

Lily pressed the play button. The footage that now came up showed a full club, people were queuing up outside in their hundreds and slowly people were being allowed in bit by bit. They watched as the video showed a man slowly pushing his way to the front of the queue, and after a short while was given entry to the club. Shortly afterwards smoke could be seen billowing out of a small side window. The same man could be seen slipping out of the door and calmly walking away from the building, whilst everyone else around him panicked and shouted. Lily clicked another play button. This time the footage began in the same way, but the date on video indicated that it was recorded the day before. Lily's Grandmother watched the same man begin to push his way through to the entrance of the bar. The camera zoomed in and locked on to his face and zoomed out again. Seconds later a security guard walked to the front of the club and grabbed the man, hauling him inside the building.

Lily pressed the off button and closed her laptop.

"What this means is that I've been able to develop the technology so that we can incorporate facial recognition. We can start to build our own database of rival society members, and pick them out one by one to prevent this kind of thing from happening. We can monitor and control who comes in to our clubs, our restaurants and our territories."

"You said that you can assist the Society in two ways. What is the second way exactly?" Lily's Grandmother asked.

Lily could sense that her Grandmother bored easily when it came to technology, so she would have to make her sell to the point to hold her interest.

"We are always looking at ways to generate income. Using the same camera technology I'm able to cloak video imaging from a remote location and replace it with another image." Lily said, hoping that she was holding her grandmothers attention.

"And how exactly would this be useful to us?" She asked.

"It's a way of protecting us whilst we gain access to funds." Lily replied.

"Funds as in…."

"Funds as in, cash." Lily finished the sentence for her Grandmother. "Potentially, a lot of cash."

"If we are able to get past all of the usual security measures in a bank, for example, cloaking the camera's is relatively simple. That gives us the flexibility to carry out the work, without detection. It would be as though we were never even there." Lily said.

Lily's Grandmother sat in silence absorbing all of the information.

"I know that we normally try and gain funds through reputable means, but Banks have insurance measures against this type of thing. So we're actually going up against the insurance company and not the bank or it's customers. We would be removing the funds from the right people." Lily explained.

"Just enlighten me with how you expect to bypass all of the security measures?" Her Grandmother asked out of sheer curiosity.

"Well, as always it's about who you know." Lily said.

"An old friend of mine works at the World Asia Bank. I think that through him I could gain all of the knowledge that I need to get into the building. I'm fine on the technology side. It's the removal of the funds that I would need help with."

"I can help you with men, if that's what you would need. That's no problem, but how will you gain access to the actual cameras, even if you can get through all of the security? I'm assuming that you would have to do something to them to get them to work as you wish."

"Well this is where fate has played a big hand. One of my other contacts that helps me on the tech side of my development has heard that the bank is planning an upgrade. I think I can bid for the contract and I'll make sure I win it. That way we can legitimately go in and make all the changes to the camera's that we need."

"I really think that it could work." Lily said, excited with her plan.

"How much income do you think this could generate?" Her Grandmother now asked.

"Enough to keep the money launderers very busy for a while." Lily replied.

Chapter 20

Motel 186

Ryan looked up at the cracked neon sign above the Motel entrance. It's flickering bright pink light spelling out the name in cursive writing, the only source of illumination on the dark street. Each flicker was accompanied by a low buzz as the electrical current surged and waned as he stood on the doorstep deciding whether to go in or leave. A few drops of rain landed on Ryan's shoulder making up his mind. Ryan pushed open the old wooden door and peered down the dimly lit corridor. The grey marble floor that led Ryan towards the reception was cracked and dirty. Litter formed small piles in unsuspecting corners. Old food wrappers, yellowed newspapers and cigarette ends made up the majority of the collection.

An old metal fan whirred overhead, its outer cage set slightly skew causing the metal blades to tap, tap, tap against the metal rods as the blades spun past.

As he drew closer, Ryan could see an old TV standing on a table top at the reception. There was no sound, just the reflection of the TV picture forming shapes, and casting shadows across the face of the sleeping Chinese security guard.

Ryan watched the old man sleep for a moment. His face was soft with sleep, but carried deep-set wrinkles. He had fallen asleep sitting upright on his chair. His feet remained flat on the floor and his hands rested gently on his thighs. His head was positioned slightly to the side and his mouth was relaxed and slack. His breathing was raspy and faltered slightly with each exhalation, as though he had something caught in the back of his throat.

Eventually Ryan shook the guard gently by his shoulder.

The guard awoke with a start. Disorientated by his sudden consciousness he looked around trying to find what had woken him so abruptly and his eyes finally rested on Ryan. The panic in his eyes changed to guarded suspicion.

"I need a room." Ryan said pointing to the keys on the wooden board behind the guard.

He spoke to the guard slowly and used his hands to mime a key turning in a door.

The guard looked to where Ryan was pointing and then back towards Ryan, his face completely blank.

"I need to sleep." Ryan said, this time placing his two hands together and resting his head on one side with his eyes closed in an attempt to make the guard understand.

LIGHTS OUT

"Ah." The Guard said and gestured back to Ryan, by showing him a key.

Ryan nodded, relieved that he would soon be able to lie down and rest.

Ryan stuck his hand into his pocket and pulled out some crumpled notes and showed them to the guard.

"How much." he said, spreading out the money on the desk.

The guard looked at the cash, then took a calculator and tapped in the amount, turning the small screen to show Ryan.

"OK, $200, that's fine." He took the two red one hundred dollar notes and flattened them out before passing them across the counter to the guard.

The guard nodded, then turned to the hooks behind him and pulled off a key with a long bottle green rectangular plastic fob with number 241 etched in white.

He placed the key on the table and pointed to a stairwell just down the hall from the reception desk. Ryan nodded.

The guard gave Ryan a toothless smile and waved him off down the corridor, before settling himself back in to his chair.

Room 241 was basic. A single bed stood underneath the only window in the room framed by heavy brown curtains that didn't quite reach the floor.

The deep red carpet covering the floor smelt musty to Ryan. He covered his nose with his shirt as he made the short walk to the bathroom.

The bathroom was not much better. Two white towels, grey with over washing, hung stiffly on a metal rail on the back of the door.

Ryan brushed his hand across them only to feel the crunchy hard fabric underneath his fingers.

A single bulb lit the bathroom sending a yellow glow across the room, and highlighting the dusty sink and low bath. The toilet lid was down, and Ryan wasn't ready to check out how clean it was. He looked at his reflection in the mirror, the dull light more gentle on his complexion than before, but he could still see the dark circles that had formed underneath his tired bloodshot eyes.

Ryan noticed a small shelf above the sink, and saw that there was at least a free toothbrush and small pot of shampoo that he could use.

He walked back through to his room. He had no change of clothes and just the few crumpled notes he'd managed to grab before fleeing his apartment.

He sat down heavily on the bed and was surprised at how soft the mattress was. Trying not to think about the smell of the carpet, Ryan lay back and covered his eyes with his forearms, pressing them closed. All that he could think about was sleep. The desire tugged and pulled at Ryan until eventually he hauled himself fully onto the bed, kicking his shoes off as he did so. He drew a corner of the bed sheet across his body and allowed himself to become consumed by exhaustion.

Chapter 21

Unable to sleep, Lam decided that her time was better spent working. She pulled herself out of bed before her alarm and quickly showered and dressed herself. She gave her dog Sasha a rub on the head before leaving, a pang of guilt sweeping over her, and a promise to herself that she'd take him for more walks once this case was solved.

She pulled up to her normal parking space in the dark. Her colleagues still had another few hours of sleep before the sun would come up.

She climbed out and scanned the parking lot. The Chiefs car was parked in its usual spot.

A bit early, she thought to herself and checked her watch. It was 5.30am.

Lam could see a shard of light under her office door. She paused for a moment and then walked in. The Chief was standing fixated. He was so engrossed in Lam's pin board that he didn't even hear her enter.

"Chief." She said, a little amused at the height at which the Chief jumped at the sound of her voice.

The Chief composed himself and smiled at Lam.

"A bit early for you Lam?" He queried, looking at his watch.

"I may say the same about you?" She countered.

Motioning to the pin board, the Chief continued.

"This is impressive Lam. When did you do this?"

"Last night. It helps me to run through the facts, try a few theories out, link things together."

"Listen, whilst I have you here, there's something that I'd like to ask you." The Chief sat himself down in her chair, rocking it back and forth slightly with his weight. Lam chose to sit in the 'guest' chair on the opposite side of her desk, not wanting to look down at the Chief when she answered him.

"Most importantly, have you been to see the Counselor yet?" This question surprised Lam, she wasn't used to the Chief being so nice, and this was twice now that she'd experienced him showing empathy, however awkward it was for him.

"I have an appointment set up for next week, but I'm actually fine." Lam lied.

"That's good. Let me know how the meeting goes." The Chief said with relief. Please to have at least asked the question.

"In fact I'm pretty focused." Lam continued. "I have a couple of new leads and I'm a step closer to our main suspect, we had his prints confirmed yesterday, and it definitely appears to be an inside job."

"Do you really think it's an inside job?" The Chief asked.

"We'll know for sure when we catch up with Harper and his buddy Black, but for now, the hard evidence is giving me a set of palm and fingerprints that match, and a staff member that is MIA from his work place."

"And what about Chow?" The Chief asked gently "Have we moved any further forward there? Do you need more people?"

Lam sat quietly for a moment.

"I have a few guys working on Chow's case Chief. How was the visit?"

The Chief shoulders slumped slightly as he remembered the stricken faces of Chow's wife and his mother. They had been perfect hosts to the Chief upon his arrival, in true Chinese tradition. When he broke the news of Chow's death, his wife rocked silently back and forth in her chair, whilst his mother howled, like any parent would who had outlived their child.

"It was as expected." The Chief replied simply, not wanting to go into detail.

Lam wanted to move away from Chow and back onto the Bank. She wasn't ready to discuss him yet.

"I think the bank job is only partly an inside job. I don't think that Harper was smart enough to set this thing up himself. Someone else planned it, and he was simply a part of it. It was very well organized, and normally when it's well organized, it usually involves our old friends. I think one of the Triad groups are involved, but I need to do some more digging first to be sure. What has thrown me is that they have included someone who is clearly not part of their normal family. They usually stick within their own kind, especially for something this big."

"I think you may be right." The Chief agreed. "That brings me on to my next subject. In fact the timing couldn't be better. I was going to talk to you about this later, but as we are both here and we have some privacy, now would be a good time."

Lam shifted in her seat. She didn't like it when the Chief just threw her a curve ball. It wasn't her style. She didn't like change, she needed to chew on things for a while, and he was giving her the distinct impression that he was about to make a change.

"I'm assigning a new partner to you from the Organized Crime Bureau. He's very experienced and specializes in organized crime. He's covered many situations like this before and I think you two will work well together." The Chief could hardly look at Lam in the eyes. He knew that she would fight him over this, but he wouldn't back down. She couldn't manage these two cases together, and he wanted someone to be there with her. Support her where she needed it.

Lam could feel the tension come into her neck and her cheeks flushing hot. She hated having new partners. She worked just fine on her own, and she certainly didn't need someone new to come and give their opinions and change the course of her investigation. She was making headway on her own. *No, no this is not going to happen*, she thought to herself.

"Chief, with all due respect" Lam started.

The Chief cut her off mid sentence knowing what was coming. "It's decided, you have no say in the matter. You need someone else on this with you. Now that you don't have Chow, you need someone to pick up the slack, and he's good. Very good. You have a case that is getting bigger and more complicated by the day. You have one dead contractor and a dead partner on your hands. Not forgetting two missing bank employees of which one we know is on the run."

"Oh, and if that's not enough, then you have to deal with me," The Chief said, pointing a finger to his own chest and stabbing himself to make a point. "I'm putting you under pressure to solve this case, and whilst I have the board of Directors and Commissioner breathing down my neck, I'll be breathing down yours." The Chief pointed a finger toward Lam.

Lam got the picture. She realized that she would have to pick her fights with the Chief. This was not one that she was about to win. She held her tongue and nodded an affirmation across the desk.

"Now, if there is nothing else, I have work to do", The Chief stood up leaving Lam's chair gently rocking backwards and forwards, and without another word he left her sitting at the desk.

Lam remained sitting, silently fuming. *I don't need anyone else on this. Damn it!* She grabbed her bag and headed out of the office, she couldn't face looking at the pin board, not now. Any chance of her focusing had long since gone. Now she had a new partner to worry about.

Lam climbed into her Porsche and sat quietly for a moment. Then she turned the ignition and allowed the car to growl under her seat. The sound of the car calmed her and she positioned the vents to blow cool air onto her face, the colour slowly disappeared from her cheeks.

She smiled to herself then. There was always one thing that helped when her head was too busy to work.

Lam pushed the car into gear, and sped out of the parking lot. Sasha would get his run after all.

Chapter 22

Lam stood staring at the pin board in front of her with her arms crossed. Refreshed from her run, she had spent the last three hours arranging and re-arranging the sequence of the last few weeks events, following up leads and chasing up reports. Her initial enthusiasm was waning as her leads began to dry up. Her theory regarding the triads were now leading her down dead end pathways and she'd hit a wall.

She had several photographs on the board, which she had separated by case. The face of the dead Chinese man was staring back at her with his black eyes. Chow had been the one to photograph his body.

So Ironic, Sarah sighed, and wondered who had photographed Chow's dead body.

She had photographs of Harper and Black, pinned up high on the board next to the old man along with Harpers finger and palm prints, the only thing that so far linked Harper to the robbery. Black, it seemed, had simply disappeared off the planet.

She was no further with the gun at this stage and there were no other fingerprints that forensics had been able to pull except from the dead man.

She looked again at the unknowing smiling face of Chow to the right of her board, and then to the picture of his body as he had been discovered. She was no closer to finding Chow's murderer. No weapon found, no traces of DNA, nothing left behind at the scene to help her.

"What had he found out that I didn't know?" Sarah questioned out loud.

"Idiot", she said under her breath looking at his picture.

"You were so keen to do well and to prove yourself that you just decided to go off on your own, now look at you."

When Lam first looked at Chow's photographs, she didn't feel shocked or repulsed. His body was positioned in such a way that he could have been asleep. His head was gently resting against his knees. It was only the awkward position of his feet tucked under his legs that gave it away.

When they had tried to move Chow his head slipped to the side revealing a grotesque and deep wound. He had been cut so deeply that he had almost been decapitated. Whatever knife the killer had chosen to use, it had been razor sharp. It would have been a forceful and swift movement, and almost certainly Chow would have died instantly.

That's the only saving grace, Lam thought to herself sadly. Death came quickly for him.

Lam was so absorbed in her own thoughts that she didn't hear her office door open.

Only when she heard a deep cough behind her, did she realize that there was someone in the room.

Lam spun around quickly to be faced with an outstretched hand and a beaming smiling face.

"Sorry, I didn't mean to startle you, I'm D.I Luk, your newly assigned partner". The man behind the smile remained with his arm outstretched waiting for Lam to take his hand.

Lam didn't offer her hand immediately. He had caught her off-guard. Lam wasn't ready for D.I. Luk. She hadn't prepared herself for an introduction so soon. Luk was younger than Lam had assumed, with so much experience she thought she'd be getting a forty-something know it all. She wouldn't put him quite at forty, thirty-five perhaps. He didn't look like a typical D.I either. Casual to the point of scruffy, she thought, observing his slogan t-shirt, worn jeans and converse shoes. Lam thought it made him look more like a student than that of a Detective Inspector. She disliked him immediately.

"Hi" Lam said reaching forward with her hand. She shook his hand quickly and dropped it almost immediately.

"I need a coffee". Was all that Lam could think to say.

"I've been looking at this board now for three hours. I'll show you where the coffee machine is." Lam said as she walked straight past an amused Luk and towards the canteen. Luk followed her, the faintest pull of a smile tugging at the corner of his mouth.

This is just how the Chief said she would be, he thought to himself as he followed his new partner down the corridor.

Chapter 23

Ryan lay on the Hotel bed and tried to get comfortable. He had tossed and turned all night, and now his back ached. He pulled the thin grey sheet across his body and tried to will himself back to sleep, pulling his knees up to his chest. But it was too late. His mind was already busy. Sleep would have to wait until later. Ryan climbed out of bed and pulled back the curtain from the small window and was greeted with darkness. He checked his watch and he groaned aloud. It was just before six am.

He had a waiting day today. He couldn't make any plans or really do anything until he had spoken to Lily, and since he had no idea when she would call, he knew that he was in for a slow day.

Ryan looked at his cell phone. He could see that he only had two bars left before his battery would run out and he had no way of charging his phone.

He certainly didn't think that it would even be worth asking at the Hotel reception, so he would need to try and buy a charger from a stall vendor or a phone shop. Today of all days he couldn't risk being without his phone.

LIGHTS OUT

Ryan dragged himself into the tiny shower. The water pressure was so low that he only managed to get a slight trickle of warm water out of the shower, but it was enough for him to soap himself down and get clean. Feeling a little better, he quickly dried himself down on the almost threadbare rough towel. *Shaving would have to wait*, he thought as he brushed his chin with his hand feeling the stubble growing through quickly. He dressed himself in the same clothes as the day before. His growling stomach reminded him that he needed to eat. He walked down to the reception and looked around. The desk was deserted. There was no sign of the old man from the night before. Rather than hand in his door key, Ryan stuffed it into his pocket and made his way outside. He walked the next few blocks to where he could see some local cafes dotted along the pavement. Even at this time of the morning with the sun just coming up, the streets felt busy. The café owners were noisily pulling up the metal shutters. Vans were busy unloading and delivering fresh supplies and newspaper kiosks were beginning to open along the road. Stacks of newspapers sat in tall pies on the pavement, tied with old bits of nylon string.

Ryan scanned the kiosk closet to his Hotel as he walked past, hoping to find an English newspaper, but there was nothing for him to read. This was too much of a local Chinese area. Ryan suddenly felt quite conspicuous. There wouldn't be too many other white men wandering around the streets at this time of the morning. Knowing that he wouldn't blend in, he tried to keep himself to himself and not draw any further attention. He walked up and down the road once, and decided upon a relatively busy looking café. It was small, but looked clean and the smell that greeted him at the entrance was enough to entice him in.

The décor was straight out of the 1960's with old wooden tables, each nestled within a private booth. The dark red plastic seats long since worn and torn along the seams looked comfortable to Ryan. The floors were covered in white tiles, and the walls had been papered so long ago that the once flowery pattern was now faded and peeling. In the top corner of the café, a small box TV had been mounted on the wall. The Chinese news channel was on, and the handful of customers that were already inside, were all facing the TV. No one paid any attention to Ryan as he slipped into one of the booths by the window. He scanned the restaurant to see what everyone else was eating. It looked like steaming noodle soup was the popular choice, so when the waiter finally came over, Ryan simply pointed to the man in the next booth and silently mimed eating the imaginary food.

By the time the noodles arrived, Ryan was starving. He realized that he hadn't eaten in over twenty-four hours, but sitting in this tiny, busy café, with all the smells and steam coming from the kitchen his appetite was well and truly awake.

The waiter placed the bowl in front of Ryan and he watched as the soup swished and slopped in front of him, a few drops landed on the table. Ryan peered into the bowl at the contents and stirred it with his spoon. The thick white noodles swam around in the steaming grey watery soup. A few pieces of chicken rose and fell in the liquid. He took the plastic chopsticks and worked his way through the noodles, scooping the soup with his spoon. Once the noodles and chicken were finished, then Ryan put down the spoon and lifted bowl to his lips and drained the contents into his mouth. He placed the bowl down on the table, and leaned back against the comfortable booth chair, satisfied and full.

Ryan thoughts moved swiftly to Rob. He imagined his friend bound and terrified. He'd been held now for three days. Not knowing where he was being held and who the people were that held him.

LIGHTS OUT

Ryan wondered for a moment whether Rob even knew that Lily was involved in his abduction, and the reason behind it.

He considered the chances of successfully getting Rob out without getting them both killed or caught. He just didn't know what to expect. He had never used a gun or knife before; he'd never been in a life-threatening situation. And here he was, hiding out in a tiny café, on the run from the Triads and the Police.

He wouldn't be much good in a fight. That much he knew, so Ryan concluded whilst he sat at the plastic covered table that at this stage, the best that he could hope for, was proof of life before turning himself in to the Police.

Ryan checked his watch. It was just before 7am, and still far too early for any of the shops to be open. Ryan raised his hand and caught the attention of the waiter. He pointed at his empty bowl and signaled for a second helping. The waiter smiled a toothless smile and nodded, quickly turning on his heel towards the kitchen to place Ryan's order.

One hour, and a second bowl of noodles later Ryan stood at a small electrical kiosk and was trying to explain to the man that he needed a phone charger. He presented his phone and pointed at the final single bar.

This time the communication was easy and Ryan walked away with the correct charger and still had some change in his pocket. As Ryan walked back down the street toward his Hotel, he felt his phone vibrate in his pocket. He quickly pulled out the phone and was relieved to see Lily's name appear on the small screen.

"Ryan, it's me". Lily said quietly as though trying not to let someone hear what she was saying.

"Hi, look we have to talk quickly, I have no battery left. Where can I meet you?" Ryan said, not wanting to waste any battery life on idle chatter.

"OK, there's a Go-Down Warehouse in Chai Wan. It's on Chai Hong Road, number 48, the Win Sun Industrial Building. Go into the building and take the lift up to the top floor. When you get out, walk up the last flight of stairs. Knock on the white door when you get there. I'll be waiting there with Rob."

"OK, I've got it. When" Ryan asked.

"Now", Lily replied finishing the call with a click.

Shit, Ryan thought. His phone was about to shut down at any moment, and now there was no time to recharge it. Ryan estimated that it would take him at least forty minutes to get to Chai Wan from his current location. Lily and Rob were close to the last stop on the underground train on Hong Kong Island and he was way out in the far side of Kowloon.

Without delay, Ryan walked a couple of blocks until he could see the nearest red and white underground sign. He then quickly entered the station and waited impatiently for the next train.

Chapter 24

Lily sat in her car in the stuffy basement of the Chai Wan warehouse. She had the car running to allow for the cool air conditioning to circulate.

She was feeling very uncomfortable with the current situation. She had heard about some of the murders and missing people, but she had never directly been involved in a planned abduction. What unnerved her the most was Ghost Face and how unpredictable he could be. She feared for Rob's life, and she was worried now that she would be putting Ryan's life at risk too.

Her Grandmother had never discussed deaths that happened within the society and Lily never thought that it was appropriate to ask. Her Grandmother appeared on the outside to deal with it all effortlessly and without remorse. Maybe by now she had just seen too much, or maybe she just didn't know.

Lily thought back to her time in Boston, the day that she received the fateful phone call. Her Grandmother was not able to make the call herself, she had been too upset, so she had one of her 'Uncles' call her. Lily had so many 'Uncles' she re-called wryly, knowing that her parents had no real siblings of their own.

She remembered being in her hall of residence. In her room, busy working on one of her papers and not wanting to be disturbed. She'd ignored the phone calls coming in on her mobile until eventually she had switched off her phone altogether. Less than ten minutes later there had been a short firm knock on her door.

With an irritated sigh, Lily had walked to the door expecting one of her fellow students, probably there to invite her to one of the student functions. Instead she opened the door to find the University Dean standing on her threshold, looking somber and oddly formal in his tweed jacket and tie. He shifted uncomfortably on each foot and asked Lily to accompany him immediately to the office. Lily new instinctively that something was horribly wrong. Why else would the Dean come and fetch someone in person, if it was not to deliver bad news.

She remembered the long walk down the narrow corridor, walking between the double doors every six rooms or so. She remembered walking down three flights of stairs and into the Hall of residence entrance. She remembered the short walk across the courtyard into the main building where the offices were situated, and she remembered being asked to sit down in the chair next to the Dean's desk, whilst he maneuvered his phone across the dark wooden desk and held out the receiver to Lily.

The Dean nodded for Lily to take the phone, and he said very gently to her, "it's your Uncle".

Lily took the phone and placed it close to her ear. "Hello?" she asked quietly.

"Lily", her Uncle Edward's familiar voice sounded both strained and relieved at the same time.

"Lily" he said again, this time his voice tailed off. Lily could hear some shifting in the background and whispers. This time a different voice came on the line.

"Lily, it's Aunt Julianna, I'm sorry, your Uncle is quite upset." She spoke more matter of fact, with less emotion in her voice.

"Lily, there is no easy way to tell you this, but I have some bad news."

Lily's stomach was knotted tightly. She suddenly felt heavy and weighed her down in her chair.

"Your Mother and Father were killed last night. It was an accident. They were driving back home after supper in the City. They were driving along the Eastern Corridor, when one of their tyres blew out. It was sudden Lily, they lost control and their car went through the barrier and into the harbour. I'm so very sorry." Her Aunt finished.

When there was no response she said; "Lily, honey are you there?"

Lily couldn't listen any longer, she held the phone out to the Dean, who took it before she let it go and he politely continued a conversation with her Aunt that Lily didn't hear.

In fact Lily didn't hear much after that. She didn't remember being escorted back to her room, or when the Doctor came into her dorm to give her a sedative.

When Lily awoke the next morning, everything had been arranged. Her Grandmother had paid for a plane ticket back to Hong Kong. The funeral would be in five days time and she would to go home to help the family prepare.

Lily went through the motions of packing her things. Everything was slow and sludgy to her, like walking through thick soup, she felt like her head was filled with it too.

She'd had been given extensions on all of her course work, and everything had been arranged by the Dean's secretary, her tutors were notified and allowances had been put into place.

It was confirmed that she would be away for at least a month.

The drive to the airport and the flight to Hong Kong was all a blur. She wasn't sure if she slept, and she couldn't remember being awake either. Food had become a thing of the past as her appetite disappeared overnight.

The first thing that she remembered about the trip was the humidity. The air was so wet, that it almost took Lily's breath away when she stepped off the plane. It was an effort for her to breathe. She waked through immigration effortlessly and swiftly to a waiting black Mercedes-Benz.

Lily was driven directly to her old family home. It was on the South side of the Island, a Mansion of a house that hugged the mountainside and was surrounded by a tropical jungle, with a direct view of the Ocean that seemed to just drop off in front of the house.

As the car drew close Lily watched through the drivers window as the familiar black security gates opened and the car swung easily into the sprawling drive way.

LIGHTS OUT

Lily climbed out of the car, whilst the driver collected her bags from the boot. She went straight into the house and yelled for her Grandmother.

"Granny, where are you?" Lily shouted as she started to walk toward the drawing room. At the sound of Lily's voice, Mrs Lui, their old family housekeeper hurried through from the kitchen to greet her. She gave Lily a tight squeeze and gently stroked the back of her hair like she used to when Lily was a child.

"Lillian, welcome back", the old lady sniffed sadly. "I'm so sorry that we have to see you again under such circumstances. Your Grandmother is upstairs in bed. She asked for you to go right up when you arrive. She's desperate to see you. Now go." She gave Lily a gentle shove in the right direction.

"Thank you, I'll go up now."

Lily ran up the staircase two steps at a time, reminding her of her childhood. She reached the landing and quickly went to her Grandmothers door. Turning the handle she pushed the door gently and peered into the room.

The room was dark, the curtains shut tight.

"Lillian, come in my dear. I'm not sleeping." Lily's Grandmother spoke quietly.

Lily duly walked over to the bed and perched herself on the edge depressing the mattress slightly. Her Grandmother had always impressed Lily. She had always been so energetic and young looking and wise and knowledgeable, but today she looked pale and old. Today she actually looked her age.

Lily leaned in to her Grandmother and wrapped her arms around her slim body tightly. She could feel every bone across her slight frame, and she suddenly seemed so fragile.

Lily pulled back gently and looked at her Grandmother.

"I don't know what to do." Lily said, almost in a whisper. "I don't even know how I should feel." Lily could feel a tear starting to escape and she quickly rubbed her sleeve across her tired pretty face.

Her Grandmother leaned forward and with her gnarled old hand, gently wiped the tears away until they were gone.

"My dear Lillian, I know how you feel right now and that will never really leave you. If we are lucky it will dull in time, but we will never forget, and you will find that at the most inappropriate time, thoughts and memories, both happy and sad, will creep up and surprise you." Her Grandmother said soothingly as she stroked Lily's hand.

"But, first we need to talk, and we have a lot to discuss. I think it's time for the truth".

Lily held onto her Grandmothers hands and nodded unknowingly.

Her Grandmother got herself comfortable in the bed, as Lily helped to plump pillows and straighten the bedding. She was instructed to switch on just one side lamp. It was already getting dark outside and there was no more natural light that could be let into the room, so she kept the curtains closed.

Lily pulled up a chair and sat facing her Grandmother, waiting for her to begin.

"You won't really remember your Grandfather" She started, "you were so small when he died, but he was a great man. You remind me a little of him." She brushed Lily's cheek.

"It was your Grandfather that provided all of this". She waved one of her arms sweeping the room to indicate the family home.

"He had his own business. It was a clothing factory, back when we could still have factories in Hong Kong. We made formalwear, cotton shirts for men and dresses for women. It was a good business. Then suddenly things started to change. China began opening up and people started to move their business over the border, customers started to work directly or through trading companies, and suddenly Hong Kong became an expensive place to manufacture. We watched as so many of our neighbours were forced to close down their factories, some of which had been in their family for over sixty years. They simply closed the factory doors and disappeared overnight. We were heading in the same direction, and started to worry about surviving the changes, when someone came to discuss a business proposition with your father.

During that time gangs in China were rife, businessmen were being bullied and businesses blackmailed, factories were being burnt down, people started paying for protection to certain gangs to stop being harassed, but it still continued. Nobody could be trusted. Some of the gangs became so big with so many members, that they no longer called themselves gangs. They formed societies. Some societies had so much money coming in illegally that they needed a way to move the money without coming under suspicion. With so many businesses closing down in Hong Kong, it seemed the perfect opportunity to use a failing company to move the money through undetected and then legitimately put it through a Hong Kong bank, when the time was right it would be transferred back to China.

Your Grandfather could see the writing on the wall with our factory, and like all good businessmen, thought through the pros and cons, and then he finally agreed.

That decision helped to keep the factory workers in employment, and kept his factory open. It worked well for many, many years and over time your Grandfather became a trusted member of the society, slowly working his way up the ladder and taking on more and more responsibilities. By the time your Mother was getting married to your Father, your Grandfather was working in so many sectors of industry for the society across both borders. Always using his old business to legitimize everything. He had Hotels and restaurants in Hong Kong and China paying protection money. A group of over one hundred security men and bodyguards worked for him. He was personally instrumental in co-coordinating the introduction of fake goods between borders, taking his cut and ensuring that both parties had police protection, or the kind that could turn a blind eye. He paid handsomely to those people that helped and supported him. Then as we reached the 1980's things became more technical slowly moving out of his realm of expertise. He realized that he needed someone young and trustworthy to work with him. This is where your Mother and Father came in. Your Father worked in computers and was dynamic and always looking for a challenge. Most importantly, he was family. It was easy to convince him to join the society and he proved to be a great asset. Next came pirated software, videos, and then mobile phones. Suddenly the business exploded and we had money coming in from every angle, and your Grandfather was controlling all of it. He knew everyone and everything. We went to parties at the Hong Kong Governors residence; we dined with the Commissioner of Police and his wife and all the other high-ranking officials. People started asking him to invest in legitimate business projects, which he started to do.

It was going well, but then something shifted. Seeing the success of the society, a rival society began to stake a claim of some of our territories, and soon a war erupted.

You may not remember this as you were still so young, but about ten years ago in Tsim Sha Tsui, there were gangs on the streets fighting. Using their hands and fists, throwing acid. It lasted for five days and the police just turned a blind eye.

We won. Even though they had tried to destroy everything that he had worked forty years to build. Your Grandfather was never aggressive, not once, he never had to be, he had thugs and other people to do that for him, but he was tough and respected, and that's what they needed to break. Your Grandfather was killed crossing the road from the Grand Hyatt Hotel. We had just had supper with your Mother and Father. Out of nowhere a car ran him down and he died there and then. I was holding his hand."

Lily's Grandmother paused for a moment, remembering the scene as vividly as if it had been the same day.

She gave a sad smile to Lily and continued.

"The next day, everyone called a meeting. There was panic within our society and no one had considered a replacement. People from China flooded across the border to pay their respects at the funeral, over a 1000 people came. It was then that the society approached me. They knew me well by then. They knew that I had the ear of all the right people in Hong Kong, and knew that I understood the mechanics of what we were trying to do. I too had gained their respect over time. I looked at your Mother that day at the funeral. She looked a little like you do today, a little lost and a little angry. That's when I decided to protect my family in the only way I knew how, and I accepted."

Lily was stunned. All these years she had no idea what her family did. She had vague recollections of people coming in and out of the house, and remembered reading about the street riots in the papers, but this was like suddenly finding out that your parent was a secret agent or you were adopted. It hit her like a train.

"I had no idea" was all Lily could manage.

Her Grandmother continued. "Your parents did a good job with you, and we all wanted was for you to have the best start in life, to have a normal life. We had discussed bringing you in so many times as you grew older, but always dismissed it. Perhaps now it is time." Her Grandmother paused again, and looked troubled, her brow pulled into a deep frown.

"Your parents death was not an accident Lillian. The rival society still hungers for our business and it appears they have now chosen to take matters a step further. They have crossed a line. Despite everything that has happened, we can never allow them to take control of our society, too much has been lost already."

Lily's mouth had gone dry and she could feel the hot anger rising up in her. She wanted nothing better than to be shown the people or person that had arranged for her parents death and for them to be pointed out to her. Her mind began to drift as she began imagining what she would say to them before she killed them.

Her Grandmother interrupted her thoughts as though she had read her mind.

"Lily, you cannot be vengeful or impulsive, you will need a clear mind from now on, not one clouded by hate."

"NO", Lily shouted, her voice suddenly bursting with emotion. I want to know who did this. I need to know who did this to our family." Lily said breathlessly as she fought the angry tears. She sat silently for a moment before continuing.

"It is time for me now." Lily said, her voice almost a whisper. "I want you to teach me everything." Lily said looking at her Grandmother. In that moment everything seemed clear to Lily, her future was set and she wouldn't falter.

Lily's Grandmother rested a hand on her shoulder and eased Lily's hunched up shoulders down until she could visibly her visibly relax.

"Lillian, you must remember this; the one who pursues revenge, should dig two graves.

There will be an opportunity for you at the right time. This situation is not something that we can react to impulsively. This is what they want. We will cope with the next few weeks first and with dignity, we owe your parents and my daughter that much". She said her voice cracking slightly at the mention of her daughter.

"I will teach you, and you will learn. First attain the skill, then the creativity comes later."

Lily had so many unanswered questions, but knew that it would have to wait. This was her Grandmothers way of telling her that she would have to go back and study.

She stayed up late that night, jet lagged and tired in her bed unwilling to sleep. She vowed to herself that when she finally found the identity of who killed her parents, she would personally avenge their death and in doing so, she knew that she would not feel any remorse.

Bringing herself out of her reverie, Lily looked at the clock on the dashboard of her car and decided that it was time to go up. She hadn't seen Rob since he'd be taken by Ghost Face, and suspected that he would be in a bad way. She had been furious with Ghost when she had first seen the Polaroid. Rob was supposed to have been taken until the robbery was over, hidden away quietly, and then simply released unharmed. Ghost Face had other plans. He saw everyone as disposable and was starting to leave quite a trail of bodies in his wake. She'd spoken to her Grandmother and raised her concerns over his recent behavior, but he'd worked for the family for so many years now, everything that he did seemed to be brushed under the carpet and accepted in silence. Their silence to him was affirmation that his actions and decisions were acceptable, with the belief that whatever he did was in the best interests of the society. Lily disagreed fervently, and this was starting to worry her.

Ryan was a different matter. Lily had hoped that he would have been picked up by the Police and be safely out of the picture. He should have been tied up in interviews and investigations, taking the heat off the rest of them. Instead he had managed to go on the run. Something that none of them had anticipated. Lily knew full well, that given an opportunity Ghost Face would ensure that Ryan disappeared for good. She would not be able to protect him for long, she knew that, but for now, she needed to ensure that Rob was OK, and that Ryan saw that his friend was alive. The rest she'd work out later.

Lily stepped in to the lift and pressed the button for the top floor. She climbed the last set of stairs leading to a white door and knocked. A camera moved just above her head to the left, identifying who was outside the door.

A buzzer sounded and the door unlatched itself and stood slightly ajar.

Lily pulled on the heavy white door and as she stepped inside was greeted by one of the Society members, a man that she recognized, but didn't know.

"I'm here to see Robert Black." She said to the young Chinese man. He recognized Lily immediately and led her down a narrow corridor to a metal door. The young man nodded towards a thin viewing slit and stepped away.

Lily silently slid across the metal shutter and peered inside the room. Rob was no longer bound. He sat on the same chair that she recognized from the Polaroid picture. He was sitting next to a basic metal bed with a thin mattress and blanket. He had his trousers back on, but wore the same blood splattered shirt, but now the blood was brown and dry. He had tried to clean his face, but still had matted blood in his hair. He looked exhausted and damaged. Lily scanned the rest of the room. In the corner was a basic white toilet and sink attached to the wall. Everything was in open view so that Rob was visible at all times, like a prison cell, *but much worse*, Lily thought. She looked down just inside the door and noticed that there was an untouched tray of food.

She looked sideways at the young Chinese man. He shrugged. "He won't eat". He said.

Hearing the sound of a voice Rob looked up toward the door. He could see that someone was looking at him through the narrow slit, but couldn't see who was behind the door. He stood up.

"Hey", he yelled suddenly angry, making Lily step back slightly.

"Hey, c'mon, how long are you going to keep me here?" he asked, his voice sounding tired and desperate.

"Talk to me." He demanded.

Lily quickly closed the slat and walked back up the corridor with the Chinese man.

"When did he last eat?" she asked him.

"He hasn't touched the last two meals. He wants to talk to someone, but I'm not allowed to talk to him. I just slide in the food three times a day.

"Any other visitors?" she asked.

"No, just Ghost Face, he comes once a day, and then one of the other guys replaces me for the nightshift. That's it." He shrugged.

Lily's mind was in conflict. Was she foolish bringing Ryan here to see Rob? What would he do when he see's his friend in this condition? Will he be convinced that Rob is OK and then simply go to the police? She thought about that. Of course he would go to the police, and then they'll come directly to the warehouse. Before Lily could change her mind she felt her phone vibrate in her pocket. She slid the phone out and looked at the caller id. It was Ryan. He was here.

She answered the phone. "Just wait outside the door".

Ryan stood outside the white door. He felt a mix of impatience and nerves and didn't know what to expect or how he would react.

The door buzzed open and Ryan stepped inside, surprised and how bright and airy the entrance was. He looked around to gauge his bearings. To him it looked like it had been newly renovated. In sections, thick clear plastic sheeting still hung from the walls covering unfinished areas. The floors were concrete but looked freshly screeded. The walls, clean and white were lit up with bright industrial metal lights dotted around the high ceiling. There was a narrow corridor running off to the right, and small windows looking out towards the Chai Wan harbour. Just as he was about to walk down corridor, Lily emerged flanked by the young Chinese man that had greeted her upon arrival.

"Ryan". Lily said. Not sure how she should receive him.

"Lily." Ryan responded curtly.

"You can see Rob, but you can't talk to him. You need to be clear on that point. This is just to show you that he's alive and well, and that's all." Lily said and motioned for Ryan to follow her.

They walked in silence down the narrow corridor until they reached the metal door. Lily turned to Ryan and pressed a finger to her lips to indicate that he needed to be quiet. Ryan nodded once.

Behind them the young Chinese man stood motionless.

Lily slid across the metal shutter and motioned for Ryan to look through the slit. He had to bend slightly to get his eyes at the correct height. He peered in and waited whilst his eyes adjusted. He took in the sparse room and then focused on the broken man sitting before him. The noise of the shutter had made Rob look up with interest. He wasn't used to being looked at so frequently and now he was alert. *Perhaps something would happen today*, he thought hopefully.

"Who's there?" Rob demanded.

"Who are you?" He spoke again, this time standing up. He walked slowly towards the door, squinting his eyes to try and see the eyes behind the slit. Wanting to know who was looking at him so intensely.

Lily looked at Ryan and silently mouthed 'No' to him, shaking her head.

Ryan looked back through the slit in the door and seeing his friend walk toward him couldn't remain silent any longer. Before Lily had a chance to respond or pull him away, Ryan was speaking through the gap.

"Rob, it's Ryan. It's OK mate, I'm going to get you out of here, just hang on." Ryan could feel Lily pulling on his shirt, but he wouldn't move from the door.

Rob ran quickly to the door now and pressed his hands against it, trying to look through the small slit.

"Ryan, get me out of here, Ryan, don't you leave me here, you have to get me out." Rob shouted, his voice was ragged with tiredness, he sounded desperate. With the little energy he had, he banged his fist against the door.

Lily was pulling at Ryan as hard as she could. The young Chinese man was already running ahead of them down the corridor.

"You idiot" Lily yelled at Ryan as she tried to drag him away from the door.

"He'll call Ghost Face. You have to get out of here, he'll kill you and Rob if he finds you here."

Ryan looked at Lily, and seeing the concern on her face, took his chance. He held her by the shoulders and forced her to look at him.

"Lily, you can do the right thing. Let Rob go. He's done his job and you've done yours. You owe him this much." He said.

Lily shook her head. Her mind was racing. She should have trusted her gut instincts. She should never have brought Ryan here. It was a mistake.

"I was a fool to agree to let you see him. You should have just taken my word for it that he was OK." Lily said. "Now you are both in danger, you have to leave now."

Lily shook herself out of Ryan's hold and dragged him with her down the corridor away from Rob's cell.

"Lily, Ghost Face is a dangerous man. Do you honestly think that he will ever let Rob live? He doesn't need Rob anymore. The job is done now. Why keep him? Why complicate things further?" Ryan spoke urgently, willing for Lily to see that he was right.

Suddenly Lily fell silent. She turned to Ryan and shushed him.

Ryan could hear the young Chinese man speaking Cantonese. Lily listened intently to what he was saying her hand was across Ryan's mouth, both of them still now.

Ryan watched Lily's face drain of all colour.

She looked at him with horror in her eyes.

"What is it" Ryan whispered. "What did he say?"

Lily looked at Ryan and then looked back along the corridor.

"Ghost Face is coming, he's almost here. We have to act quickly." She whispered.

"OK, how do we get Rob out of that room?" He questioned.

Lily thought quickly. She knew that it was only minutes until Ghost Face arrived.

"There's only one way. We need the door code." Lily said. She nodded her head in the direction of the young Chinese man that was now walking towards them.

"He and Ghost Face will be the only ones with access to the room." She said under her breath.

Ryan stood just behind Lily and watched as she carefully slid her hand behind her back and pulled out a handgun. She rested her hand on the back pocket of her jeans, keeping it out of sight.

"I'm sorry Miss, I cannot let you leave. Ghost Face will be here any moment and he wants to talk with you."

Lily looked at the young man for a moment before responding.

"Look, I know you are just doing your job, but I have another appointment to get to, we really do need to leave." Her voice friendly, almost soothing in her tone.

She took a step forward.

"Stop." The young Chinese man said. Lily ignored him and walked another step closer.

"I want to talk to Ghost Face myself." She said, taking another step towards him.

Ryan stood back, not sure what he should do.

LIGHTS OUT

In the background he could hear Rob still calling out his name.

"Ryan, are you still here?" Rob's voice was faint, as Ryan concentrated on the situation in front of him.

"OK, but I'll make the call." The young Chinese man took out his phone, keeping his eyes on Lily. Lily waited for the right moment. She watched his eyes carefully, and knew that he would need to look down at his phone to dial the number.

Then she saw his eyes flicker down to the keypad. She took the last stride towards him and before he could react pressed the cold muzzle against his cheek.

She heard him take an intake of breath as she pressed the gun against him. She quickly patted him down for his weapon. She knew he would have one. She quickly found it pushed into the side of his waist belt and passed it to Ryan.

"Nice job". Ryan said, astounded that she had been able to do it so easily.

Lily leaned into the young Chinese man and instructed him to walk down the corridor.

Ryan followed behind them looking at the gun in his hand. He'd never handled a gun before and had no idea whether it was ready to fire or whether the safety catch was on or off. *Where is the safety catch?* he thought as he turned the small weapon over in his hand.

Once at the door, Lily jabbed her gun harder into the young man's cheek and told him to open the door. He looked at Lily with stubborn determination, and she jabbed him again, this time pulling back the trigger on her handgun.

The sound of the click was enough to move him into action and he quickly punched in the code.

There was a buzz as the door was released and Ryan quickly grabbed the young Chinese man by the arms and roughly bundled him into the room. Lily aimed the gun at the young man.

"Stay." She said simply.

The young Chinese man sat heavily down on the bed and watched them in silence.

Seeing the door open, Rob took his opportunity and stepped out of his prison cell into the corridor, to where Lily and Ryan now stood. Ryan quickly closed the door behind them, relieved when he heard the click as it locked back into place.

"About time" Rob said to them both, giving them a wide grin.

"Would either one of you like to tell me what's going on?" He asked looking from one to the other.

"There's no time to explain." Lily said to Rob, her voice now serious. "You and Ryan have to leave right now."

Lily started down the corridor, her walk picking up to a run with Ryan and Rob keeping up behind her.

Before they reached the end of the corridor, Lily suddenly screeched to a halt. She listened again and heard a click as the heavy main door opened.

"No", she said under her breath. She pushed her handgun back into her jeans. "He's here." She said flatly. Her stomach flipped as the adrenaline began to pump through her body.

Without needing to be told twice, Ryan pushed a bemused Rob behind the plastic sheeting closest to them. He looked at Rob and motioned for him to be quiet. Rob looked frightened but understood, and nodded to his friend.

Lily continued to walk along the corridor until she reached Ghost Face. His face was hard and pale. He looked less like a ghost today, she thought, more like a killer.

"What took you so long?" She said breathlessly trying to appear flustered. "They've escaped and they've locked the guard in the cell." Lily turned and started back down the corridor trying to encourage him to follow her.

Ghost Face eyed Lily suspiciously and scanned the corridor. There was certainly no sign of his man. He walked slowly behind Lily toward the cell. As he drew closer he could hear him calling out. He picked up his pace. When he reached the door he whipped back the metal cover and peered through the slit.

"Chang." Ghost Face barked.

"I'm sorry Sir." The young Chinese man replied, his eyes to the floor.

"You fool." Ghost Face shouted into the room before slamming the metal cover closed.

He turned and glared at Lily.

"You let this happen". He spat.

Hearing the commotion Ryan looked at Rob.

"Let's go." He said.

They slipped from behind the plastic and ran as hard as they could towards the exit.

Hearing the footsteps echoing behind him, Ghost Face spun on his heel and started to run at full speed. Still running he pulled out his handgun and prepared his aim. Then he saw them.

Ryan turned mid-run to check his rear. Ghost Face was almost upon them.

Ryan looked ahead, they only had another twenty meters to go and they'd be at the door. He looked across at Rob.

"Don't look back." He said breathlessly to his friend as they ran on.

Ghost Face had Ryan's back perfectly in his sight. He slowed down to a walk to steady his arm. He was less than ten meters away from them. He carefully pressed his finger on the trigger releasing the bullet.

The sound of the footsteps chasing them disappeared completely. The urge to look back was now too over powering for Rob and he snatched a glimpse behind him. Ghost Face was taking aim. Rob moved on instinct. If he'd had time to think, perhaps he would have done something else. But now, he did what came natural to him.

"Ryaaaan." Rob yelled as he pushed his friend out of the way. As if in slow motion, Ryan felt his body lose balance as his shoulder ricocheted off the wall and sent him tumbling to the ground. He pulled himself up and turned to Rob who was frozen to the spot. Ryan watched in silent horror as the bullet that was destined for him tore through Rob's cheekbone, shattering it instantly. He saw a tiny glint of metal as the bullet exploded out of the other side of Robs face and embedded itself into the opposite wall along with a splatter of bright red blood.

Rob collapsed at Ryan's feet, his body twitching as blood oozed out of the open wounds in his face. He looked up to see Ghost Face striding toward him closing the gap between them with every step.

Ghost Face was shaking his handgun in frustration. It was jammed. He kept trying to cock the trigger, but he couldn't pull it back.

Ryan was rooted to the spot, he couldn't move. His friend lay at his feet bleeding. He had his blood and flesh all over him.

Lily's scream ripped Ryan out of his daze.

"Run," She screamed at him. "Run".

It was enough to get Ryan to his feet and he bolted to the door. He slammed his hand onto the exit button and the door buzzed open. He pulled the door closed behind him, hoping that it would give him valuable seconds to escape. He ran down the staircase four steps at a time to the lift. He was in luck. Since Ghost Face's arrival no one else had used the lift. It remained on the top floor as if waiting for him. Ryan pressed the open button stepped inside and stood impatiently jabbing at the *G* button and the *Door Close* button simultaneously willing the big metal doors to close. He heard shouting as Ghost Face followed him down the stairs and to the lift door. The doors closing just in time. Ryan heard a fist slam against the outside of the metal doors. As the lift descended the noise became just a muffled low din.

All that Ryan could hear was his own breathing. He tried to slow everything down and catch his breath. He leaned forwards hanging on to the metal rail and forced himself to take slow breaths. Eventually he could feel his heart slow down and his breathing returned to normal. His stood and watched the digital number change as he descended lower and lower to the ground floor of the building. He just hoped that when the doors opened that no one would be waiting for him. He didn't have the energy for another chase, least of all a fight.

Ryan held his breath as the lift arrived and the doors slowly opened.

He carefully peered out and quickly scanned his surroundings. It was quiet. He took a tentative step out of the safety of the lift and walked quickly towards the exit. When he turned the corner he ran as fast as he could out of sight.

Upstairs, Ghost Face was pacing. He'd tried to catch Ryan before he entered the lift, but he was too late. For now Ryan had managed to escape him, but he would track him down.

Lily was now his biggest problem. He needed to find her, and quickly before things started to fall apart. He walked back in to the building and made a quick search. Of course Lily was nowhere to be found, she was sassy enough to know when to make herself scarce. He could hear the young Chinese man yelling in the room and pounding on the door to be let out.

Ghost Face calmly stepped over Rob's dead body and walked to the door. He punched in the code and released the door. The young Chinese man sprang out of the room almost bumping into Ghost Face. His eyes looked past him along the corridor and rested on the dead body of his capture.

Ghost Face looked at the man before him and narrowed his eyes.

"Because of your stupidity, Black is dead and Harper has escaped. And Lily…" He trailed off exhaling slowly.

"I will deal with Lily." He said quietly to himself.

Ghost Face checked his watch. "Assuming that Harper has notified the police, we do not have long." He said and nodded to the direction of the body. "Make it disappear. We were never here".

The guard nodded in silence hardly able to take his eyes off the dead body lying in a pool of blood.

Lily had sped off in her car, her mind in turmoil. What had started out as a simple plan was turning into total chaos. Rob was never supposed to be killed. Ryan was supposed to be arrested, placed under suspicion until such time that they had moved the money, laundered it and moved on.

Her Grandmother was expecting her. She wanted an update from her and from Ghost Face. Luckily he didn't yet know where she had placed the money from the bank. She needed to convince her Grandmother that he was dangerous. She needed to get to her Grandmother before he did. From now on, she knew that she was going to have to watch her back. The members may be loyal to her Grandmother, but some were as loyal to Ghost Face and now that Rob was dead and their only other witness was on the run, she knew that the blame would be turned to her. He would stop at nothing until she disappeared. Or worse yet, branded a traitor to the Society. That frightened her above all else. If all members of the Society agreed, even her Grandmother would not be able to save her.

Chapter 25

After her parents funeral Lily had done exactly as her Grandmother requested and went back to Boston.

She felt different now. Something inside her had changed since her parents death and she knew that she would never be the same person again.

She managed to get back into her work and studied furiously. She stopped going out and became almost reclusive. Most people that knew her put it down to the loss of her parents, a natural grieving process. Friends that would normally have pestered her to go out allowed her to grieve in private and eventually stopped asking altogether. Everyone that is, except for Rob.

Rob by now had heard about Lily's personal loss and had traveled down to Boston to see whether he could coax his old friend to get out of her Hall of Residence and to start living her life again.

Refusing to return Rob's calls, Lily was a little taken aback when he appeared on her doorstep out of the blue.

Her first reaction was to dismiss him and send him back to New York, but knowing how far he'd traveled, and the sentiments behind the visit; she softened and allowed him to take her to supper.

She didn't talk much that night, but with Rob she didn't need to. He did enough talking for the two of them, and it suited her. She could just sit and listen to his funny stories and antics with his friends, and Lily found herself becoming absorbed and really enjoying his company. It was the first time since her parents died and her Grandmothers revelation that she found herself not being swamped by it.

That night Lily decided that she could have one friend, and it would be Rob. He wouldn't bother her during the week, but if he wanted to come and visit, or if she needed company, she knew that she had someone to turn to.

Lily did a good job of keeping her secret. She managed to almost separate her life in Boston and her life in Hong Kong. Then, a few months before she matriculated, Rob told her that he was leaving.

It had been on the cards for some time. He was keen to move up the corporate ladder, and most of his peers had worked off shore for two to four years, returning with big promotions, and equally big salaries. Rob wanted the same, but he would have to move country to achieve it.

Lily was almost at the end of her studies and knew that she would be going back to Hong Kong soon afterwards. Rob knew this too, and something in the back of her mind told her that he had engineered his transfer to coincide with her eventual move.

Rob left first and they stayed in touch. She was actually looking forward to having a friend in Hong Kong. Most of her other friends that she'd had as a child had slowly fallen by the way side. Rob could be her one normal friend amidst the chaos that would help balance her life as a triad.

Lily's last few months in Boston went by in a blur. Her studies blended into one another seamlessly as her life became a series of exams, sleeping and occasionally when she remembered, eating.

Lily's Grandmother had prepared everything for her arrival.

Her old room had been newly decorated and her parents' room had been transformed to accommodate guests. It saddened Lily to see this, but she knew that it was the right thing to do. Otherwise she would be seeing too many ghosts.

Before Lily could start learning the ways of the Society, there were many formalities that she needed to go through.

To join a Society at any rank meant that she had to be acknowledged by the other Masters and be sworn in.

During her first week back home, her Grandmother took Lily to an old temple in Kowloon. The ceremony would take place at midnight and Lily had been told to wear all white. She'd selected her wardrobe carefully, not wanting to make any mistakes, and wanting to appear professional. She wore a long sleeved white cotton shirt with a high Mandarin collar and white linen pants. She had simple white ballet pumps on her feet. At the suggestion of her Grandmother, she wore her hair in a traditional knot at the nape of her neck held into place by a single gold pin.

The old temple was closed to the public after 8pm every night. The ceremony would be a private affair. To be sure, two security guards stood at the entrance to keep watch.

Upon entering the temple, Lily felt overwhelmed. She'd been into so many temples throughout her life, but this one was quite spectacular. She stepped over the stone threshold and was immediately hit by a wall of burning incense. Lily found it intoxicating. Hundreds of ochre yellow incense spirals hung from the ceiling. Long lengths of red string holding them in to place. The smoke, thick and grey, danced and spiraled up to the high ceiling. Piles of incense ash covered the floor, turning it black underfoot.

Lily walked past the incense spirals and continued as directed into the next room. She stepped across another threshold and onto some giant grey flagstones. The ceiling was high and vaulted, and huge red pillars stood in all four corners holding up the heavy tiled roof.

She took in her surroundings. The temple had obviously been chosen for the elaborate centre piece, an impressive grey stone altar, consisting of a flat large stone, which stood in the centre of the room. It was flanked on four sides by life-size wooden carved gods, each wearing a bright red piece of silk that had been carefully wrapped and tied around their heads. Behind the alter, toward the back of the room, was a large recess. Inside was a red painted bowl filled to the brim with grey ash. In every available space brown incense sticks burned, making the air thick with smoke. The smoke rose in one continuous spiral and escaped through tiny outlets before dispersing into the night sky.

Lily looked back toward the wooden carved Gods, all brightly painted and intricately carved. She recognized one as the God of the Sea, and another as the Goddess of Mercy. Lily smiled to herself. Just like her Grandmother, she was named after the God of Mercy. Lily saw it as a good omen for the ceremony and relaxed a little.

Lily's Grandmother represented the head of the Society in Hong Kong, and with her were eight other senior members, all with the designation of Master. Lily recognized them all; she had grown up oblivious to everything and everyone around her, now it all started to make sense.

One of her Uncles was to carry out the ceremony.

Lily noticed that by his feet, he had a bamboo cage with a rooster inside, it was a tiny cage, hardly enough room for the bird to turn in a circle and it had started to squawk and fidget, trying to fluff it's wings, but unable to do so.

Each of the eight members stood in a circle inside the four Gods with Lily in the centre. They each held a bunch of incense sticks, which her Uncle proceeded to light with a single wooden burning stick. Once the incense was burning well and the smoke started to ascend, the Masters began to chant whilst fanning the incense around Lily, shaking their sticks up and down, chanting low under their breaths.

Lily watched as her Uncle took the rooster from its cage holding the wriggling animal upside down with its feet. The bird flapped and squawked it's way to the stone alter. With one hand he pressed his arm and hand across the bird keep it down, and with the other withdrew a long sharp sword that glistened in the dark smoky room. The chanting increased in volume, whilst Lily remained in the circle, she found the smell was over whelming, slowly engulfing her in incense smoke.

The chanting grew louder still until it reached a high pitch, then her uncle swiftly brought down the knife slicing the roosters throat in one powerful sweep. The body of the rooster twitched and shuddered. He held it down until it subsided. Lily stood rooted to the floor as she watched the dark red blood form a pool in the basin of the stone. Her uncle filled a narrow glass with some of the warm sticky blood. He held the blood up to the two gods and bowed a deep bow. The circle had now broken, and a gap had been made for her Uncle to bring the glass to her. He took a step down into the centre and when he reached Lily he looked straight at her.

"Are you ready?" he asked simply.

Lily's heart was racing. The loud chanting and incense smoke had bewitched her. She felt light headed and strange. She hadn't expected any of this. It was never spoken of, and she would never be allowed to speak of it after this evening, not even with her Grandmother.

She nodded numbly at her uncle.

He dipped one finger into the blood and drew a symbol onto her forehead. Lily could smell the blood. It smelled of metal to Lily. The feeling of him drawing on her forehead was an odd sensation. His finger felt hot and the pressure in the centre of her forehead made her head buzz. She tried to keep her focus on her uncle and stood still whilst he finished his task. Next, he lifted the small glass to Lily's lips and said quietly to her; "now drink".

Lily closed her eyes and drew the liquid into her mouth. She tried to block off her nose. The thick warm red blood swirled around her mouth and she almost gagged. She screwed her eyes up tighter and drank some more, her Uncle each time raising the glass to let the contents slip into Lily's mouth.

Lily took a last gulp and opened her eyes and blinked. She felt flushed and a little unsteady. She looked around at all of the nine faces surrounding her. Her Uncle took away the glass, placing it back onto the stone alter, and opened a black wooden box; he withdrew a small book from inside.

He walked back to the centre of the circle where Lily stood and gave her the book. The book was covered in red silk, the colour faded with age. It was slightly dog-eared on the corners and Lily wondered how many times it had been used over the years. She tried to imagine her father doing the same rituals, but couldn't picture him.

"Now read the Good Fortune Harmony oath', her uncle said to her gently. "There are thirteen in total."

Lily cleared her throat, wishing desperately that she could drink some water to free her mouth from the metallic taste that was still so pungent. But she knew better than to ask.

She looked around her. All members were now silently waiting for her to begin.

She opened the book, and taking a deep breath, she proceeded to recite the contents to her audience.

"The thirteen Oaths of the Good Fortune Harmony Society", Lily read out loud, her voice echoing slightly around the temple. She continued.

"1. After entering the Good Fortune Harmony Society I must treat the parents and relatives of my sworn brothers and sisters as my own kin. I shall suffer death by five swords if I do not keep this oath.

2. When my sworn brothers and sisters visit my house, I shall provide them with board and lodging. I shall be killed by myriads of knives if I treat them as strangers.

3. I shall not disclose the secrets of the Good Fortune Harmony Society, not even to my parents, brothers, sisters, husband or wife. I shall never disclose the secrets for money. I will be killed by myriads of swords if I do so.

4. I shall never betray my sworn brothers and sisters. If this oath is broken, I will be treated as a traitor to the society and will receive one hundred cuts to my body.

5. I must never commit any assaults on my sworn brothers and sisters, or the family of my kin. I shall be killed by five swords if I break this oath.

6. I shall never embezzle cash or property from my sworn brothers and sisters. If I break this oath I will be killed by myriads of swords.

7. I will take good care of the family of my sworn brothers and sisters entrusted to my keeping. If I do not I will be killed by five swords.

8. If I am arrested after committing an offence I must accept my punishment and not try to place blame on my sworn brothers and sisters. If I do so, I will be killed by five swords.

9. If any of my sworn brothers or sisters are killed, or arrested, or have departed to some other place, I will assist their family who may be in need. If I pretend to have no knowledge of their difficulties, I will be killed by five swords.

10. If it comes to my knowledge that the Government is seeking any of my sworn brothers or sisters. I shall inform him in order that he may make his escape. If I break this oath, I will be killed by five swords.

11. I shall not appoint myself as Deputy Mountain Master without authority. After serving the Good Fortune Harmony Society for five years the loyal and faithful ones may be promoted by the Mountain Master with the support of his sworn brothers and sisters. I shall be killed by five swords if I make any unauthorized promotion myself.

12. I must not take advantage of the Good Fortune Harmony Society in order to oppress or take violent or unreasonable advantage of others. I must be content and honest. If I break this oath, I will be killed by five swords.

13. I must never reveal the secrets or signs of the Good Fortune Harmony Society when speaking to outsiders. If I do so I will be killed by a myriad of swords."

Lily finished the last oath and looked towards her Uncle.
"Now just the last paragraph." He nodded to Lily and indicated that she must finish in full.
Lily turned to the last page and continued to read.

"After entering the realms of the Good Fortune Harmony Society I shall be a loyal, faithful and true member. I promise to follow the path of the Society and I endeavour to keep true to the Oaths that I have spoken.
I will worship our precious God; Guan Gong and will incorporate the six qualities of the humble man into my life.
Humanity. Righteousness. Ritual Obedience. Wisdom. Loyalty and Trust."

Lily closed the book and passed it back to her Uncle, who, for the first time since starting the ceremony, smiled at her. Lily looked around her. All of the members were nodding in acknowledgement. She turned to her Grandmother who reached forwards with her hands to take Lily's. Lily stepped forwards quickly closing the gap between them and held her hands out.
"Congratulations Lillian", she said looking up at Lily.
She withdrew her hands and carefully twisted off a gold and jade ring from her bent finger.
She took Lily's hand and slipped the ring onto the middle finger of her right hand, it was too big and swung around loosely.
"What's this", Lily whispered rubbing the cool jade stone with her fingertips.

"It shows that you are a member. Only members of our society can wear them. It's one of our signs. This one is over thirty years old. A good piece of Jade." Her Grandmother said.

"But what about yours?" Lily asked, "Shouldn't you still wear one?"

"I have one." She stated and touched Lily's cheeked with her old fingers. "This was your fathers, you can have it made smaller to fit you. But it's very much yours now."

Lily smiled at her Grandmother and looked around the temple. It was such a surreal setting; the lighting was low, mostly candles surrounding the stone altars. Smoke still poured out of the incense tips and twisted and spiraled above their heads causing a haze. The walls were all painted a deep red, making it feel like they were inside a cave. This was truly a life changing moment for her. She had read the Oaths, and knew how important they were. She would honour them all and learn from her elders, and when the time was right, she would avenge her parents' death.

"Time to eat." Lily's Uncle clapped his hands together breaking the moment. He guided them all to the exit and they stepped out onto the quiet Hong Kong street.

Chapter 26

Sarah was sitting at her desk when the call came in. At first she didn't register, the voice was talking so quickly it made it hard for her to understand.

"Who is this", she asked, squinting as she tried to push the phone closer to her ear so that she could hear properly.

"He's dead, they killed him, they had him and killed him, he's dead, and I have his blood all over me. He's dead." Ryan panted as he spoke.

Sarah recognized the voice of Ryan Harper, it was clearer now.

"Ryan, is that you? Where are you?" She asked standing up. With her free hand she grabbed her suit jacket off the back of her swivel office chair and started toward the door.

"Ryan what happened, talk to me. Who's dead?" She asked, striding now down the corridor toward the exit, trying to keep Ryan engaged and talking at the same time.

"I'm in Chai Wan," He said. This time his voice sounded calmer.

LIGHTS OUT

"My battery is low, I might get cut off." He said.

"OK, tell me the road name and I'll come and get you right now".

"Shing To Road" Ryan managed to say just before his phone battery died.

Ryan slumped down onto the floor. He had hidden himself down a narrow side street and would just wait. He knew that it would take Lam about twenty minutes to get there, so he would just sit tight until then.

His head was swimming. He didn't know what to think anymore. His world in the last week had been turned completely on its head, and his life was clearly in real danger. He thought back to the shooting. He could see vividly Rob's face explode in front of him. It happened so fast, one second his friend was there, pushing him out of the way. The next he was twitching and squirming on the floor, blood pouring out of his head and face.

Ryan looked down at his clothes. They were covered in speckles of blood and flesh. Ryan gagged; he leaned over to his right and vomited. Supporting his weight on his hands and knees he continued to heave, even though there was nothing left in his stomach. He coughed until his throat was raw, and then shaking, he moved himself back into a sitting position slightly further down the alleyway, away from his mess on the floor.

Ryan wiped his mouth with the back of his shirt. He wanted to claw his clothes off and shower, but he couldn't, he had nothing else to wear. He would have to wait.

He was suddenly so thirsty. His mouth dry from vomiting, he desperately wanted to drink some water. His head was throbbing so hard now that he could do nothing except press his palms against his forehead and close his eyes tight.

He was still in this position when he felt a hand gently touch his shoulder.

It gave Ryan a start, and he jumped to his feet unsteadily.

"It's OK Ryan", Lam said softly taking in the man before her. Even in the dim alleyway she could see that he looked so disheveled and pale. His unshaven stubble had particles of what looked like vomit, and his shirt was covered in what was clearly blood. He smelt terrible, she thought.

"Thanks for coming," Ryan said, his throat husky and dry, realizing for the first time in days how relieved he actually was to see her.

"Before you ask, I'm not coming in." Ryan stated as they walked slowly back down the alleyway. "I'm innocent."

"I won't force you to Ryan, but to clear your name, you are going to have to be interviewed. Your prints are all over the bank. You ran Ryan. It's a clear sign to us that you have a reason to run." Lam said. She wanted nothing more than to bring him in, but in her experience she could see that he was frightened of something and she needed to know what that was.

They walked together slowly down the dark narrow alleyway and stepped onto the pavement. It was bathed in bright sunlight making Ryan squint and shade his eyes. They continued a few more steps until they arrived at Lam's car. She'd driven her 1985 Porsche and parked it on double yellow lines close to the alleyway where she had found Ryan.

"Whose blood is that?" Lam asked, testing the water and nodding towards his shirt.

"It's Rob's, he's dead." Ryan said matter of factly, as though she'd asked him what aftershave he wore.

"I can tell you everything that you want to know, but I'm not coming in yet. I will, I'll promise you that. But if you force me to come in now, I'll be dead within twenty-four hours. They have people everywhere. Even part of the Police force." Ryan said, brushing down his shirt in an attempt to get rid of the drying debris.

"You need a change of clothes." Lam said. Looking at him now in the bright sunshine, his appearance was even worse than she initially thought.

"I know. Can you drive me somewhere. I can run in and quickly buy something, then we can talk.' Ryan said.

Lam thought things through for a moment. If she insisted that she bring him in, he would most probably run again, and she really didn't want to shoot him in the leg or have to bring him down. What she wanted was to find out what happened. She wanted to nail the bank robbery and find out why Rob had been killed.

Lam turned to Ryan.

"OK, here's the deal. I'll get you cleaned up, and then we're going to find a place to talk. You are going to tell me everything that has happened, from the beginning, nothing left out. I want names, places, everything." She said. "and I want it on tape. It needs to be submissible." Lam continued. "I can forcefully bring you in, but I'm not going to do that. I can see that you are scared, and I believe that you don't trust anyone right now, including the police, so I appreciate that you want to talk to me. But once I have everything secure at the station, I'll ask you to come in, and I'll need you to make another statement and be interviewed by another detective, not just me. I do have just one other question." Lam said.

"Are you completely innocent in this Ryan?" She looked at him. His eyes had dark circles around them and his lips were cracked and dry.

"Yes." He said, his voice ragged and tired. "Yes, I am."

Lam nodded.

"No more questions for now. Let's get you some clean clothes." Lam looked at her car interior and then at Ryan, and for a second contemplated what she should do.

"Luckily it's leather." Lam said with a sigh.

Ryan forced an apologetic smile and climbed in to the passenger seat. For the first time in a few days he felt safe. He sat in silence as Lam pulled the car into gear and sped off leaving the empty warehouse behind them.

Twenty minutes later Lam eased the Porsche into an underground parking lot and found a space in the far corner away from all the other cars.

She turned to Ryan.

"Give me your sizes, you can't go out in public looking like that, you look like you've just killed someone." She said.

Ryan looked at Lam, taken aback by how accommodating she'd been since arriving in Chai Wan. He thought she may try to coax him in, or force him, but she had been patient and seemed to understand. He wondered how much she knew already.

"OK, well I'm a size Large top, 42" chest, and 34" Waist and 34" Long on the leg for the pants. My shoes are fine. But I could do with some deodorant, shampoo, and a toothbrush if you don't mind." He said, feeling a little awkward.

"And, thanks." He said before she climbed out of the car.

"Give me 30 minutes. You look as though you're about to crash. Why don't you sleep? I'll be back soon." Lam said as she stepped out of the car, trying not to worry about her leather interior, and how she would get rid of the smell afterwards. She looked in one more time at Ryan, his eyes were already heavy and closed. She locked the car and pushed the key deep into her pants pocket and quickly made her way to the shopping mall entrance.

When Ryan finally opened his eyes, he didn't know where he was. He quickly glanced to the side and saw Lam driving. She glanced sideways and smiled at his expression of horror.

"It's OK". She laughed. "I'm not taking you in. I'm taking you somewhere where you can get cleaned up." She told him reassuringly.

Ryan sat up in the passenger seat and looked out of the window. Finally he recognized where he was. It was close to his own home in Mid Levels. Lam took the next turning to the left and pulled into what Ryan recognized as Bowen Road.

"Where are we going?" Ryan asked, a bit puzzled.

"My place." She said looking at him. "It's probably the safest place to be right now. I figured that anywhere public that I took you, it would be too obvious. No one will think to look at my apartment. You can clean up, take your time and we can talk without being worried about anyone listening in. It's totally secure." She said. "You don't have to worry."

Ryan sat quietly thinking about being safe. It seemed like such a long way away. He didn't know if he could ever feel completely safe again.

Lam parked the car and led Ryan into the building and up to the third floor.

She let herself in and immediately had her dog Sasha bounding up to her and jumping up.

"Get down boy", Lam said, gently chiding him and pushed him into her kitchen and closed the door.

"He gets a bit excited, especially when I have new visitors", she said apologetically.

"Come in." Lam opened the door fully so that Ryan could step inside.

He glanced around at her apartment. It was big and spacious. It looked like an old 1950's apartment with beautiful high ceilings and polished parquet wooden floors.

He took in the old tan leather club chairs, well worn on the arms. The walls of bookshelves stuffed to the hilt with books. An old wooden dining table took up most of the space, making Ryan think that she must like entertaining at home.

Lam pointed Ryan in the direction of her guest bathroom.

"You'll find fresh towels, and shampoo, and shower gel in the bathroom", she said as she handed him the shopping bags.

"Just take your time." She said.

Ryan took the bag and walked to the bathroom, closing and locking the door behind him.

It was a clean and modern bathroom. Over size white tiles on the walls, and pale marble tiles on the floor. There was an old roll top bath in the centre of the room, and an open shower in the corner. The tiles had been laid to

LIGHTS OUT

allow the water to drain towards the corner so as not to flood the rest of the bathroom. *Clever*, Ryan thought to himself. He located the guest towels and the shampoo in a vanity unit. He took the plastic bag and carefully emptied out the new clothes and toiletries onto the top of the toilet seat lid to keep them dry. He placed the plastic bag on the floor and started to undress.

He carefully peeled off his shirt taking care not to drop anything horrible onto the floor and turned it inside out, dropping it onto the open plastic bag. He noticed that the blood had changed from bright red to dark brown making the fabric feel stiff. He took off his shoes and placed them neatly together at the door, then removed his socks, his pants and finally his boxer shorts, dropping them all into a pile near the door. He walked over to the mirror and looked at himself.

He hardly recognised the face looking back at him. He never went more than a day or two without shaving. Now he'd gone three days and his stubble was starting to turn into a dark beard. It was itchy and course. His face had speckles of dried blood, smudged in places across his forehead and matted into his hair. Ryan felt suddenly exhausted as he looked at himself. He was fatigued beyond what he thought was possible, and yet he still kept going.

Ryan opted for the shower for fear of falling asleep in the bath. He turned on the large tap, and let the water run over him. His whole body felt tired. He stood like that for five minutes until he felt that every bit of bloody flesh and sweat had been washed away. Then he spent another five minutes scrubbing and washing his entire body until his skin was pink and raw.

The towels here felt like pure luxury after the grey scratchy towels in the Hotel. He dried himself down and looked at his new pile of clothes.

Everything was neatly folded still with the price tags in place. He took out the pants first. Jeans, his size, exactly right. He rummaged through the pile and almost laughed out loud, when he saw that Lam had even bought him underwear. Plain black boxers. *She's so practical,* he thought to himself.

He took all the labels off and pulled the boxers on, then the jeans. Both fitted perfectly and felt good on his clean body.

He went through the rest of the pile and pulled out socks, and a t-shirt. He put the socks on, they were a little short, but after all he hadn't told her his foot size, so she'd had to make a guess.

The t-shirt was marl grey jersey cotton with a picture on the front depicting a Hawaiian surfer with "surfs up" on the reverse. Not really his thing, Ryan thought, but it was clean and his size. He pulled it over his head and smoothed it over his torso.

He looked around the bathroom and located some toothpaste and spent a long time cleaning and brushing his teeth, swilling and washing out his stale mouth until it felt refreshed.

When Ryan finally stepped out, with his dirty clothes rolled up and inside the plastic bag, he was greeted by Sasha the dog, still very excited at the sight of a new guest, but no longer jumping up. He followed Ryan dutifully toward the kitchen where he could hear Lam banging and clanking around.

When Ryan popped his head around the corner it made her jump.

"Oh." Lam said. She was on her haunches digging out what looked like a mug.

"Coffee, tea? Lam asked Ryan, holding up the mug.

"Coffee please, milk and sugar."

Lam stood up and looked at Ryan. For the first time since they had met, she considered that he was actually quite good looking. Feeling her face grow hot at the thought, she quickly busied herself with the tea making.

"Make yourself at home, just go and grab a chair, I'll bring the drinks out." Lam said.

Getting the hint, Ryan walked back into the lounge and chose one of the comfortable leather club chairs close to the window. The view was amazing. Not quite the three sixty that he had, but spectacular all the same. To the right palm trees swayed in the breeze along with century old bow trees and rubber trees all so dense and green. It was like a having a private jungle for a garden. Several white parrots circled around the trees before settling themselves on the branches of one of the massive rubber trees. It was stunning, and felt so colonial. The water from the top of the peak ran down into a ravine next to the building. Ryan could hear the faint sound of a waterfall. The view directly in front of Ryan swept down the mountain towards the CBD and he could clearly see his bank, then beyond out into Victoria harbour and to the ocean. He suspected that at night time the view would be even better, probably also having a birds eye view of the light show that took place in the harbour every night.

He was pondering this when Lam came through with two steaming mugs.

She placed them on the coffee table in front of the two chairs and went to her bag to get her moleskin notebook and pen that she always carried with her.

Ryan settled himself into the chair and took a sip of his coffee. It tasted so good.

"OK", Lam said. "We have a lot to go through, so let's start from the very beginning, everything that you know."

Ryan nodded, then proceeded to tell Lam everything, starting with the morning of the shooting at the bank.

Every now and again, Lam would interrupt Ryan to ask a question, or to clarify a date or a time.

When they got to the point when Ryan first met Ghost Face, she interrupted him.

"Where did you meet? Lam asked.

"I'd asked Lily to come with me to the Café in Tsim Sha Tsui". Ryan explained.

"When you realized that Rob had been kidnapped, did you ever consider that he might also be involved? He knew Lily after all, and introduced you both" Lam asked Ryan, looking for his response her pen poised above her notebook.

Ryan thought this through for a moment, and then dismissed the notion.

"I really don't think so. I don't think he ever had a clue who she really was. I think they were very good friends. I don't believe that she ever thought that Rob would be killed. She wouldn't have had that as part of her plan. That I'm sure of." Ryan said, taking another sip of coffee.

"Do you think that Lily planned it all?" She asked.

"For sure this was very carefully planned, and successfully executed. They just walked straight out." Ryan stopped and corrected himself and with a wry laugh said, "I mean WE. We walked away with twenty million US dollars in cash." He continued. "She's very clever, and she is definitely the brains behind it all, but I don't think she's a natural killer. I don't think she ever thought that anyone would die. It was just about the money."

"Who do you think she is? Who does she work for? Lam asked.

"I think she's part of some kind of Chinese Triad gang." He said. "To be tied up with a man like Ghost Face, and robbing an International bank, using every sophisticated method possible, requires funding and support. Where else, or who else would want to be a part of something like that." He asked Lam.

"We also suspect that the local triad gangs are involved." Lam stated. "That's an avenue that we are exploring." She refrained from saying too much else on the subject of what they were working on.

"Go on" she prompted Ryan.

"Ghost Face was definitely in control. Lily was the organizer, she had everything planned to a 't', but he made sure that it went through without a hitch. He seemed to have every angle covered. It was a very smooth operation."

"So how did you get the money out? I understand about the camera's, that's very clever, but how do you simply walk out with all of that cash?" She asked.

"We didn't," Ryan said. "That's the beauty of what she had planned. "We didn't have to. We deposited all of the money into rubble sacks and left them on the fourth floor where all of the construction work is being carried out."

Ryan laughed to himself. "It's actually brilliant. Every morning at 7am, a construction truck comes and parks along Bank Street. They have a special permit and one hour to unload materials and pick up the previous day's rubbish. There's a rubble shoot, a big plastic tube that is directed out of one of the big windows and down into the back of the truck. They throw the rubble bags down the shoot. Once they are done, the tube gets packed away, the window closed and secured, and the truck drives off."

Ryan sat back in the leather chair. "It's amazing really." He said.

Lam was astounded. They'd been looking for witnesses who could tell them if they'd seen people carrying large duffle bags, or suitcases. She couldn't believe that no one had seen them. They had wasted time questioning hundreds of people there that night. But now she knew. Of course no one had seen them. The money was still inside the bank. Safely hidden in rubble bags, and before anyone even knew that the bank had been robbed, they would be loaded and dispatched somewhere else. *So clever*, Lam thought.

"Look Ryan, I need to call my colleague and ask him to start checking the fourth floor, and also to contact the construction company. Somebody somewhere knows something about the rubble bags. Do you mind?" she asked digging in pants pocket for her phone.

"OK, but no mention that I'm here?" Ryan asked sternly.

"Don't worry." Lam stood up and dialed a number. She walked into another room and Ryan could hear muffled talking as she was telling someone about the robbery.

She came back into the room and looked at Ryan as she sat down.

"Thanks', she said brightly. "This is all really interesting. Please go on."

"Well that's where my role ended. Once we had managed to get back out again, I was taken back to the car and then knocked out." Ryan turned his head to show Lam the cut on the base of his skull.

"I woke up hours later, I was really groggy. I think they must have given me something to sleep that long and to feel that bad. There were sleeping pills on my coffee table. That's when I heard the knock on the door and panic set in when I saw who it was. I knew that Rob's life was at stake and if I ended up in custody, then I wouldn't be able to help him." Ryan said truthfully.

"How did you find Rob?" Lam asked trying to keep her voice calm.

Ryan described his phone call from Lily, the warehouse and the young Chinese man. He talked through how he and Lily managed to release Rob out and then his lucky escape. He skipped the part of when Rob was shot.

Lam pushed Ryan gently. "How did Rob die?"

Ryan sighed, knowing that he had no choice but to re live his friends' death. He slowly explained the sequence of events of the fatal shooting. How Rob had pushed Ryan out of the way saving his life. He remained still for a moment remembering his friend.

"Why did Lily suddenly decide to help you and Rob. Why would she risk everything? She would have known that the guard would make a call and Ghost Face would immediately know that she was involved."

"I've also thought about that." Ryan said, "Rob truly was her friend, and I think she knew in her heart that Ghost Face wouldn't let him live. I think she had no choice. She did the right thing." Ryan said.

"You're a liability for them both now, especially now that Rob is dead. You could identify Ghost Face, and you know Lily already. You could expose a triad gang." Lam finished.

"I know", Ryan said. "That's why I'm not ready to come in. If he wants me dead, then he'll do it any way he can, whether I'm in Police protection or not. I'm better on the run for now, I can lay low for a while."

"What happened to Lily?" Lam asked.

"I don't know, I ran, I assume she did too. I don't know where she lives, or where she would go, but she'll be a target too. He'll want her dead for sure."

'Where will you go now?" Lam asked Ryan.

'I have a place to go and I still have my phone, so we can stay in touch, although I need to charge it." Ryan said fishing his phone out of his new pants. "Do you have a charger by any chance?"

"I think I have a spare that you can have." Lam said getting up.

Lam went into her bedroom to rummage through her drawer where she was sure she had a spare charger. "Give me a minute." She shouted through to the lounge. There was no answer. Lam stood up and padded back through to where they had been sitting. Ryan was gone. She walked through the apartment, and into the guest bathroom. No Ryan.

He'd slipped out of the apartment as quietly as a mouse.

Lam stood for a moment with the spare charger in her hand, wondering which lead she should follow up first.

Chapter 27

Lam was in a taxi on her way to the Station after dropping her car off to be cleaned. It would be ready to pick up at 7pm that evening.

She'd already briefed forensics to go through the fourth floor of the bank with a fine toothcomb, whilst her new partner Jimmy went to the construction company to see what he could find out about the driver and truck used the morning after the robbery.

She headed straight to the forensics lab as soon as she arrived.

The lab always impressed Lam. It was the latest addition to the station and gave them serious kudos amongst the other stations. Not only was the lab state of the art, so was the forensics team. If there was something to find, then they would find it. She trusted their results and view implicitly, and they respected her for it.

Lam swiped her security card at the door and breezed into the lab looking for Cheng. She found him hunched over a microscope in his white jacket. He was the lab whizz kid. Always in skinny jeans and the latest Adidas shoes, always wearing some form of designer t-shirt. The only formal thing about Cheng was his white lab coat. An essential that he couldn't get away with not wearing. His hair was thick and straight and had been worked up into a messy Mohawk and held stiffly into place with hair putty, the latest in Japanese hair technology.

Lam watched him for a few seconds before interrupting him.

"Cheng" she said her voice low, so that she didn't startle him.

"Oh hey Sarah," Cheng said smiling brightly at her. He liked Lam. She was tough, he knew that from some of his other colleagues, but she'd always treated him well, and was always pretty friendly, so he shook off the bad vibe that his colleagues gave him when they talked about her, and was friendly back.

"I don't have anything yet for you. Two of the guys are still at the bank, they'll be done in about an hour." He said apologetically, knowing that that's what she was chasing him for.

"It's OK, as soon as you have anything for me, then please just call me, OK?" She asked pausing to look over Cheng's shoulder.

"What are you working on, she looked past Cheng and across at the clear glass slide underneath the microscope.

"We're still trying to find something concrete on the prostitute killings. This is the third death in the space of a couple of weeks, he's busy, and he's thorough. We managed to get more of the semen this time, and we're still running a DNA match through our database. Nothing yet. Normally he doesn't leave a thing behind. He always wipes everything down, and he always showers before he leaves. It's the same M.O." Cheng shrugged disappointed.

"If anyone can find anything, you can." Lam gave Cheng a hopeful smile.

"Thanks Sarah, let's hope so." He said truthfully.

Lam smiled. He was the only person on the team that called her Sarah, and she let him. She liked it.

'Is Detective Wong still handling the case?' Lam enquired, curious to know if he was.

'Yeah, he's working night and day to catch this guy. No-one seems to care because it's prostitutes, but he does.' Cheng said, a little impressed.

After thanking Cheng again, Lam wandered back to her office. One thing that she despised most of all was men that fed on women. That used their strength and violence to control and violate in the worst possible way. Then after everything to just kill them afterwards, it was vile. She'd quite like to get her hands on this one herself, she mused.

She arrived back at her office and sat down at her desk ready to go through the robbery file but with fresh eyes. The information that Ryan had given her had totally opened up her case, but she still needed to get more on Ghost Face and Lily. They would lead her straight to the money and also the Triad gang.

She started to work through the reports. She turned the first page and started to read. She had a lot to follow up on, and now more than ever she was missing her old partner. He was always so good at this part of the job. She missed Chow and thought about him for a moment. The investigation was still ongoing. The Chief had given the case to another team to follow up on, freeing Lam to continue with the robbery investigation, especially now that she had so much to work through. She had been interviewed and they pulled together everything they had on Chow, it didn't amount to much. The Chief was desperate to nail this killer. "One of his own." He had said to Lam. But they had nothing. There was no evidence left at the scene after the overnight down pour, no fingerprints, and no weapon. Just Chow's almost decapitated body. She didn't know why he was there, or what he'd been working on. He had nothing on his body when they found him, his wallet and ID was missing. They concluded that it may have been a tragic case of a mugging gone horribly wrong, but there was something about the way that Chow had been murdered that didn't sit well with Lam.

Lam sat drumming her fingers on her desk. Then she stopped suddenly, her fingers raised, hovering above the desk as though she had been momentarily frozen.

"*Oh my God.*" She whispered slowly under her breath. She quickly grabbed her moleskin and scanned through her roughly scribbled notes. After flicking through the pages, she stopped and turned back one page. There it was in black and white.

8th August, Ryan meets with Lily and 'Ghost Face' at a Café in TST.

The realization dawned on Lam, like having a glass of cold water thrown on her face, bringing her to her senses. The Café in Tsim Sha Tsui, which Ryan described, was directly opposite the alleyway and the 7Eleven where they found Chow's body.

Chow was watching them, Lam thought horrified. *He had a lead, he knew something and they killed him for it.*

'What did you know?' Lam said out loud. As though Chow was in the room in front of her.

"I don't know, what did I know" came the reply from behind her.

Lam jumped, swinging her chair around quickly to face Jimmy Luk. The very last person that she would discuss Chow with.

"Nothing," Lam said straightening up her back and closing her notebook quickly.

"Any news for me?" She asked abruptly.

"Well that depends. " He teased. " I may have a bit of information that you might be interested in."

"OK, I'm waiting," Lam responded, irritation seeping into her voice.

Jimmy walked over to Lam's board showing all of the crime information so far. She hadn't yet updated Rob's or Ryan's status, she'd do that later after Jimmy had left.

"You were right. The rubble bags definitely were full of the cash. Twenty-six rubble bags were sent down the disposal shoot that morning from the bank. Only 16 bags were delivered to the construction site to be disposed off. The vehicle has been taken away and put in the pound. I've arrested the driver and he's here, ready to be interviewed. He seems eager to talk." Jimmy finished. Giving Lam wide smile as though he expected her to tap him on the back or give him a well-done sticker.

Lam nodded, the best that she could muster, and stood up.

"OK," she said. "Let's go and chat to our driver."

The driver sat in the interview room looking absolutely petrified. He was young, somewhere in his mid-twenties and wore jeans and a long sleeved t-shirt. Lam could see tattoos just showing around the wrist area below his t-shirt. His hair was cropped short. She noticed that he was sweating.

Both DI's sat down opposite the driver. Lam switched on the tape recorder. She spoke first.

"Please could you state your name for the recording".

"Anthony Choi', he said nervously, wiping his forehead with the back of his hand.

"You have been brought here because you are thought to have information regarding the Bank Robbery of the World Asia Bank four days ago. Do you understand?" Lam spoke slowly and clearly as she always did during recorded interviews.

The young man nodded.

"Please speak so that we are clear of your understanding."

"Yes, I understand," he said.

"Please can you talk us through August 9th, starting with loading up the truck with the rubble bags." Lam said.

"My job that day was to load the bags of rubble, take it back to the yard, then once we've sorted it we dispose of it in one of our land fills. It normally take a few hours from start to finish." He said.

"And what was different this time." Lam prompted.

"I was asked to make an unscheduled stop." He said.

"Who asked you to make the stop?" Lam asked

"A – A Woman", he stuttered a little embarrassed.

"Did she ask you in person, or over the phone?" Lam said.

"In person. That morning I was waiting for the bags to be loaded and she just climbed into the cab next to me. She really took me by surprise." He said, clasping his hands in front of him on the table to keep them from shaking.

"Go on" Lam prompted.

"Well, she went into her bag and showed me an envelope. She said that if I gave her a lift to a particular road, which was on my way to the yard, I could have the envelope. She opened it to show me. It was stuffed with cash, a lot of cash." He said, his voice trailing off.

"I just thought it was my lucky day. A beautiful woman climbs into my cab, and offers me money to drop her on the way to the yard. So I said OK. I was stupid." He said, casting his eyes down.

"So you took the woman with you, and did you drop her where she asked?" Lam said.

"Yes, it was all a bit weird really. She wasn't very chatty at all. She just made one phone call, I assumed to her boyfriend, and so after that I put the radio on so that it wasn't too quiet. Then once we got close to her drop off, she guided me down a wide off ramp and into a disused quarry. There was a van waiting, I just thought it was her boyfriend or something. But then four men got out, and I got scared." He said.

"She told me not to worry, and to just stay in the truck. She said that they just had to pick up something that belonged to them, and before I could argue they had jumped onto the back of the truck and were throwing off the rubble bags. I thought it was so odd. Why would they want rubble? They took ten bags and loaded them into their van. Then she handed me the envelope, climbed out of the truck and she was gone, they were gone. So I just drove back to the yard and unloaded as usual.'

"How much money was in the envelope?" Lam asked.

"Fifty thousand Hong Kong dollars. A lot." He said.

"Do you know what was in the bags?" She asked.

"I think I do now," he said.

"I saw the news later in the day, and I kind of thought that's what it probably was." He said.

"I didn't really know what to do. I'd taken the money, and was worried that if I came forward that the police may think that I'm involved." He finished, shrugging.

"Do you need to have the money back?" he asked earnestly.

"Yes, we'll need to check the money and the envelope for finger prints. It's also probably part of the stolen cash from the Bank." Lam said.

"We'll only know that once we can cross check the serial numbers."

"I have it still, I didn't take anything out. I was too scared to use it after seeing the news, so I was planning to wait and maybe use it later, you know, once things had died down."

"OK, I'll need you to give a detailed description of the van, the woman and the other four men that got out of the vehicle." Lam said. She turned to look at Luk, who had remained silent throughout the interview.

"Anything else that you would like to ask?" She said.

"No, I think that covers everything. " Luk replied offering her one of his best smiles.

He leaned in toward the recorder and said.

"Interview with Anthony Choi finished at 15:32hrs." He clicked off the machine and turned to Choi.

"Come with me and I'll take you to one of the officers to take down the descriptions and write up a report." He stood and waved for the young man to follow him leaving Lam sitting in the room.

A few moments later Luk returned to the room.

"Is everything alright?" he asked her.

Lam turned to look at Luk, thoughtful for a moment.

"It's all very, very clever." She said. "Luk, come with me, I want to show you something." Lam stood and led the way out of the room and down the grey corridor to her office.

They stood in front of her board looking at everything involving the bank case so far. They scanned the pictures, starting with the dead contractor, through to images of the vault and Bank exits.

She looked again at Chow's picture, her partner, and she signed and shook her head.

"What is it?" Luk asked noticing her mood change.

"Oh, it's nothing" she said pointing towards the smiling picture of Chow.

"Just such a waste of his life."

Not wanting to get morose, Lam quickly changed the subject.

" I think I'm getting closer to finding out the sequence of events, and this is where I'm going to need your expertise and knowledge of the Triads and which gang may be responsible for this." She said, moving towards the left hand side of board, and the dead contractors picture.

"We always wondered why this old man", she said tapping the picture with her finger, "would attempt to get into the bank. He was never going to be able to rob it. But that was never the intention. I've gone over this hundreds of times. It was to see if he could get to the fourth floor undetected. To see how far he could get before someone official stopped him. That's all." She said blinking at the board.

"But that doesn't make sense, he was bound to get picked up, his card didn't work for a start." Jimmy countered, not following Lam entirely.

"That was their only flaw. The swipe card didn't work. Had it been working as intended, he could successfully have got through the security entrance and he would have been in the building, undetected. He could have made it to the fourth floor and exited and it's possible that he could have done this without being stopped and questioned." She said.

"But other security camera's would have picked him up moving around the building, stepping into the lift. He would have been noticed." Jimmy said.

"No, he wouldn't. The camera's we're all down that morning, remember? They were being upgraded. There was no footage whatsoever recorded during the first few hours of that morning. That's why we could only take eye-witness accounts of the security officers and Ryan Harper into consideration. There was nothing to verify what happened, where or when." Lam finished, deep in thought now, she moved along the back wall and stopped at an image of Ryan Harper and pressed her hand against the wall.

"She pointed a finger at Ryan's image." He was the key to all of this, but he didn't even know it yet." She said, drumming her fingers on his forehead on the paper picture, whilst she was thinking.

"In the background his girlfriend was planning the robbery with meticulous accuracy. Every fine detail covered off. This has been planned for a while. Her pseudo electronics company had successfully negotiated a contract with the bank. They installed all of the new equipment exactly one week before the robbery.

Her intended target was always going to be Ryan Harper. He had the security clearance to get them through every area of the bank without triggering an alarm or unwanted attention. She worked him and he naively took the bait. So they started to get to know each other, meanwhile she's planning the whole event. But I think she needed security to make sure that he would definitely be a part of the robbery. She wasn't convinced if she could bribe him with money, or other promises, so she used collateral, she used his closest friend in Hong Kong, which also happened to be her closest friend.

This is where Robert Black comes in. The unsuspecting innocent in all of this. He never knew of Lily's involvement until just before he died. He was supposed to be released shortly after the robbery, but this was taken out of Lily's hands.

"Poor guy. I hear her got a bullet in the face." Luk said.

"That's right." Lam responded, then paused. Temporarily stuck in her own thoughts.

Shaking it off she continued. "The timing was just perfect. The bank is undergoing upgrades to their security cameras and systems and renovation work inside the building in also being carried out. Contractors are coming and going, there's lots of noise and disruption. It's clever, because staff are less cautious, they don't question when they see a new face, assuming that it's all to do with the renovation work." Lam said, on a roll now.

"Then they had cover of the City's 'Lights out' campaign. The whole of Hong Kong being thrown into pitch darkness couldn't be more perfect. It gave her the ideal opportunity. A chance to get in undetected both supported by a black out, and camera's and motion detectors that could be easily switched on and off. They had Ryan with them, their 'key' and obviously enough people to help carry the money out." Lam continued.

"She knew that she didn't need to walk out with the money causing them unnecessary risk. She could simply load up the rubble bags. She already knew they would be collected the next morning at the same time that they always were. It was the perfect way to get something out of the building unnoticed and undetected. It was hidden in plain sight. No one even knew that the bank had been robbed at that stage. The money was well and truly gone by the time the alarm had finally been raised. She used her charm and guile to get the truck driver to drop her off at a pre-determined destination, so that the bags could be removed. It was so easy for her to bribe Choi. It was too much of a temptation for him and probably more money than he could earn in three months." Lam was about to continue when Jimmy interrupted.

"Actually it would be four months salary." His comment was greeted with a glare from Lam.

"I asked him earlier today", he muttered under his breath.

"They still had Ryan with them straight after the robbery." Jimmy asked Lam. "So what happened to him. Why not simply kill him, so that he couldn't identify them later?"

"They needed him to be the scape goat. He was already under suspicious by us, and they knew his prints would be found everywhere. It would buy them enough time to move the money, probably by laundering it, and release Robert unharmed. He would verify that he didn't know who had kidnapped him. Ryan would already have tried to exonerate himself and would have given descriptions of Lily and the other men involved. Our whole process would be too slow for them. They are professional and are experts at covering their movements and tracks and have been for years."

Lam finished and looked for a response from Jimmy.

"So where is the money now?" Jimmy asked.

"I don't know, and I suspect only Lily and a few loyal people will know at this stage."

"So, how do we find Harper?" he asked.

"Harper I'm in contact with, but he's running scared. He's very high profile target right now, so it'll be hard to get him to come in and talk to us on the record."

"Hold on, you've been in touch with Harper?" Jimmy asked, a trace of irritation in his voice.

"You're supposed to keep me in the loop here, Lam." He said, crossing his arms in front of him, showing her that he was annoyed. "How am I supposed to help you if you keep things hidden from me?"

"Look I had the opportunity to chat with Harper in private under his conditions, that's all, and he ran again. He doesn't trust the police." She said, almost as though she felt the same way. "I don't blame him at this stage. The triads have infiltrated us in the past, they could easily do it again." Lam said. "Also, Lily is not the only person involved in this." She stated.

"Go on", Jimmy said.

"Harper told me that Lily called him after she heard that he'd escaped the police and was on the run. She'd agreed to let him see Robert, to check that his friend was at least alive. They met, and he persuaded her to do the right thing and release Robert. Then another man came in, the same man from the robbery and the café. They call him Ghost Face. He tried to shoot Ryan, but Robert got in the way." Lam said, picking up her black marker and drawing a cross through Robert Black's name on her board.

"So now we have two dead bodies on our hands." Jimmy said.

"What do you know about Ghost Face?" Jimmy asked, more interested now.

"Harper described him to be in his mid-fifties, slender, but strong with incredibly pale skin. He had cropped black hair, going slightly grey at the temples. Whoever this guy is, he managed to not only convince Harper to be a part of the robbery, by intimidation and kidnapping Rob, but he has also shown himself to be very adept at killing."

"Do you know him?" She asked Jimmy hopefully.

"No, no. Not one of the names that I'm familiar with." he said confidently. "But it's possible that he has another name, most Triads members do?"

"Well can you do a search of other known names or anything similar?" Lam asked.

"I can, but if he was a leading triad member, then I would know him already, and I don't recognize the description or the name." Jimmy said flatly.

Lam continued. "Harper didn't think that it was Lily's intention for anyone to get killed. The contractor was unplanned, Rob's murder was totally avoidable, had they kept to their side of the bargain and released him straight after the robbery. But it's clear that something has changed, and there is a shift in the relationship between Lily and this man, Ghost Face." She turned to Jimmy.

"This is where you come in. You know everything there is to know about Triad gangs in Hong Kong. From what Harper has told me, and looking at everything we have. This is definitely triad related; I'm 100% sure about that. What's the likely outcome between Lily and Ghost Face if they are both part of the same Triad family?" She asked Jimmy.

"What's the triad protocol when two members disagree over something?"

"It's not good. A lot depends on hierarchy and it sounds as though Ghost Face is probably either more senior or more respected. There are not many women that we know of in triad societies. The odd one or two have come up in the past. There is one main female that has become quite a legend in Hong Kong, she's an unknown to us, but we have learned over the years that she heads up one of the biggest gangs. She's been able to stay anonymous for years. She's very well protected from all sides and very well respected within the Society." Jimmy continued.

"Triads have rules, the same way that we do. If a member has gone against one of the triad oaths, or has put one of the gangs into a situation where they may get exposed, then it's likely that person will be branded a traitor. If this happens, a hit will be ordered by the head or by the triad masters collectively, and that person will killed outright." He said matter of factly. Continuing his thread, he said "and it's not a nice death. There's an old ritual killing for traitors that some triad groups still use."

"What can we expect?" Lam asked.

"Well, firstly the death is very slow. It starts with cuts to the body using a large knife or sword. None of the cuts are lethal, so death is painful and drawn out. Normally we would expect to find a total of exactly one hundred cuts, if we find a body at all. We've been told in the past that sometimes the person carrying out the murder will bury the traitor alive. It's a horrible way to die." Jimmy finished.

Lam was absorbing everything that he was telling her.

"That's not good. We need to find out more about these people before we get another body on our hands."

"We haven't been able to trace the money yet. But I'm assuming it will be laundered somewhere known to the triads. Do you know any of the money laundering routes? Are there places that we can start to investigate, and people that we can talk to?" She asked Jimmy.

"It's not that simple. I'll have to do a bit of research and digging, I don't want to discuss this too much in the open. I'll be cautious and discreet and see what I can find out. We first need to find out which triad group we are dealing with here. Other groups will be aware, and may know things, but we need to be careful how we approach this." He finished.

Lam thought for a moment.

"We need to find Ghost Face. He's the dangerous one, and without him, I'll never get Ryan to come in. He doesn't feel safe whilst he is still out there." She said.

"I need you to find out as much as you can about Lily and Ghost Face, see if any of your contacts have heard of them, or seen them." She said.

"OK, but I think you should try and get Harper in here, we can offer him protection. He'll be safe here. If we can interview him again, there may be other things that he can tell us about these two people that will help us to close the net." Jimmy said. "I can show him pictures of some of the triads and see if he recognizes anyone."

"OK, I'll do what I can, but he was quite adamant about not coming in." Lam stood back and took in the contents of her board. It was starting to form a story, but she still had so many holes and she knew that Jimmy was right. Without Harper, she knew she couldn't pull everything together.

"I'll make a call." Lam said, picking up her phone.

Chapter 28

Lily drove out to the New Territories to the house that she kept there. She'd taken the property on her Grandmother's recommendation about two years ago. Some money had come in after the death of her parents, and she'd been advised to buy a place that was well away from the City, a safe house that she could use if she ever felt that she needed protection, or just timeout from the Society.

Her Grandmother also had a house, but hers was in China. It served the same purpose and many times had assisted her Grandmother when she needed to lay low.

Only her Grandmother and her lawyer knew the location of Lily's secret place.

It was situated close to the ocean in an area called the Gold Coast. All of the properties that ate up the sea front were modern condominiums, garish and ugly, but Lily had managed to find an old stone village house, slightly higher up the mountain offering uninterrupted views of the ocean and of the road that snaked and twisted it's way up to the mountain to her front door.

She had bought the house outright from an elderly Chinese family that were happy to take the cash. The purchase agreement had been drawn up in another name, which her lawyer had been able to wrangle somehow, so it could be never be located through public records or deeds and tied back to her.

She'd spent three months working with an architect, flown in from overseas, on every aspect of the property. Tearing it down to its bare bones, and re-building it sympathetically back to how it would have looked ninety years ago. The architect had done a good job of mixing the old features with new modern amenities. Her living room joined a huge decked terrace which dropped down a few steps into an eternity pool, all overlooking the ocean and beyond, with Hong Kong Island in the distance.

Security throughout was of course was state of the art with no expense spared. Lily had rigged up the house incorporating her new digital camera systems covering every aspect and angle of her home. She could monitor this from her laptop remotely at any time.

Lily felt safe here, and for now it's where she needed to be until she decided what her next move should be. She knew that she had to speak with her Grandmother. If Ghost Face got there first and managed to speak to all eight Masters then her fate could be decided upon without her even having the chance to defend herself. She knew that even if her Grandmother decided against the ruling, that if all other eight Masters agreed, she would be over ruled.

Chapter 29

Ghost Face sat on the gold brocade couch in the heavily ornate drawing room. He didn't like being kept waiting, and certainly not by someone that he had no respect for. He had come directly to the house after leaving the warehouse, knowing that he only had a short time frame to have this discussion. He had been waiting for fifteen minutes.

He wondered if the girl had called ahead, which was why the old lady was taking so long, but then dismissed the idea. She was running scared he knew that. When she had time to think about the events of today, she would realize that she had broken one of the oaths. She was a traitor to the society and he would take great pleasure in informing her beloved Grandmother of the truth. Once the girl was taken care of, by him, he so dearly hoped. Then he would be well positioned to take over. He would have to be cautious. He couldn't just allow her to disappear too soon after her Granddaughter. He didn't want it to be too suspicious. It had to feel like a natural take-over, intuitive. No different to any other business, a merger of two great societies of which he would become The Great Mountain Master.

LIGHTS OUT

The sound of the drawing room door distracted him from his thoughts and he turned to watch the frail old woman walk in to the room. It was laughable he thought, that she of all people could be in charge of such a powerful entity, that she even had respect. Behind her came another man. This surprised him. He had expected a private audience; certainly that is what he had requested when he had made the call. He didn't want a baby sitter present.

Ghost Face stood momentarily to show his respect and bowed his head as she seated herself in her usual armchair. Silently behind her chair stood the unknown Chinese man. He was dressed all in black. His hair slicked back, and his skin dark and golden. His head was bowed, so Ghost face couldn't see his face clearly.

He looked from the man to the old woman.

"Ghost Face," The old woman spoke with such a gracious air that it captured Ghost Face's attention immediately. He had forgotten how commanding her voice could be.

When he settled his gaze upon her, she continued.

"Ghost Face, you requested to see me in private, do not be alarmed or feel unease by Mr Ng's presence." She smiled, fully aware that the unease he felt was exactly her intention. "He is here by my request, my personal aide. He is discreet and invisible". Lily's Grandmother continued.

"It's been a very long time since you have been here to see me. What occasion is this?" She asked.

Ghost Face, moved himself closer to the edge of the couch and toward the old woman. He wanted to see her face in detail when he told her that her

Granddaughter was a traitor to the society.

"Dear Madam, I am here under very unusual circumstances and to bring news that affects our society greatly." Ghost Face spoke softly, causing the old woman to move her face toward him, to hear him more clearly.

"Go on", she said.

"We have a traitor in our midst, someone who we both trusted. Someone who has placed us in such an exposed position that it is likely that our Society will be critically damaged. We cannot allow this person to remain within our group, and I urge that the Masters conduct a hearing immediately to resolve the matter in a swift and appropriate manner." Ghost Face finished, his head theatrically bowed to show his respect.

"Exactly who and what is troubling you so, Ghost Face?" The old woman asked.

"Your Granddaughter." Ghost Face replied, lifting his head to watch the reaction.

The old lady's back stiffened, but her faced remained stony and calm, free of emotion, disappointing Ghost Face. He had hoped for at the very least a gasp or a verbal outburst. But she showed nothing except the very smallest of flinches.

"Tell me more." She said.

"Your Granddaughter appears to have an affiliation with the man that we used for the Bank Robbery. Along with him, she tried to release our only negotiation card, the man that would ensure that Harper would carry out his duties without difficulty. Yet after the event, your Granddaughter decided in her wisdom to help them both and tried to release him without consultation. She has betrayed us Madam and she must be punished. " Ghost Face paused.

"Casualties?" The old woman demanded.

"Yes, one. Robert Black, the friend. He is dead. Harper is on the run and so is your Granddaughter." He continued. "She has broken one of our most cherished oaths, and she cannot be trusted." He stated. He began to feel irritated at her apparent lack of concern. This is not how he had planned it.

He raised his voice, so that she could truly understand the gravity of what he was telling her.

"She has broken an oath and must be punished accordingly." He said.

"Oath number four states; *"I shall never betray my sworn brothers and sisters. If this oath is broken, I will be treated as a traitor to the society and will receive one hundred cuts to my body."*

"It is clear," he carried on. "It is a clear disregard for the privacy and secrecy of our society." He stopped now. Aware that she was now watching him intently. Her eyes reduced to narrow slits, her brow in a deep frown. It was a look that he hadn't experienced before. He remained silent and waited for her to speak. After a few moments, she did, so quietly and calmly, that Ghost Face had to lean in to catch what she was saying.

"Ghost Face. I appreciate your devout loyalty to the society over many, many years. At least thirty I think. However, as much as I am indebted to you bringing this to my attention, I was very happy to hear that you were coming to see me today. As it happens, I was planning to pay you a visit myself, but you made it possible for me to see you here, in the comfort of my own home. So I thank you." She said and gave him a small bow of the head, which Ghost Face returned back to her.

"Now it's your turn to listen." She said, her voice hardening. "Over a year ago, we had a tragedy within our own kind. Loved ones, well respected, members of our society were killed, almost provoking a triad war, of which we did everything in our power to prevent. We have managed to do so, until now. We have eyes and ears in many places, as you well know Ghost Face. The Government, the Police, the Bank, the list goes on and on, and we also have eyes and ears inside other societies." She paused to allow what she was saying sink in.

It was his forehead that was set in a frown now, and his skin, she was sure, had turned an even paler shade of white.

She continued. "Our good friend has been feeding back to us for over twelve months, and some interesting things have been brought to light. Things initially that we disregarded as not possible. Things that we didn't want to believe. But slowly the truth has unfolded, and now those things are no longer hard to believe. They simply leave us feeling cold. A wise Englishman once said, that being forewarned is being forearmed. I think that is a very true statement. Wouldn't you agree Ghost Face?" The old woman smiled slightly, her thin lips pulled tight across her mouth showing her old brown teeth, making her look suddenly ugly. There was no humor in her eyes despite the smile.

"I'll go on. It is not my Granddaughter that is the traitor, Ghost Face. It is not she who has thrown this Society into turmoil and uncertainty. Trying to strip it of all its values and respect. Trying to push it into directions that we do not intend for it, or wish it to go. Slowly killing off members one by one, until there is just an old lady left to protect and guard the oaths that we once all swore to abide to. It is not she who murdered her Grandfather,

Mother and Father in cold blood and made it look like an accident." She paused to catch her breath. Her cheeks were flushed now, the oxygen rising to the skin as her heart pumped fresh blood around her body giving her a youthfulness and energy that she had not experienced in some time.

Dropping her voice, to a mere whisper she continued, forcing Ghost Face to lean in even more to catch her words.

"It is not she, who is trying to overthrow our society and pull us into a black hole of corruption and murder of war and terror. No. It is not Lillian. There are thirteen oaths, of which all have been broken. If there were a myriad of swords in this room, they would all be pointing at you, Ghost Face. The man who sits before me and tries to take advantage of an old lady, thinking foolishly that I will simply accept your lies and respect and honor you. No, I will not. I have lived too long and seen too much. Age gives you strength and knowledge that youth cannot offer, it prepares you for death, so that when it comes, you accept it graciously and with open arms, not bitterly and with fear." She paused and settled herself in her chair. She turned her head the side slightly to acknowledge the man behind her.

Ghost Face was silently in turmoil. All that he wanted to do was lean forwards and place his two hands around her neck and to squeeze the last bit of life out of her, enjoying the look of terror and helplessness on her face. He had to fight hard to stop himself, knowing that her protector would be on him in a second. He could feel his temper rising.

He needed to get out of this house. Thirty years of visiting as a guest had made it familiar to him. He would never get out of the front entrance, so he would need to go through the kitchen and out the back. Then he could then make his way through the garden and over the fence. He was still fast and agile, and was sure that he could out run anyone on his tail if he had a head start. Ghost face gently ran his hand down his leg and pretended to scratch it, whilst feeling for the hilt of his knife hidden by his trousers. It calmed him immediately. He always carried it strapped onto his lower leg for exactly these situations. When the security guard had patted him down upon arrival, they had only removed his gun. Luckily for him they had missed the knife.

Suddenly the sound of the old woman's voice quickly drew him back into the moment.

"How many woman have you murdered Ghost Face?" Her eyes were full of distaste now and hatred.

How did she know that? He thought. His mind worked quickly. *She'd had him followed, that must be it*, he thought. Whilst he was under suspicion, she had someone follow his every move. They must know about the police too, his mind quickly started to scan events over the last year. He looked at the old woman. She looked like a stranger to him now.

"You know the answer already, so why do you ask?" He replied simply.

"You are pure evil." She stated. The old woman tapped her hand gently on the armrest of the chair. Her signal to the protector that this meeting was now over.

Ghost Face pulled out his knife and had it pointing to the old Woman's throat before the protector could react. He heard the old woman breath in as she focused her gaze, not on the knife, but on him. Her protector had his gun already aimed at Ghost Face at point blank range at his temple. They were in a catch-22 now. If he stabbed the old woman, the protector would shoot him dead. If he ran, he would be shot in the back. He had to take out the protector to stand a chance of survival. Making his mind up in a second, he quickly ducked in front of the old woman and moved himself next to the protector before he even had time to shift his gaze toward Ghost Face. The knife was plunged deep into the left side of his chest between the ribs and straight into his heart. The protector didn't make a sound as he slumped to the floor, his legs buckling beneath him as he did so.

Then the screaming started. Her voice surprised Ghost Face. There was such a force behind it that it didn't belong to an old woman. She pushed her self back in her chair momentarily caging Ghost Face into the corner, but his strength was too much for her as he pushed the chair over to the side throwing her out onto the carpeted floor in a heap. Physically she was frail, and he watched her pathetic body as she tried to pull herself up. This kill would be so easy, he thought arrogantly as he stepped over the protector's lifeless body and stood over her. He was sure that he could see fear in her eyes. He wanted to see fear, as he felt the heat in his body rise.

There were footsteps, many footsteps. He scanned the room and chose a window. It was too late for the kitchen exit, he had to get out now. Picking up the chair in front of him he ran and thrust it as hard as he could against the window, shattering the glass. He shook off his jacket and placed it over the broken glass jumping through onto the deck below. He heard the drawing room door burst open and raised voices. He ran through the familiar grounds and onto the street and kept running until he reached the first street corner. He stopped and walked down the road, more casually now, not wanting to draw attention to himself. He glanced behind him. There were no signs that he was being followed.

He twisted his neck and cracked the bones on both sides, making him feel better. He did the same to his knuckles and released the pressure in his shoulders. He slowed his pace down to a stop and waited for a taxi. He didn't have to wait long.

He slid into the back of the car and gave his instructions to the driver. The sun was starting to set and he looked out the window and watched the lights of Hong Kong flicker and turn on. *Now there will be a war*, he mused and allowed a thin smile to spread across his pale lips.

Chapter 30

Ryan leaned against the pier railing for a moment, watching Victoria Harbour stretch out in front of him. There was a gentle breeze against his cheek and it ruffled his hair making the humidity seem less intense, but it was still hot. The sky was clear today and the sun had started its descent as the long afternoon began to turn into evening. He watched all of the water traffic squeeze and jostle for position down the narrow thoroughfare that separated Hong Kong Island and Kowloon. Giant 3000-ton container ships, slowly glided by, silently flanked by old wooden junks, catamarans and ferries all in its wake. Occasionally there would be a Cruise ship or military war ship docked somewhere along the harbour side, but not today. There was nothing stationary on this busy route.

Ryan was planning to take the Star Ferry across to the Island and to his meeting point with Lam. It was cheaper and arguably quicker than a taxi at this time of the late afternoon. Already much of Tsim Sha Tsui looked grid-locked in the direction of the cross harbour tunnel, plus Ryan's finances were starting to grow thin, so he thought that a dollar fare of $5.30 was much more achievable than a taxi fare of $100.

Ryan looked at his watch. It was 4.30pm. During his brief conversation with Sarah Lam and after some convincing he had eventually agreed to meet her on the Hong Kong side of Star Ferry terminal. He still had thirty minutes to spare.

Despite Ryan's current mindset, he always loved the Star Ferry journey and never tired of it. Once on board it gave him ten minutes of silence away from the hustle and bustle of the City where, under normal circumstances, he would read a newspaper or just enjoy the view.

Ryan watched one of the Ferries, the *Celestial Star* slowly make its way across the harbour. Bobbing gently on the dark jade green water and swaying side to side when other high-speed vessels rushed past, it expertly worked its way between the traffic, like an old workhorse ploughing a field.

The ferries had not changed in over 100 years. They still had the classic wooden hulled construction. The only difference being the addition upper deck that had been added eighty years ago to allow more passengers on board and the modern update from a steam engine to a more efficient diesel-electric engine.

The lower deck was painted in the traditional dark green and the upper decks were always painted bright white surrounded with a necklace of white life buoys with the *Star Ferry* logo stenciled in black on each one.

Ryan looked at the spectacular backdrop across the harbour, making the ferry look somewhat small and misplaced against the giant glass and metal high rises, however it had more right to be there than anything else surrounding it. The Star Ferries had earned their right of passage and their place in Hong Kong history.

As the *Celestial Star* drew closer to the pier, Ryan decided to take the same ferry back on its return journey. He estimated that he still had around six or seven minutes to pay and board before it would depart again. Plenty of time, he thought. He walked past a newspaper stand and came upon a legless beggar in the centre of the path, head bowed down, with his arms outstretched, tapping an old red plastic cup on the dirty floor. The man was topless, with just rags wrapped around his waist. His legs finished in stumps where his thighs should be. His hair was jet black and matted and his skin dark and golden brown. His upper body and back showed sinewy muscles developed over years of pulling himself around. He had no wheelchair close by, and Ryan wondered what happened to him at the end of each day. For that moment it made Ryan's situation seem less serious. He dug in his pocket and found a $10 coin. As he walked past the beggar he dropped the coin into the plastic cup and walked on, hearing the muffled and hoarse *m'goi sai* behind him.

Ryan came to the entrance of the ferry terminal, and the old fashioned turnstiles where he dropped in enough coins until he had paid the full $5.30 amount. The metal turnstile clicked as the last coin went in, and he pushed his way through.

The ferries were double decked. As a passenger you could choose to travel on the upper deck, or the lower deck, which for years had been considered less appealing and normally reserved for the common workforce or the poor. The lower deck was more closed in and less comfortable. The seats were crammed in to allow more space for passengers and it was also situated closer to the engine room, which made the journey across a noisy one. Ryan had opted for the upper deck, which gave him open sided views across the harbour, and a more comfortable and peaceful journey.

Having travelled on the ferries many times, Ryan was always amazed that they still kept going. Constructed to last, these old wooden vessels had survived typhoons, when even the piers had collapsed and the Japanese occupation with only one ferry casualty, which had been bombed and sunk in the harbour by the American forces. Now there were twelve left in the World and they managed to cross the harbour without incident over 120 times a day, seven days a week.

Ryan found a good seat next to the side railings on the left hand side. He sat on one of the old wooden benches with a back support and white painted seat, with a star punched out of the wood.

Ryan watched as the mooring ropes were loosened and released and the gangplank was hoisted up and locked into positioned. He looked around. He noticed that the ferry was full of a mixture of commuters and tourists. The difference between them was obvious. Local commuters were either reading a newspaper or texting, and the tourists were all armed with cameras. As soon as the ferry began its journey, the tourists were up on their feet, leaning over the side barriers to get clear shots of the harbour. One lady leaned across Ryan completely to get the shot that she wanted, only apologising when the ferry swayed and she landed awkwardly in Ryan's lap. He helped her to steady herself and offered to switch places so that she could photograph the view in relative comfort.

Across the harbour, hidden by a staircase and the shadows stood Jimmy Luk. He had the meeting point in full view and was carefully scanning the crowds, watching every single person as they exited the Star Ferry terminal. He had been standing here for the last ten minutes. His eyes, every few moments, darting up to the main clock tower and monitoring his own wrist watch as the minutes ticked by. Jimmy had covered all eventualities. In case

LIGHTS OUT

Harper had decided on taking a taxi, Jimmy also had a clear view of the drop off taxi rank, and of course if he came by foot, he had a clear view of the adjoining paths leading up to the tower. Checking his watch again, Jimmy knew that he only had a slim window of time before Lam would show. He needed just a few seconds to get to Harper before Lam arrived and this would all be over quickly. If Lam was early, or if Harper didn't show, then he would have to make alternative plans for Harper, but getting him before he entered the safety of the Police Station was the priority. At this point he felt confident that Lam didn't know of his involvement, however, he still wanted to get this over with and get Harper out of the picture and Ghost Face off his back.

Jimmy smiled to himself. If he did manage to pull this off, he could even continue to work with Lam and she would never even suspect him. He was pleased about that. Killing Harper was one thing; he didn't really want to kill Lam, unless he had absolutely no alternative.

As Jimmy's thoughts drifted to his future as Lam's new partner, something caught his eye. Suddenly he was alert and scanned the crowd once more. His heart sank as he glimpsed Lam. She was pacing. She walked over toward the pier and lent on the railing looking across the harbour, confirming to him that Harper was indeed coming across the old fashioned way.

Jimmy started to think, he somehow had to intervene before Harper exited the ferry terminal and made it to the meeting point. He'd have to go into the terminal without Lam spotting him and be ready for Ryan the moment he stepped off the ferry.

Ryan sat on the seat, next to the female tourist totally unaware of what lay ahead of him.

He was grateful to be sitting in the open air for a change, and took advantage of it by closing his eyes and taking in deep breaths, but his mind kept pulling him back to slow motion replays of Rob's head exploding in front of him. He knew then that this was something that he would never be able to block out entirely, but hoped that with time it would be pushed back to the far recesses of his memory. For now, it was at the forefront, and every time Ryan closed his eyes the images danced and flashed making it hard for Ryan to escape them.

He opened his eyes and saw that the ferry was close to the pier. He looked at his watch. It was now 4.55pm. Five more minutes and he would be meeting with Lam, and this nightmare that he had endured would soon be over.

Lam looked across the railing towards the incoming ferry and hoped that Ryan was onboard. The ferry was full with tourists pouring over the sides snapping away at the skyline behind her obscuring her view of the other passengers.

She looked at her watch and then looked up at the clock tower.

Five more minutes. Lam exhaled, as she realized that she had been holding her breath.

She scanned the crowd around her again for signs of Jimmy sure that he would be here somewhere. She knew. The moment that Jimmy revealed to her that he had knowledge of how Robert Black had died. Only someone who had a contact within the society could have known that it was a bullet in the face that has killed him. She had never disclosed that information. His body had not yet been recovered so there was no other way that Jimmy could have known.

Her gut instinct was telling her that she was right. It was all starting to make sense. He was the Triad Guru after all. He knew everything, but it wasn't through years of study and experience. It was all inside information. He may have started out as a good cop, but somewhere along the way he had been bribed or pressured and had buckled. He was theirs. She knew that now and if Harper was someone that they needed to silence, they would use all of their tools and assets, including Jimmy to ensure that he couldn't speak.

Ryan stood in anticipation of the ferry docking against the pier. He didn't feel like being jostled and shoved, so if he could step off first, then he should be able to avoid some of the commuters that had a lack of awareness, like the lady he had spent the journey sitting next to.

He stood in front of the red gangplank next to the deck hand. The ferry heaved and rolled as the driver attempted to slow down all 164 tons. Slowly positioning the ferry next to the dock, the mooring ropes were thrown over the side and the ferry was pulled to a final halt with just a gentle rocking against it's own wake as the gangplank was released. Ryan strode ahead onto the concrete slope that led up to the turnstile exit. Around him bustled 300 other passengers all with their own destinations in mind. But Ryan was only looking for one person, Sarah Lam, so when a tall Chinese man stood in front of him blocking his exit it took Ryan a moment to register that he was being blocked on purpose.

Lam stretched her neck to get a glimpse of the people exiting the ferry, but pillars, staircases and now floods of people hampered her view. She decided to head back towards the clock tower to avoid missing Ryan. It frustrated her that he wasn't answering his phone. She would just have to be patient. She paced for a few moments, pausing to re-adjust her shirt and tuck it back into her pants and subconsciously brushing her holster to remind herself that her gun was there. As the last trickle of people came through the turnstile, Sarah started to feel uneasy. In the distance she could see another ferry on it's way, but the time had now ticked past 5pm, and for some reason she didn't think that Ryan would be late unless something at happened. Lam's mind was now in turmoil. She had no way of contacting Ryan and had to make a decision how long she should wait. Suddenly the decision was made for her. Out of the corner of her eye she saw a blond haired man walk back onto the ferry on the lower deck. Sarah ran toward the railing and squinted at the gangplank to get a better look. All of the passengers had now boarded the ferry and the deck hands were starting to reel in the ropes. Sarah started to walk the length of the pier towards the terminal and turnstile, picking up her pace as she did so, all the time scanning the ferry. She squatted down to look through the railing to the lower deck. Most people were standing, making it hard for her to see through the crowd. Then two people moved, and she saw him. Ryan had his back to Lam facing away from the pier. Then to his left was the unmistakable silhouette of her colleague, Jimmy Luk. He was standing so close to Ryan that Lam guessed that he must be holding a gun at his side. She stood up and was suddenly in motion. She sprinted down the remaining length of the pier towards the turnstile. Already with her hand at her waist belt she ripped off her detective badge and waved it at the surprised turnstile attendant as she bolted over the top of it. By the time she reached the gate the entrance was closed. She stood up on tiptoe to see the ferry head back towards Kowloon side.

Lam looked around at her surroundings. She had ten minutes to get to the other side before she would lose them both for good in the congested streets of Kowloon unless she could get the ferry stopped. She ran quickly back up towards the turnstile and looked at the wide-eyed attendant who was blinking back at her with shock. It wasn't an every day occurrence to have a female Police Detective clear the turnstile in one athletic jump.

Lam spoke quickly as she asked the wide-eyed Chinese man to contact the ferry in question to see whether it could be stopped. It took the man a few seconds to register what was being asked. He nodded and fumbled through the papers on his desk until he located the correct emergency number. He picked up his phone and dialed through to what Lam assumed was his superior. He chatted on the phone for a few seconds causing Lam to grow more impatient. Eventually, patience getting the better of her, she grabbed the receiver from the attendant and spoke with as much authority as she could muster.

"This is Detective Inspector Lam, I need to have the Celestial Star stopped immediately. There is an armed man on board holding a man hostage." Sarah paused waiting for the gravity of what she had just told the man on the end of the receiver to sink in. It had the desired effect.

"Detective, I'm the Star Ferry Senior Manager, Mr Lo, we have a protocol for this kind of thing. As the ferry is already past half way, it's better to dock at the other side and we can have some police waiting as soon as it stops". Mr Lo said.

Lam thought for a moment.

"Is there any way that I can get across in time to meet it?" She asked, thinking that a speedboat might work.

"Yes, I'll arrange for you to be picked up in a couple of minutes. In the meantime I'll contact the police and ask them to wait in Tsim Sha Tsui. Our driver will be told not to dock until everyone is in place." He said.

"Thank you, and please hurry". Lam wondered whether she should call the Chief, but decided against it. If she had the back up of Kowloon police officers then she should be well covered.

Lam paced up and down inside the waiting area as new commuters started to filter in.

Business as usual, Sarah thought.

Ryan stood motionless, his mind trying to reconcile that last ten minutes. He was so close to meeting Lam when he was stopped dead by a tall Chinese man. They both stared at one another, and then suddenly Ryan had a strong feeling that this was intentional. Ryan tried to step to the side and was immediately blocked again. He looked at the man in front of him.

"Can I help you?" Ryan asked, not wanting to hear the answer.

"Turn around slowly and don't say anything and I won't kill you." Jimmy said to Ryan. Ryan hesitated, then feeling the hard cold muzzle of a gun digging in his side reluctantly did as he was asked and turned around ready to get back on the ferry.

Who was this guy? He thought as he tried to suppress the panic now rising in his chest.

They walked forwards with the rest of the commuters queuing up for the return journey. Ryan felt the gun being pressed into his side at every step.

Once on board, Ryan was maneuvered toward the centre of the ferry on the lower deck. It was much louder down stairs. The engine room was right next to them, and Ryan could feel his head start to throb as he breathed in the mixture of air and diesel. He stole a glance at the man next to him and studied his profile for a few seconds. He was clean-shaven and wore expensive clothes. Not quite what he would have expected for a Triad.

Reading his mind, Jimmy Luk turned to face Ryan. He sounded almost sympathetic when he spoke.

"We can't let you talk". He said simply, almost confirming Ryan's fate there and then.

"So what will happen now?" Ryan asked, fearing the worst.

"For now you need to just be quiet and do what I ask. You have caused us enough problems."

Jimmy turned his face away from Ryan and continued to dig his gun into his side. At this point, Jimmy only had a vague idea of what he would do when they reached the other side. He had been told to take care of everything, and now he needed to find a quiet location where he could do just that. He thought about quiet areas, close to the ferry terminal, but there were so many tourists today, that he may expose himself unknowingly. The sound of the ferry horn quickly pulled Jimmy back to the present as he felt the ferry roll slightly. Continuing to press against Harper he bent down slightly to get a better view of the cause of the horn.

To his horror he could see a slate grey police boat heading in their direction. He could feel the adrenaline start to pump through his body as his eyes followed the boats route. It was no mistake; it was definitely working its way toward them.

Ryan sensed that something was wrong and turned to follow Jimmy's gaze. His eyes rested on the same Police boat and he saw something vaguely familiar. He squinted, and this time he could make out the long hair, blowing in the breeze and the resolute stance of Lam. Ryan felt surprise and relief all at the same time. He looked across at Jimmy, and saw his face twisted in an angry disbelief. Ryan allowed himself a faint smile, and for a second was able to push away the thought that he may not make it.

The thought quickly dissolved when Jimmy grabbed Ryan's waist by his belt and pulled him closer against the gun. He leaned in toward Ryan's ear and whispered.

"If you make a sound, a noise, I will kill you on the spot. Now move forwards toward the middle of the crowd." By now Ryan could feel that the ferry had slowed down. They were maybe just a couple of minutes from the pier, but this ferry would not be doing its normal docking procedure. Ryan moved forwards slowly trying to decide what to do. He knew that any moment the police boat would be up against the side of the ferry and that Jimmy would need to make a decision about what to do. For sure they wouldn't make it to the pier.

Lam could feel the breeze on her face as her hair whipped around her head like Medusa as the boat sped along the water. She stood at the front of the police boat holding on with one hand. With the other she was holding and talking into a walkie-talkie. The Star Ferry manager had been fast and efficient. Within a couple of minutes they had contacted and updated the *Celestial Star* driver, notified the Kowloon Police and arranged for a police boat to pick her up. She was impressed, and felt encouraged that they would be able to intercept Jimmy and retrieve Ryan before anything untoward happened.

The boat drew closer and she felt like a wolf circling a sheep, pushing it into a corner until it had nowhere else to hide. She just hoped that Jimmy didn't do anything stupid in a panic to save himself.

The engine was still on and the noise, coupled with the sound of the speedboat, was getting louder and louder. Ryan could sense the unease in Jimmy and he shuffled from one foot to the other trying to decide what his next step would be.

Jimmy was furious with himself. He felt trapped and hadn't given Lam enough credit to intercept him. He was running out of options. If he killed Ryan now it would be in plain sight, and he would never get off the boat alive. The only option was to take Harper as hostage to keep himself alive. Once on dry ground he would think of something else.

A loud haler crackled and jumped to life, making everyone on board the ferry turn their heads towards the police boat.

"Luk, you need to give it up and let Harper go. We have police waiting at both Piers. Drop your weapon and slide it across the floor." Lam spoke into the loud haler.

Two Police officers had their weapons trained on the ferry, pointing in the direction of the lower deck.

The whole ferry erupted in whispers as people started to look around at the person next to them, fearing that they were standing next to an armed man. People started to move towards the opposite side of the boat causing the ferry to tilt slightly to one side increasing the fear amidst the passengers.

Jimmy gripped Ryan tighter placing his arm around his neck and across his chest, and pushed the gun at Ryan's temple with his other free hand. Ryan sucked in a breath as he felt the cold steel against his head. His breathing was becoming laboured with Jimmy's arm restricting the airflow.

Jimmy's blood was pumping wildly now and he could feel his heartbeat in his ears. In his head he was already picturing his twenty-year career collapsing around him. He knew that he had stepped over the line this time. It was over for him.

The pressure across Ryan's throat was increasing making it hard for him to breath properly. In desperation Ryan grabbed Jimmy's forearms and tried to release enough of the grip to allow him to get a full breath in, but Jimmy's grasp was surprisingly strong. He could feel the pressure of the gun on his temple and closed his eyes momentarily to try and compose himself. The panic he felt was shutting down his mind section by section. He was worried that if his heart beat any faster that he may pass out with the stress.

"NO" Jimmy yelled out to Lam, "It's never too late. If you don't stand down I will kill him right here, right now. Don't push me Lam". Jimmy shouted, his voice cracked with the strain.

Ryan could feel the heat off his body. *He's stressed.* Ryan thought. *Not a good sign.*

Lam hadn't expected that he may take Ryan hostage, she thought that being found out and the trained officers with their guns on him would be enough. He knew well enough how these things worked. He knew that if he didn't stand down, that she would have no option but to shoot him. It was protocol. He would be ticking it off one by one. Lam was torn. Maybe he wanted her to shoot him, but she didn't want him dead, or to shoot Harper in the process. She decided to negotiate one last time.

"There is no way out Luk, you need to put the gun down and let Harper go. It is too late. There's nowhere for you to go. It's over." She said firmly.

Jimmy started to shuffle Ryan towards the front of the ferry, all of the passengers had now stepped away from them terrified that they may get caught in a cross fire, they had their heads down and most were curled up on the floor to protect themselves. Parents huddled over the backs of their children, couples wrapped around each other. Ryan could hear a few young children sobbing quietly, as their parents whispered to try and sooth them.

Lam continued. "I know everything. I know it all. Your involvement with the triad gang. Your agreement with the Society. Your dealings with Ghost Face. All of it. You need to talk to me Luk. I'm your only chance now."

Lam's voice crackled through the loud haler echoing over the ferry. Jimmy's mind was racing. He couldn't believe that it was over. If they charged him, he would never survive prison. The triads would get to him there. He was a dead man either way. Lam's bullet would be quick and accurate. There would be no beatings, no torture that would leave him begging to be killed quickly. This was the better option. Finish it all now.

Ryan's survival instinct had started to kick in. He forced himself to calm down and to think rationally. What could he do? If he pushed back toward Luk he might inadvertently cause Jimmy to shoot him in the head, so that wouldn't work, but if he pushed himself down, it may give Lam enough of an opportunity to shoot Jimmy, or be able to disentangle himself enough to wrestle the gun away from him. It was risky, he reasoned, but maybe that was his only option. He could sense that Jimmy was planning something, the way that he was being forced toward the front of the ferry.

Ryan slowed down his breathing and looked ahead towards the police boat. Lam had put the loud haler down and now had her gun trained on Jimmy.

Now it was a stand off, Ryan thought.

Suddenly there was a loud click next to Ryan's ear as Jimmy engaged the trigger. It was now or never Ryan thought. He took in a deep breath and with all his strength he pushed his hands upwards forcing his body down toward the wooden deck. Jimmy's forearms loosened enough to release Ryan's neck. Momentarily Jimmy was left standing exposed from the waist up.

Two shots cracked overhead at the same time, Ryan covered his ears with his hands and stayed low waiting to feel a bullet rip through his body at any moment, but it never did. Around him there were screams and shouts and scuffles as people moved as far away from them as possible. Ryan heard a muffled cry of pain behind him. Uncertain what may greet him, he turned to see Jimmy lying on the floor holding his right arm with his left hand. Blood pumped through the gaps in his fingers as he lay there gasping and whining like a small child. Ryan stood unsteadily and scanned the floor for the gun. He located it a few feet away and moved quickly to pick it up. With a shaky hand he pointed the gun at Jimmy.

The police boat was now up against the side of the ferry and Ryan glanced sideways as he watched Lam jump easily onto the lower deck and stride quickly over to his side, all the while her handgun trained on Jimmy.

One of the other officer's came up next to Ryan and relieved him of the gun. Ryan was thankful and let the officer take it. He patted Ryan gently on the back and motioned for him to go toward the police boat. On his way past, Lam turned to Ryan.

'It's OK now', she said, slightly breathless, 'you did well'.

Ryan gave an awkward smile and followed the Police Officer to the boat.

Lam looked down at Luk writhing on the floor in pain, the blood pooling under his arm as the colour started to drain from his face.

"It's just a flesh wound, you'll live." Lam said, her voice deadpan and void of any sympathy. "And for the record, next time you take a shot at me, you'd better make sure that it hits."

Jimmy glanced up at Lam and through the mist of pain in his eyes he could just make out a bright red scratch mark across her cheek where his bullet had struck her.

In the final moments Jimmy had shot at her on instinct and missed. His aim not as good as it used to be. As for Lam, Jimmy realized that she would never have killed him, her aim was perfect, her reputation of never missing a target, intact. Jimmy groaned and laid his head back on the wooden floorboards. He closed his eyes for a moment and wondered how long the Society would allow him to live. He gave himself two weeks.

Chapter 31

Across the hall from Sarah Lam's office, Detective Wong sat hunched over his desk, his forehead creased with stress. He was under pressure from the Chief to solve the murders of the three dead prostitutes. He sat with all three files laid out before him, three pairs of dead eyes staring back, hoping that something would jump off the page and give him the lead that he so desperately needed.

They had received so many calls from the general public after they released the details to the news channels and the newspapers. Typical media headlines like *Serial Killer Stalks Hong Kong Hookers*, *New killer appears as fear spreads across Hong Kong* and *Killers slays sex workers*, had done little to stem the widespread panic both amongst the locals and within the industry. But so far they had received nothing relating to possible suspects. People were calling in because they were scared and lived in the local area. Local women were worried about being accidently mistaken for a sex worker, or they themselves had their own *one-woman* brothels and wanted to know how they could protect themselves. The police had already spoken to their regular targeted brothels and advised the women to take extra security measures and precautions, maybe have a security camera fitted or an alarm that could be triggered easily. All of this was good practical advise, but unrealistic for the women in question.

One-woman brothels were the only legal form of prostitution in Hong Kong provided that there was only one women per apartment, if more than one woman was found at an establishment, the police were then able to prosecute, it was a catch-22. The lone sex worker was becoming popular choice among 18 to 30 year olds, and kept dedicated police departments busy. Historically connected to the Triads, sex trafficking and organized brothels were becoming a thing of the past now that women could legally work out of one-room apartments offering a range of sex services in a homely environment. Advertising was easy and cheap, online ad companies like Sex 101 offered monthly packages, making set-up costs and overheads low.

There were now brothel districts spanning from the Island, across Kowloon and far into the New Territories bordering China.

The three locations of the recent murders were set apart from one another, but all well-known areas by the police. Yuen Long, Mong Kok and now Tsim Sha Tsui were highlighted in red marker pen on Detective Wong's map of the City.

For the client it was easy too. With little chance of being recognized, a man could have privacy and confidentiality and could avoid possible public embarrassment. Normally there would be a yellow light bulb, a well-known colour symbol, placed above a doorframe, or a marking above a doorbell, normally of a phoenix, to provide a hint to the client that they were at the right address.

The Police knew most of the prostitutes and canvassed all of the brothel districts. The main concern for the police these days, apart from a serial killer on the loose, was the influx of illegal immigrants, normally from the North that would filter into the City on short-term tourist visa's and set up one-woman brothels. This was happening more and more and one of the dead prostitutes was found to be a young immigrant from Qingdao.

With little or no money most of the one-woman brothels had limited resource to make their homes safer. It meant that the women continued to accept appointments with both regular and new clients, and they simply prayed that they would survive the night.

The police had been asking the prostitute community to highlight any regular clients that showed aggressive or violent behavior, or anyone that seemed to be acting strange or out of character. The police had a slim hope that perhaps the killer was actually known to one of the women. After days of door-to-door enquiries, not a single person was willing to identify a client or freely offer information. In the same way that patients enjoy Patient-Doctor confidentiality, the same theory seemed to apply to prostitutes and their clients. Detective Wong wasn't that surprised with the outcome, after all it was their bread and butter, and if it leaked out that a sex-worker had spoken to Police about one of her clients, her career would be over in an instant. The police had many doors closed in their faces and would continue to do so.

This left Detective Wong with nothing but the physical evidence at the scene, and the offender profile that had been written up by their in-house expert Dr Eric Ng.

Detective Wong took a sip of his weak, warm coffee and started to review the paperwork.

All three murders so far followed the exact same M.O. The killer was neat and meticulous and left nothing behind except his own DNA inside each victim. Whilst this was enough to nail the killer once they had him. They first had to physically catch him and he seemed very inept at staying in the shadows.

The brutal murders had been carried out over a three-week period, with the time span between each murder becoming narrower. There was concern that the killer would not stop now until he was caught and he didn't want a fourth victim on his hands.

There had been no forced entry, telling him that the killer was a client and easily gained access to the apartment where the killing took place. It was always late at night, normally after midnight. There had been no caretaker or guards at the building entrances.

All three murders were sexually motivated.

Usually the killer showered thoroughly and cleaned up the room using the victims' own towel, which was always missing. They had found cotton yarn threads at two of the locations indicating that this was the case.

The body was always left on the bed in position. The victims had been found either naked from the waist down or completely naked. The way the clothes lay, it appeared that the victims had consensually removed their own clothing. All three victims had been strangled and raped.

Detective Wong shuffled through the papers until he got to the Psychology report.

He read through it trying to picture what kind of man could do something like this.

Reading it again, he started to build a picture in his head.

The killer is a sadist, who derives sexual gratification through the pain of his victims.

He is most likely a Chinese male who has had a series of dysfunctional relationships with women.

He is intelligent with a high IQ, however it's likely that he is socially inept and prefers solitude.

He has fantasized and rehearsed the crimes in his mind before hand.

His victims are most likely strangers to him, however he is not a stranger to using prostitutes and most likely uses them on a regular basis quite possibly showing rage or aggression.

He has absolute control over his victims and is physically strong, rendering possible escape as futile.

He is organized and methodical in his sequence of events.

He knows the Kowloon district well and finds it easy to get around.

The final act of strangulation offers the killer his sexual gratification.

He is most likely 40 to 50 years old.

He is likely to kill again.

This last point always made the hairs on Detective Wongs arm stand on end. This was the point that he dreaded the most. Not knowing the when, the who or the where. All he had was the how.

Detective Wong finished the report and absentmindedly ran his fingers through his hair. He imagined the fear in the three women upon realization that they had let a monster into their homes. Wong found the reports grim and disturbing and more than anything wanted to catch this killer before he struck again. He had requested more police patrols around the known brothel districts, but he had limited funding to do this long term and door-to-door enquiries were becoming fruitless to the point of futile.

He had to hope that if the killer struck again, that he would somehow become over confident and leave a clue behind. For now all he could do was wait.

Chapter 32

Lam was back at her desk pressing a white towel filled with ice against her burning cheek. She had refused to go to the hospital to get it checked out, and instead accompanied Ryan to the station, whilst Jimmy Luk was carted off in a different direction to a nearby hospital. The bullet fired by him had brushed past Lam so fast that it wasn't until moments later that she felt the stinging sensation across her face. She had heard the whoosh as it swept just below her left eye, grazing her in passing, before narrowly missing the top of her ear. Her cheekbone was bruised and swollen now and the skin raised and angry. She was lucky. One or two millimeters to the right would have left her with half a face, if alive at all. There was no question that his shot was intended to kill. He now lay in a hospital bed with a shattered elbow, not quite the flesh wound that she had promised him. It was the next best thing to shooting him outright, but she needed him alive. She knew that as a last resort she would have killed him if Ryan had not managed to take himself out of range. That was quick thinking on his part. Now she would have to wait for Jimmy to come out of theatre and wake from his anesthetic before she could question him in detail. But she at least had Ryan in one piece, and he was at the station under police protection.

With her one free hand, Lam pulled open her desk drawer and fished around for some painkillers. She always had some on hand. Locating the packed, she expertly pushed two pills out of their foil wrapper and popped them into her mouth, chasing it down with some cool water. Another fifteen minutes or so and the pills would work their magic, erasing the headache that was threatening to turn into a migraine. She shifted in her chair trying to get herself comfortable whilst she took out her case file. Her lower back was sore, and she absentmindedly rubbed it with her thumb. She located her old raised scar on her lower back and massaged it trying to ease the ache that was working its way slowly up her spine.

For that brief moment the scar triggered old memories. She was no longer sitting at safety of her desk at the station. She was lying on the cold stone floor of a disused warehouse. Her nose was bleeding heavily now, and her whole body ached from the fall. She had landed awkwardly and thought that perhaps her wrist was broken. She heard a movement close to her left, and with the small amount of strength that she had, she forced her body to sit upright, and then to stand. Lam looked around her in the dark to try to get her bearings. She couldn't see Ko, her partner, she hoped that he had managed to survive and would soon be coming down the steps to find her. She blinked away the pain and half walking, half jogging moved deep into the shadows and out of sight. Lam felt her side for her gun, but it must have fallen out of her hand during her fall, she didn't recall hearing it clatter anywhere close by. She moved deeper still into the shadows whilst she regained her breath and her location. It was silent all around her now except for the faint footsteps of someone walking down a metal staircase, she couldn't be sure if it was Ko, surely he would call out for her if it was. She strained to see if she could work out the direction of the stairs, her head still foggy, but it was so dark.

It had been a tip off. It should have been a major drug bust, probably the biggest that Hong Kong had experienced. Lam and Ko had been working undercover with two detectives from the Narcotics Bureau. A team of four, they had been told, by one of their well-oiled informants that this is where the hand over would be. They were expecting at least 38 kilo's of Cocaine, along with one of Hong Kong's biggest Drug Lords. It was the end of a trail that they had been following for months now. They had already successfully carried out a raid one month before, the same gang involved, but that time the ring leaders had slipped away, leaving behind just a few kilos in their haste, each one kilo brick of cocaine embossed with their well known symbol of an eye inside a triangle. Sarah felt cold and tried to stop herself from shivering. They had sat for hours outside the disused warehouse in an old car hidden between a parked truck and an empty skip, watching and waiting. They were in the middle of typhoon season, so the rain had been heavy all day long, switching between tropical downpours and intermittent light drizzle. Eventually their patience had paid off. At first it was a silver van that had pulled up about fifty meters in front of them. Two men had climbed out and moved around to the back of the van, where they had removed two heavy black duffle bags. Trying not to get wet, they had grabbed the bags and ran straight into the warehouse entrance, letting themselves in via a small metal door set inside a larger oversize metal gate.

Within minutes a black Mercedes had pulled up behind the van. The man that exited the drivers side stepped out with confidence and grace. He opened up an umbrella, and strolled toward the small metal door as though he had all the time in the world.

Ko spoke to his colleagues on his radio. 'We are green'. He said simply, the pre-arranged code to say that they were going in.

They had firstly moved up to the black Mercedes and the van to check the interiors, ensuring that there were no other people waiting inside that could jeopardize the bust. Satisfied, and giving each other a silent signal, they quickly ran across the broken tarmac towards the small metal gate. Lam rested her ear against the metal door, but with the sound of the rain behind her it was impossible to hear anything on the other side. Nodding at Ko, she silently counted down with her fingers visible for Ko to see. Three, two, one. She twisted the metal door handle and pushed open the door for Ko, he slipped in quietly with Lam entering behind them. They were grateful for the rain. Any noise that the door would have normally made was muffled by the noise. The warehouse was pitch dark. Closing the door behind them, the last of the light was shut out. It took a few seconds for their eyes to adjust to the darkness. Lam could now make out a metal staircase and then the open mezzanines on each floor, leading up three full flights. Ahead of them toward the far corner of the warehouse she could make out the shape of a large metal box, she motioned to Ko using her hands, and signaled for him to follow her. They worked around the side of the large space without making a sound. As they drew closer Sarah could see now that the box was a container that had been converted into a makeshift office corrugated metal sides, no windows and a basic door cut out of the side. A slither of light shone under the door indicating that someone was inside, but there was no sound, not even a murmur of conversation. A wave of uneasiness flowed over Lam now as she considered their next move. She looked at her watch. It was strange that her narcotics colleagues had not yet responded or joined them. She had expected them to be close behind. Now almost at the door, Lam shot a glance at Ko. Their eyes locked and they silently agreed the next move. After so many years, it was so easy to read each others mind. This time Ko indicated that she should enter first. Their handguns were ready, the safety catch off. With Kos spare hand he leaned in and held the door handle. Lam silently counted down again with her fingers; three, two, one.

What happened next, they would never have imagined. The door swung open and Sarah stepped in with her gun steady, her muzzle now pointing directly at the terrified eyes of the two narcotics officers, gagged and bound on chairs.

'Shit,' she said under her breath, quickly placing her gun in her holster.

She turned to Ko, 'cover me, I need to untie them.' 'Shit' was all that Ko could say in response. She frantically untied the two men, and as soon as their hands were free they helped her to untie their legs and remove the gags.

"It's a trap', one of the officers said, a younger man, who looked frightened and now much younger than his years. 'We have to get out of here.' The other said. "They took our guns and our radios." 'They have weapons, we saw pistols and a shotgun'.

'OK, OK', Lam said, trying to think what they should do next.

'Ko, kill the lights. We need some cover to get out of here', she kept her voice low, but now sure that they were being watched.

Ko switched off the wall light sending them all into darkness. All that she could hear now was everyone around her breathing. She motioned for one of the officers to go with Ko, and one with her. She went first. As soon as she stepped outside of the metal room, the first round of gunfire went off.

They ducked and swerved toward the exit as the bullets sprayed and ricocheted off the metal pillars and stairs surrounding them, momentarily lighting up their whereabouts. Realising that they wouldn't make it to the exit alive, Sarah turned sharply and ran at full speed towards the staircase the other three men following closely behind her. At least the metal railing may afford some kind of cover, she thought. Taking two steps at a time, she bounded up to the first mezzanine level and quickly moved back into the shadows the second officer right on her heels. Lam could hear that Ko was close behind her when she heard the same spray of bullets bouncing off the staircase. Just as Ko reached the top, the officer behind him let out a yelp as a bullet tore through his shoulder. He collapsed against the railing, unable to pull himself forwards. Ko turned and grabbed him by the collar dragging him the remainder of the way and into the corner. Blood was pumping from the wound as Lam and Ko tried to stem the bleeding. The other officer was in shock and unable to do anything except stare. They didn't have to wait long. With a loud gurgle and a final explosive spluttering cough, the injured officer's stiff body suddenly relaxed, his last breath pushed out of his body as his head fell back onto Kos knee and his legs and arms relaxed onto the cold metal floor. Then there was silence.

'We're fucked', Ko said under his breath, alarm now in his voice. 'They have us like cornered sheep. This is a fucking set up.' He said as he gently pushed the officers head off his knee resting it on the cold floor. He looked down at himself and could see the dark stains across his shirt. He tried to wipe some of the blood onto his trousers to get it off his hands.

'What now?' he hissed to Lam who was squatting silently in the corner trying to gather her thoughts.

Ignoring Kos question Lam considered their options. She had never been out of control before, and this was not common territory for her. Blocking everything out she tried to focus and keep her mind steady and her wits sharp.

Finally she turned to Ko and the young officer.

'We need to lure them up.' She said, matter of fact. 'The second we try and go down, we are sitting ducks, they'll just take us out one by one.' She whispered.

'And how do you suggest that we do that?' Ko had replied, hoping that she would have a better solution.

Lam had never seen Ko panic like this before. He was normally calm and steady, they both were. She needed him to shape up, quickly.

'I'll show you." Lam grabbed Kos radio from his belt and turned the knob until it was on the right frequency.

'DC this is Detective Lam, over.' The radio jumped and crackled to life, the interference was noisy and Lam made sure that the volume was up as high as possible.

'I have three officers down, repeat, three officers down, in need of immediate assistance, over."

'What?' Ko mouthed.

'If they think we are all injured they'll be more confident that they can finish us all off.' She whispered back. 'I think they come up. It's worth a try'.

The radio blared to life again, this time with a reply.

'Detective Lam, reading you loud and clear, please confirm your location, over.'

Just as Sarah was about to respond, she heard a loud clatter as something dropped on the metal floor, and it sounded close, too close. Like lions ready to pounce on their pray, both Ko and Lam were in position, legs slightly flexed, gun ready and arm steady. The young officer stood close behind them feeling naked and useless without his weapon, desperate to get out of their predicament and ready to follow Lam.

Without warning there was gunfire upon them again, the bullets were closer this time. The three of them sprang into action and ran as fast as they could to the next level of stairs, Ko was the first up with the young officer close behind and Lam keeping up the rear. The spray of bullets rang around their heads, and Lam heard the whoosh close by her body reminding her that this was life or death. Behind her she could hear two sets of footsteps as she was being chased up the stairs and they were closing fast. Just as she was about to make it to the second level she felt someone grab her foot and yank her back. The pull was hard sending her off balance and making her fall face first onto the edge of the metal step. There was a sickening crack as she felt her nose explode as it took the brunt of the fall. She yelled out in pain, and twisted her body around to face her assailant kicking with her feet as she did so. He looked like a thug, with his shaven head, his eyes narrowed and determined and staring her down. He was strong and wouldn't release his grip on her foot despite her stamping on his hand. She pointed her gun into his face and as she did so heard a shot being fired from above her. It was Ko. The face in front of her disappeared as the body, now limp released her foot and fell backwards onto the level below hitting the other man and pinning him to the floor. There was a loud yell, this time from her right as more shots were fired. Forgetting the searing pain across her face, Lam scrambled to her feet and made it to the second mezzanine and to safety, finding Ko and the young officer both in the shadows catching their breath.

'Are you OK' Ko asked noticing the deep cut at the bridge of Lam's nose.

'I'll live', she responded, wincing as she touched her face. 'Thanks, I owe you one.'

'One down, two to go.' Ko said, this time seeming a little more relaxed.

'You OK Tsang' Lam motioned to the young officer visibly shaking in the dark.

'I'm good', just happy to still be alive." He whispered somberly.

Before they had a chance to get their breath back, a serious of bullets now sprayed them from the side. Whoever was firing, they were blindly trying to take a shot at them now, clearly angry that one of their men had been killed. Luckily for the three of them, the aim was way off course, bullets spraying around them randomly. Lam wondered how long they should wait now before their next move.

Lam rolled silently to the left of the mezzanine to see whether she could take a clear shot. Carefully stretching her body toward the edge, she peered over the side of the railing. She could just make out two figures below on the first floor.

'I think we have to go back down.' Lam said, not happy with the idea, but seeing no other way out. 'But I'm open to suggestions'. She said to both men.

Tsang and Ko exchanged looks, neither of them with any better suggestion.

'OK, Ko, you take the left hand side of the staircase, I'll cover the right. Tsang, you stay low and in the middle. We'll all go on three and then start firing. Make each shot count'

'OK, three, two, one' with a silent nod, the three of them launched into action, they ran down the staircase at high speed firing left and right as agreed and made it to the first mezzanine, as they turned to regroup in the shadows, one of the men stepped forward, taking them by surprise. In a blur of bullets and screaming, Tsang was shot at close range; he slumped down to the floor, clearly dead. Someone else grabbed Sarah, knocking her gun out of her hand and she felt herself being lifted effortlessly off the floor, suddenly her stomach lurched as she realized what was about to happen. She clawed at the man holding her, but he was too strong, she felt her centre of gravity shift momentarily before he released his grip, and then she was falling. In that second, she was sure that she heard Ko shouting, 'Nooooo' as the shooting began again.

She must have blacked out briefly upon landing, and now she was back in the shadows, horribly injured and without a weapon.

The silence seemed to be closing in on Lam as she weighed up her options. She scanned the darkness for her weapon, but couldn't see anything from where she was situated. Then she thought of her radio, and patted her belt for it, but it was gone. Probably in the fall, she thought. She tried to slow down her breathing, so that she could hear any movement or footsteps. Then she heard it again; the unmistakable sound of feet walking slowly across the concrete. Whoever it was, they were getting closer now. Her heart was beating hard in her chest as she tried to see which way she should go, but she had lost her bearings in the fall and couldn't remember which direction the exit was. She shook her head to try and stay focused, pushing away the thoughts of sleep that had started to smother her brain.

The footsteps now were getting louder. Lam would have to run; it was her only chance to get out of the building, then to her car. Once there, she could get help. Taking in a few deep painful breaths, she steadied herself. The footsteps sounded as though they were coming from her left, so she would head right. Ignoring the searing pain in her wrist and her head, Sarah slowly took a few steps out of the shadows. Feeling that the time was right, she took off at full speed. Her lungs were burning in her chest within seconds; she pushed herself harder now aware of footsteps directly behind her. She looked around for the exit, but could only see empty space. As she turned the next corner, she could just make out the metal container in the far corner and she knew that she was close. She forced her legs and arms to move faster, ignoring the blinding headache that was taking over her entire head and the throbbing in her temples. Then she heard it, the cocking of a gun and the rip roaring sound of a bullet being fired. Lam had never been shot before. She'd seen plenty of gunshot wounds, and often wondered how it felt. Was it painful immediately, or did the pain only show itself later, once the brain had registered what had happened to the body? Now she knew first hand, the pain was instant and it stopped her dead in her tracks. As though someone had taken the legs from under her, Lam landed once again face down on the floor. One of her teeth was knocked upon landing out and it rolled lightly across the floor stopping just a few feet away within her line of sight, bright white against the darkness. Her body felt heavy now and the pain, even though intense was starting to move through her body in sickening waves. 'Maybe this is what it's like', she imagined that death would come quickly, but her chest was rising and falling and she somehow kept breathing.

Now the footsteps were upon her, and she knew for sure that it would not be Ko. Unable to move, and now only able to breath in shallow pants, Lam could do nothing to defend herself.

Her killer moved to her side and bent down to look at Lam's blood covered and mangled face. A pool of dark blood was starting to seep around her waist forming a moat around her body. Lam tried to keep her eyes open as she tried to focus on the face swimming in and out of her vision. All that she could see was a ghost, her mind was playing tricks on her now, she thought, *but it must be*, she reasoned. His face was so pale, so white that it almost glowed in the darkness and then it was gone.

Lam had learned only later the details of her rescue. Her radio call had placed her stationed team on red alert and they had rushed over to the stake out location arriving just in time. The two narcotics officers and Ko had been found dead. Ko shot between the eyes at point black range. He didn't stand a chance. There were two other bodies, later identified by Lam as the two men in the silver van that had carried in the black duffle bags.

Lam had been unconscious and barely breathing when they found her. No one could believe that she had survived. The bullet had entered her lower back and lodged itself into her spine. She needed 12 hours of surgery to remove it, and only weeks later would the Doctors know if she would make a full recovery. She remained unconscious for almost three weeks, missing the funerals of the two Narcotics Officers and her partner of eight years, Ko. Slowly her broken nose and broken wrist mended, and her dentist fixed her missing tooth.

It took Lam six months of rehabilitation before she could go back to work. By then it was like being the new girl all over again. The staff treated her differently, with kid gloves and she hated it. The Chief was the only one who knew how to behave around her, he acted as though nothing had happened and she silently thanked him for it. As far as she was concerned it was business as usual, except this time, she was working solo. Every few months the Chief would try and give her a new partner, and every time Lam would refuse, until eventually, two years later and without consent, he had given her Chow.

Lam could feel her headache lift, and she removed the towel and the ice from her face.

She grabbed her file and headed towards the interview room. It was time to find out what Harper knew before anyone else was killed.

Chapter 33

Lily felt numb as she entered the Chinese restaurant. She sensed that her meeting with the eight Masters could easily go either way. If they believed Ghost Face, then it was likely that her sentence would be severe. If they listened to her, then she would have the chance to prove herself and to express her fears and concerns about his actions.

Lily hovered outside the familiar door and could hear the voices debating inside. She took a deep breath and rapped loudly.

Silence was immediate, followed by a voice that boomed through the walls, 'Enter'.

Lily stepped into the room and surveyed it quickly. They were all there, all eight Masters, including her Grandmother, and the Master of Ceremonies; her Uncle. They were all seated around a large round table. Up until the moment that Lily entered the room, they had been debating relentlessly. Now there was absolute silence, just eyes that followed her movements. Her Uncle was the first to stand and move toward her, but he wouldn't look at her face. Instead he ushered Lily silently to the only empty seat among them, and then sat himself beside her. Lily looked across the table and what she saw shocked her. Her Grandmother's right arm was bandaged from the hand up to the elbow and was resting on the table in front of her. Her face was bruised, also on the right side making her face look distorted. It was clearly swollen. Her Grandmother registered Lily's concern and she shook her head slightly, the shake of the head telling Lily that now was not the time to discuss the reason behind her injuries. She sat as tall and as proud as her weak body allowed, her eyes still on her Granddaughter. But for the first time ever, as Lily looked at her, she couldn't determine which emotions were running behind them.

Lily sat still, momentarily closing her eyes, taking in a deep breath to prepare herself for the worst. A few moments later, her eyes suddenly flicked open as she faced her silent audience, now ready to accept whatever the Masters had to say.

Her Grandmother began the proceedings and spoke only to Lily.

"You have been brought here today in front of the Society Masters to review the allegations against you and to decide upon your fate. Do you understand that the decision made here today is final and cannot be challenged or revoked?"

Her Grandmother locked eyes with Lily to ensure that she fully understood what she was being told.

Lily gave a simple nod, and straightened her back as she replied. "Yes, I understand."

Facing the Members and with a somber tone, Lily's Grandmother addressed them all.

"For some time now, we have had reason to believe that there is a traitor among the Society Members. It's not uncommon for members to switch between societies, especially between the lower and younger classes, some of you yourselves, many years ago, joined us from other societies, however it is highly unusual for a senior respected ranked member of our society to switch sides and one that we have considered unwaveringly loyal from the very beginning. We have never had a case such as this.

Our doubts increased just a few months ago, when we had heard, through a trustworthy source, that one of our members intended to move from us to the Society of the Golden Eye. We all know this group well and they have been our long-standing adversaries over these last few difficult years. Up until the deaths of my late husband, beloved daughter and son-in-law, they had remained at arms length, our fights never that serious. Since then they have made their intentions very clear to us, and now they are a direct threat. They want our Society, our members, our land, our money and our submission. They have increased their aggression toward us and are threatening the very values of our Society."

Turning again to Lily, she continued.

'Lillian, after the death of your parents, we debated long and hard as to whether you should be brought into the Society. Your Mother and Father were against it, and yet it was their whole life and ultimately the reason for their death. Upon my death, your Father had already been selected by the very Masters that you see before you in this room, to be the one to take over."

Lily was pleased that she was sitting down. She hadn't expected this at all, and now all she could do was stare in disbelief at what she was hearing.

"You had showed us early on that you were capable of handling yourself, that you understood the importance of our beliefs and that you would be a loyal and trusted member. I had planned to train you myself; to arm and prepare you with everything that you could possibly need, so that when the time came, you would be ready, like your father, to take the lead. To bring young blood to the table and to ensure the safety and longevity of our Society.

We control a myriad of businesses here in Hong Kong, throughout mother China and across the globe. Some of our ventures are legitimate. Some are not accepted within the realm of the law and even we do have limits to how far we will stretch for monetary gain.

We do sell sex and we do it well, we have brothels all over Hong Kong and the mainland, yet we only use local girls in each region, and we don't deal in any way or form in human trafficking. We offer security in every possible guise. To Hotels and restaurants, brothel owners, clubs and drinking establishments, we protect these people from people like the Society of the Golden Eye, and they pay us well for it. We offer protection to Government officials, travelling dignitaries and celebrities. We are the ones that people come to when their child is kidnapped or when their lives are in danger, and we deal with it all, discreetly and professionally. We have maintained a respect within our industry by abiding by the Society rules and by our Oaths.

We are becoming more sophisticated in our means for attaining funds. We have an elaborate and untraceable method for money laundering, managed by a team of specialists employed by the Society. Through them, and with their guidance we legitimately purchase property and land and have built an impressive and highly performing stock portfolio. We have another team that works solely on credit card fraud on a global scale, buffered by worldwide insurance companies and banks, and now we have another new route, one that enables us to enter a major Bank and walk out with millions of Hong Kong dollars in under eight minutes.

We have the knowledge and the expertise to do all of these things, and to do them well.

We will not deal or distribute drugs, we will not deal with human trafficking, or prostitution against will and we will not deal in the theft of religious or historical relics from the mainland. Those things we will leave to the Society of the Golden Eye, where they are willing to compromise their rules and what the oaths stand for, to use old fashioned and barbaric ways to get what and who they want.

If they manage to gain power over our society and yolk all of this knowledge, then our Society is finished and everything that we value and have worked for would have been in vain. We cannot allow this to happen.

We have waited long enough, and now we must strike fast at those who challenge us."

She sat back heavily in her seat, exhausted by her monologue and drained by the darkness of the subject matter.

The room was silent. Not a single member had interrupted her speech, no whisper or word uttered quietly under breaths. However, throughout the quiet room there was a tangible affirmation that swept across the Masters as they all nodded and agreed in unison.

Continuing from her seat, Lily's Grandmother looked again at Lily. Her voice calm and her demeanor now softened and relaxed.

"So now I will explain to you. Your challenge was a hard one. We pushed your skills to see whether you could be an asset to us, and whether, under pressure you could perform. Not only were you able to bring your plan to fruition, a feat that I must admit I had my doubts. But you managed it successfully, the collateral damage, under the circumstances, will later be considered minor.

You are still under suspicion by the police, but the authorities do not know your true identity and after a time we think that you will be able to continue your work for us here. Until then, we feel that to be safe, that you should return to the United States until such time that we deem it appropriate for you to return. Your new passport and documents will be ready within the next few days."

Lily didn't know what to think. She didn't like the idea of being sent away. She felt that she had only just come home. But she knew better than to argue. In some ways she knew that the decision was the right one, but she also knew that her future lay in Hong Kong and with her Grandmother.

"Before you go, there is one final job for you." Her Grandmother said. The statement made Lily sit up and take note. Curious as to what the Society would have her do now before she left, she listened intently.

"You know well who I have been referring to within our ranks. Ghost Face cannot be trusted. He is a dangerous man, a traitor to us and able to murder in cold blood, and will stop at nothing to get what he wants. For sure, having him killed by one of our own will spark another triad war within the City, which we want to avoid at all costs. However, through Ryan Harper, we think that you can lure him in. We can arrange for the police to arrest him. He will never be charged for triad related crimes, he is too clever for that, but he can be charged for the serial murder of prostitutes, and for that, he will never again be a free man."

Lily was shocked by the revelations. She was trying to process all of the information that her Grandmother was now revealing.

"But how do you know that he has carried out these crimes, it could have been any man?" Lily asked simply.

"For a long time now I have had my concerns, which I have buried deep. When we brought you in, his distaste for you was made clear and my worries were brought rapidly to the surface. I arranged for him to be discreetly followed. Sadly, after three such occasions, the day after a young woman, a prostitute, was found dead. There can only be one explanation. His affinity for young woman has been one that we have been forced to live with, but no longer. He is not a man to be trusted, and we will no longer harbour him."

Lily nodded in silence, once to her Grandmother, and turning slowly, once more to the other Masters. All eyes were on her, and she suddenly felt a huge responsibility weighing down on her, more so than she had ever felt before. She knew that Ghost Face was the poison that had to be removed and she was the one to do it. Asking to be excused, Lily stood up from her seat and hurried from the room. Her mind already spinning out of control, she was suddenly very aware that her window of opportunity was narrow and if she played this wrong, her life would be very much at risk.

Chapter 34

Lam looked through the window separating the interview room and one of the main offices. This room had no secret two-way mirror or glass and it even boasted a small window that let in just a small shaft of natural light into the room. This is where they placed low-risk people that were not likely to escape or cause harm. Lam felt that Ryan had earned his place here.

She tapped on grey metal door out of courtesy, which made Ryan jump a little. He must be so tired. She knew his world had been turned upside down in the space of a few weeks. His colleague and friend murdered in front of him forcing him on the run. He had done well to keep things together as well as he had, she thought. She looked at his clothes. His attire hadn't much improved since she had seen him last. He wore the same outfit that she had given him and it now looked almost as dirty as the first set of clothes that she had found him in. He'd even managed to get some of Jimmy's blood onto his shirt, which had dried now to a reddish brown. She entered the room silently and gave Ryan a wide smile. It was good news for him. Based on what Ryan had told her in her apartment, the police had managed to confirm his story of how the bank robbery took place and how he was blackmailed. They verified the kidnapping of Robert Black and Ryan's innocent involvement with a female triad member, Lily. Which of course was not her real name. The pieces missing were surrounding Ghost Face. He was a threat to the police, the triads and Ryan and seemed to be the missing piece to the puzzle. Jimmy Luk would be the one to shed more light on this character. From Ryan, all that Lam wanted was loose ends tied up.

Lam pulled out a chair and sat down facing Ryan.

"I didn't think I'd be so happy to be sitting in an interview chair again," he said with a crooked half smile. He was too exhausted to offer anything else.

"Well, you get a window this time, so things are looking up", Lam replied.

"Thanks for earlier" he said earnestly. "I was starting to lose the will to live there."

"How's your cheek?" he said motioning to her face. With the ice bag now gone, the swelling had reduced leaving a bright red scratch, but the skin was not broken.

"I'm lucky", Sarah replied. "Had he been a good shot, it would have been a different Detective sitting here right now," she said, touching her cheek.

"We've followed up on everything that you told me previously. The way in which you described the bank robbery, this was validated by our team as well as John McIntyre from the bank. The money has not yet been recovered. As for Robert Black, unfortunately we have not been able to find his body yet. By the time our team arrived at the warehouse, someone had sent in a cleaner. There was nothing there, no prints, debris or sign that someone had been killed. Our teams are still investigating the surrounding area". Lam continued.

"There are two people that we still need to find. One is Lily. She has managed to disappear into thin air. As far as our records show, she doesn't actually exist in this Country. We followed up on the company that she owns and it never existed, she did a good job of covering her tracks. We have no way of tracing her or her movements. When you told us that she met Black whilst in the states and that she attended M.I.T, we contacted the authorities there, and we've been unable to trace her, she definitely would have been under another name. Lily is clearly a very intelligent woman, who has managed to not only pull off a sophisticated bank robbery, but also engineer a state of the art security system enabling her and her team to enter and rob a major bank undetected. Then, just when things were going well for her, you decided to wake up and run." Lam paused and looked at Ryan for a moment to make sure that he was taking everything that she said in.

"Do you need a coffee or something, or am I good to continue?"

"No, keep going, the coffee can wait." Ryan said, suddenly far more awake than he had felt for hours.

"I am guessing that Lily engineered this crime, so long as it didn't involve any unnecessary deaths along the way, which is why she probably negotiated that you were knocked out and left in your apartment for the police to find, rather than killed after the robbery was finished. It was a risky move on her part. She knew that you would be able to identify her if caught, and would also be able to tell the police how the robbery took place. So she couldn't have been too concerned about that. What did concern her was the use of her good friend Robert Black, who she believed would be released as soon as the robbery was executed successfully. I truly believe that she would never have negotiated her friends' life over this otherwise. I think that this is where her plans began to change significantly, as well as her relationship with Ghost Face."

Ryan nodded for Lam to continue.

"What we have on Ghost face is very limited. Thanks to our friend Detective Jimmy Luk, Ghost Face has successfully been under the radar for what we now assume is years of criminal activity. Until we have Luk in a condition where he can be interviewed we only have what you can tell us." Lam said as she leaned back in her chair and crossed her arms. Indicating that it was now Ryan's turn to add some meat to the bones of Ghost Face.

"OK, well I only spoke to him just a couple of times before the robbery, and then for the first time face to face at the Café, when he showed me the picture of Rob tied up. I got the impression that Lily was not very happy about Rob, but by now she was in far too deep to alter the course of events. Ghost Face was definitely the muscle and the driving force behind the robbery; Lily was the tech in this case.

The next time I saw him was when I tried to get Rob out. This time things had clearly gone sour between him and Lily. Had we stayed there, for sure all three of us would have ended up dead. He wanted no loose ends, and that also included her. He was angry and violent. We only had minutes with Rob before he died. He said that he was sure that the police were involved, that he'd heard conversations through the door. That's all I know. I've had no contact with Lily since then. I don't know where she went. I don't know where Ghost Face is. But for sure he knew I was coming in to see you. Jimmy would have handed me over, and I would have been killed, I feel sure about that." Ryan said flatly.

"Lily is in far more danger than I am right now."

Lam picked up the thread.

"If she's a triad member, then she's a new one. Probably enrolled for her expertise in engineering and computers. Ghost Face is old school. We've seen his type before. He will stop at nothing to complete a task. He'll have powerful allies and friends that he can call upon. He'll be able to threaten and bribe his way out of anything." She said, disappointed at the thought of losing this fish.

"I need you to try and contact Lily. She's our only link with Ghost Face."

Ryan nodded. "Unless he has managed to get to her first." He said.

Lam walked back to her office and sat down heavily in her chair. She needed a lead, just something small that would give her the break she needed. Something to sink her teeth into.

Just then her ancient computer did it's usual sound as the screen came on bringing it out of it's hibernation. An icon flashed in the top corner of her screen telling her that there was a message on the internal intranet. Lam clicked on the icon and entered her six-digit password to allow her to gain access to the site. Once in, she saw a message waiting for her from Detective Wong, who she knew was trying to crack the prostitute murders. It was normal for detectives to share information about cases and also to cross-reference between departments. In this instance it was relating to footage just in of the serial murderer. Detective Wong was asking all departments to review the footage and to brief their Detectives that if they come across this man, then they would need to bring him in. Lam clicked on the large play icon, and the short thirty-second footage began to play. It was black and white and grainy and she had to squint to make out what she was looking at. Eventually it became clear that a street CTTV camera was positioned towards a shuttered shop front, which then lead into a narrow side street. The first few seconds played and there was nothing to see. The top right hand side of the video displayed the date and time in green. Just when Lam was wondering why Detective Wong had sent her the footage a figure emerged into the streetlight. It was momentary, and fleeting. But it was clear. A man dressed in a dark suit walked down the alleyway toward the shop front. Lam felt the hairs on her arms stand up. She quickly rewound the footage. She pressed play again. This time she leaned in closer to try to get a better look, but there was no mistaking the face, she would have recognized it anywhere. She watched as the smooth white-faced man walked down the alleyway again. His skin so pale against the dark night, that he could have been a ghost.

Breathless Lam grabbed her desk phone and punched in the Chief's number, tapping her fingers impatiently on the desk.

"Chief Inspector's Office", the female voice spoke politely on the other end of the phone.

"Where's the Chief", Lam barked, more forcefully than she meant.

"He's in a meeting this afternoon. Is that Detective Lam?" The voice purred, knowing full well that it was.

"Yes, yes. Please ask him to call me the second he comes out of his meeting. It's urgent." Without waiting for a reply Lam had replaced the receiver and tried to gather he thoughts. She had been waiting for this moment for a long time. She knew that she would recognize his face again if she saw it. She had dreamt about what she would do if she ever found herself face to face with the man that killed her partner and left her for dead. More than anything she wanted Wong to find this man. Not for the number of women that he had murdered, not for the safety and protection of others, but for her. Her own selfish vengeance in its purest form.

Lam dialed Wong's extension number and was tapped through to his voice mail. She left him a message to call her, and leaving her cell number replaced the receiver again. This time she was calmer. Needing a distraction, she stood and grabbed her jacket and car keys. She decided that it was time to pay Jimmy Luk a visit and see whether he was out of his anesthetic and ready to talk to her.

Chapter 35

Ryan held the mobile phone to his ear and listened to the ring tone, this was the fifth time that he had tried Lily's number in the last two hours, but with no answer. It didn't click on to voice mail, it just rang out, until a recorded message asked him to try and call again later. Thinking that perhaps Lily would be screening her calls, he tried to text her.

Lily, it's Ryan, I really need to talk to you, please call me or text me. Thanks Ryan.

He didn't expect a response. She was probably long gone now, probably not even in the Country. The phone disregarded or destroyed, her traces well covered. If he were in Lily's shoes, he would probably do the same, so he couldn't really blame her. He somehow didn't see her as the big villain anymore. Ghost Face had filled that position quite well, and made anything that Lily had done look positively minor. His feelings right now were not as he had expected and he wanted nothing more than to see her again. To sit with her and listen to her side of the story, learn what had driven her down this path, and why things ended as they had. He knew, the second that Lily came within distance of Sarah Lam or the police, that she would be arrested immediately. She would be charged with masterminding the bank robbery, kidnapping, manslaughter on two counts, then there would be charges of extortion and money laundering and black mail. The list would go on and on. If she was loyal, then she would be the one to shoulder all of the responsibility. He didn't put her down as the type that would allow other people to take the blame. She wouldn't negotiate a lighter sentence, he thought, she would just accept it all.

Suddenly he didn't want her to get caught. He wanted to warn her and protect her. But he didn't know what he could do or offer.

He grabbed his phone again and started typing.

Lily, I have some information about Ghost Face, you really need to call me.

He hoped that if she did read her messages, that she would be curious enough to contact him.

Lily sat on the edge of her couch looking at her mobile phone. She kept it switched off most of the time, she didn't want her location tracing, and tried to keep the time short. It had been a few hours since she had last checked her messages. She pressed the black on button at the top of her phone, and waited patiently for it to go through its start up sequence. Eventually the phone was on, and she had a good signal. Within seconds her phone started beeping as messages began to come in. She scanned the small screen. She had two from the same number and one from a number that she didn't recognize.

The first two she read were from Ryan. She knew that he'd been picked up by the police and suspected that he had been interviewed already. They would have a good description of her by now and would have done their homework on her business activities and past history. There would be a warrant for her arrest, so getting out of the Country would be more difficult that her Grandmother had perhaps anticipated. She didn't even know if the messages were really from Ryan, or whether they were simply from his phone, and the police were trying to catch her out by typing on his behalf.

The third message confused her. She read it again for a second time.

I need your help to catch Ghost Face. We can do a deal.

Lily switched the phone off again and sat back on the couch. *That's strange*, she thought. If the third message is from the police, then the first two messages must be from Ryan. She thought through her options. Lily needed Ryan to get close to Ghost Face. She would have to take a few risks, she knew that, but if she was arrested before she had the opportunity, then for sure there would be a triad war, and she would have failed her Grandmother.

She switched the phone on again, and waited for the signal to show. As soon as the seven signal bars were showing on the screen, she pressed the call button and held her breath whilst the call connected and the dial tone rang in her ear.

She didn't have to wait long. By the second ring, Ryan had picked up the call.

"Lily, is that you?" He said, a little surprised that she had called.

"Yes, it's me. Where are you?" She asked quickly, not wanting to stay on the line too long.

"I'm at the station. Lily, they want me to help to get Ghost Face, and I need you to help me. But the second you come anywhere near they'll arrest you.

You can't come in. The police are corrupt too Lily. One of the Detectives was working with the triads, no one can be trusted." He was talking quickly now, his voice staying low, so that his conversation could be private.

"OK, I understand, but I also need Ghost Face. He is a traitor and he killed my friend. I will find him." She said, sounding more courageous than she felt.

"You don't need to call me again. I'll call you if I need anything."

"Watch your back Lily". Ryan said.

"I will." With that she finished the call and switched off the phone. The call had lasted thirty-five seconds. She didn't know exactly how long it took to trace a call. Landlines were instantaneous these days, since the telecom world had switched to digital, so when she renovated her house she had decided to keep everything remote, including her phone. For cell phones, she knew that the speed of a trace varied greatly depending on the phone unit, as well as the location where the call was coming from. Even though her home was remote, her signal was strong which meant that it was easier to trace her calls, and quicker. She estimated that it would take well under a minute, and she would need to keep calls under forty seconds to protect herself.

She switched her phone on again, this time to call whoever had offered her a deal. She would need the help of the police to get Ghost Face, and maybe this person would be able to help.

She dialed the number and waited. This time the call rang through for a long time, until eventually the call connected and a womans voice answered.

"Detective Lam", was the response. Lam sounded impatient as though she didn't have time to be taking unimportant calls.

"This is Lily, you sent me a text message." Lily said simply.

There was a moment of silence whilst Lam scrambled to her feet and signaled through the glass to her colleague to trace the call. She took in a deep breath and sat down in her chair.

"Lily, thanks for calling me. I'd like to talk to you for a moment about Ryan Harper." She said, thinking of ways to keep the call going until she had the green light from the other room.

"Please keep it quick, you have twenty seconds." Lily responded.

Lam rolled her eyes and signaled for the team to speed up the trace.

"Do you think I can persuade you to some into the station? We need your help to catch Ghost Face and I'm prepared to cut you a deal. You know him better than anyone, and we need inside information to catch him." Lam's voice was genuine.

Lily looked at her watch, just five seconds to go.

"We can switch to email." Lily said.

"Lily@anonymousspeech.com, that's Lily with a y." Lily clicked the off button and closed down her phone.

Sarah sat for a moment with her mobile still against her ear. *Clever girl*, she thought. There were so many untraceable emails these days that even leading FBI and CIA agents had been unable to hack into these sites. Their security was so tight and so complicated that they had become favourites within criminal networks.

This website was one of the big ones. Given that a member didn't need to offer any information and that it was an internet site, it made the whole process utterly remote. Lily could be in a café, at the airport or out of the Country and feel safe corresponding by email.

She turned in her chair and pulled up her email.

Her colleague leaned in through the door. "Sorry Lam, we were five seconds short of getting her location. She's still in Hong Kong, that's all we know."

"OK" Lam said indicating that there was nothing more to say as she started to type to Lily.

Lily.

We know that Ghost Face is responsible for all of the murders. We know that your involvement was purely to rob the bank, and that you had no intention for Robert Black to be killed. I know he was a good friend of yours.

If you come in and help us catch him, we can reduce your sentence and cut you a deal. We can remove the manslaughter charges. But you will have to face the bank robbery charges. With good behaviour, you'll serve ten years at the very most.

If you don't come in we will find and arrest you. Then you'll be charged for the whole thing, and it's likely that once the judge is done, that you'll be looking at life.

Think it over.

Detective Sarah Lam

Lam signed off and kept the screen open. Within seconds a reply came through.

LIGHTS OUT

Lam,

No deal, but I'll help you to get Ghost Face. I need Harper. Ghost Face wants him dead, he can identify him. We'll set up a meeting place with Harper. Ghost Face will come, and then he's yours.

You should know something, if you haven't worked it out already. He murdered the three prostitutes. You'll never get anything else to stick with triad related charges, he knows that and can implicate too many influential people, but for the prostitutes, you may have a chance.

Trust no one.

L

Lam stared at the screen and read the message again. She could see his face so clearly. His pale skin, his cold dark eyes and his cruel twisted mouth. He had haunted her dreams for so many years, and now in the space of a day, he had been thrust upon her a second time.

Lam had spent the last two hours with Jimmy Luk in the hospital pushing him for information. At first he was reluctant, frightened even. He didn't trust anyone, even her. But slowly he had started to talk. He was in so deep now. It had started innocently enough, years before. Lam believed that as a member of the police force there would be a time in everyone's career, where you could be compromised, and you would be forced to make a decision and to choose a path. Maybe it would be something minor; using your status for some form of gain, a better seat at a restaurant or a free bottle of wine. Perhaps accepting a bribe that should rather be disclosed. Everyone has a choice to either allow oneself to be drawn in, or be the bigger person and do what's right. She had always felt that the hardest path to follow is the righteous one and she didn't want to judge Luk too harshly, but he had come to that fork in the path, and instead of standing up to what was right, informing his Chief of what was happening, he had submitted to fear and greed allowing himself to be corrupted. Lam had listened in silence as Luk told her his story.

He had been sent down to a Wan Chai brothel after reports that a triad gang was harassing a woman in the street. It was just at the time when the Government had changed their laws and had banned whorehouses, only allowing one-woman brothels in the City. This had left triad-run organizations in a difficult position and the women, now seeing that they could legally sell sex and from their own homes, were starting to leave their 'illegal' employment. Even with the triads threatening their workers, it didn't seem to make a real difference and the Government was praised with its new policy and control of sex workers. When Luk got to the scene, the woman was still shouting in the street at three men. She had been badly beaten, her hair crazy and knotted, her dress ripped and Luk could see bruises fresh across her chest and legs where she had been kicked and punched. One of the men was yelling back to her.

"You are so ugly, no one would pay for you now. Look at you, you are nothing but trash." The man shouting was laughing as he taunted the woman. "You will starve on your own, how will you feed yourself? " he jeered, "And when you come back begging for us to help you, to take you in when you are at your lowest, the door will be closed in your face." He spat on the floor in front of her.

Luk didn't like the scene that was unfolding. He and his colleague stepped out from the shadows and Luk pulled out his badge. The sudden movement made the men turn. Seeing Luk immediately resulting in the men fleeing in different directions. Shouting orders to his colleague, Luk targeted the man that had been doing all the talking. He made chase, following him down back streets and between restaurants, over garbage bags and bins, dodging people and cars. The chase led Luk towards the Wan Chai playground. An open area in the middle of the city surrounded by high rises, where kids could play soccer or basketball on hard grey tarmac. It was a known area to the police for drugs and gangs. The walkways surrounding the playground had pillars and high metal fences, making it hard for Luk to see clearly in front of him. He slowed down to a fast walk and discreetly pulled out his gun, keeping it at his side to avoid any panic from the public. He scanned the playground and the people walking past him, looking at their faces. He walked towards the top corner of the playground. As he drew close he felt the sharp point of a knife in his back and a hiss in his ear.

"You and I are going to become good friends, unless of course you prefer it otherwise", the voice said as the knife was pushed a little harder, causing Luk to suck in some air as the pain started to register. He was relieved of his gun as it was expertly slipped from his hand and placed into the man's jacket pocket.

Luk nodded silently as he was guided down a narrow side street between two high rises, to a hidden doorway. His attacker opened the door, still keeping the knife pressed against his side, and opened it ushering Luk to go ahead. Once inside it took Luk a while to adjust his eyes. The room was dark and dingy with a strong smell of mould and an acrid smell of urine. There was a dripping noise to his left where he could make out the entrance to a toilet. In the middle of the room was a small table and two chairs and in the corner a stained mattress on the floor. It was clearly a drug house, the place where people came to shoot up in privacy. The urine stench was so overpowering that it made Luk gag and he covered his mouth.

"Cozy isn't it", his attacker said pushing Luk toward one of the chairs.

"Make yourself comfortable" he said.

Luk sat down with a thud on one of the old metal chairs. The beads of sweat across his forehead from his recent run were now turning cold making him shiver in the dank room.

"I knew we would be friends when I first set eyes on you Officer…?" he probed for Luks name.

"Luk", he said simply.

"Officer Luk. I've been missing a police friend for a few months now and I think you are going to be perfect." His attacker stated, stretching a thin smile across his ugly mouth.

"Did you know Officer Liu? Such a shame. He started out well. He helped us a lot, and of course we helped him too. His wife was delighted with their house in Clearwater Bay, three bedrooms, and a nice garden. But then he made a few mistakes, put us in a difficult position and, well, we don't like mistakes." The attacker finished menacingly.

Luk wracked his brains. He had heard of Officer Liu. He'd been killed a few months earlier. He couldn't remember all the details, but the message was clear. He could feel a sickening surge in his stomach and he tried to repress the urge to vomit.

"Today you'll go back to the station, because you didn't manage to catch any of the bad men. But you will hear from me very soon. We'll look after each other and you'll start to see the benefits. Your work won't be difficult."

Luk assessed the man before him. Clean cut in his dark suit. His collar was undone at the top button and his black tie slightly loose at the knot. Luk thought that he was maybe in his early forties. He looked fit and had managed to outrun Luk easily. In the dark room he stood out. At first Luk thought it was because of his white shirt, but then he realized that it wasn't that at all. It was his pale skin. He almost glowed.

"And if I refuse?" Luk said.

Within a second Luk was bent over the table on his back, a hand pressed tightly around his throat cutting off his breathing and the sharp tip of the knife was hovering millimeters from his left eye. He could feel the man's rancid breath and see the rage in his attackers eyes bearing down on him. It was the look of a man unhinged, prepared to do anything, including kill a police officer.

Suddenly Luk found himself released and he slumped back into the chair, allowing the air into his lungs as he rubbed his throat. He watched as his attacker wiped the saliva from his mouth with the back of his hand, panting as he did so. His hair had flopped forward out of its slicked back style and he pushed his fingers through it, tidying himself up. Once composed he looked again at Luk.

"If you refuse, my dear new friend, it will be the last thing that you do."

With that his attacker slipped out of the door, leaving Luk alone in the dark room. He was shaking uncontrollably now. No longer able to suppress the nausea, Luk stood and vomited next to the table. He wiped his mouth, and exited the room, relieved to be in the narrow alleyway. Glad of the rush of fresh air as he stepped outside. He scanned the alleyway in front and behind him, but his attacker was gone.

He didn't say anything when he met up with his colleague. Just that he had lost him in the chase. They went back to interview the woman, and did their paperwork.

Luk only had to wait two days before he received his first message. It came in a bouquet of flowers, delivered to his desk. There was no note, just a card with a phone number.

He called the number and waited.

"Ah Officer Luk, so nice of you to call. Did you like the flowers? I thought yellow was your colour. Let's meet, shall we say, thirty minutes at the Blossom House dai pai dong? Don't keep me waiting, I hate being kept waiting." The same voice that had hissed in Luks ear, now made him shiver. Then the phone went dead.

Telling his colleagues that he had a Dr's appointment, Luk left and made his way to the Dai Pai Dong.

The first few meetings were all the same, Luk would sit and listen and his attacker would talk. He still didn't know his name. Then on the third meeting the first request was issued. One of his men had been arrested, an extortion charge, the evidence was backed up against him and the hearing was coming up soon. He needed the evidence to become inadmissible.

Luk didn't sleep that night as fought with reason. Eventually he had decided to look into the case, and if he thought he could do it without compromising himself, then he would.

It was easier than Luk thought. He re-wrote a couple of the statements, and removed one of the pieces of evidence. It took him less than twenty minutes to destroy a case that would have for sure sent the man to jail.

That night, when he arrived home, Luk dialed the number.

When his attacker answered he simple said. "It's done", and switched off the phone.

Two days later a delivery arrived at his home. It was a parcel, wrapped in brown paper addressed to him. He quickly ripped it open, and was stunned when he saw that it was a traditional Chinese tea set. It was exquisitely presented in a lacquered box. It had a bright yellow silk inlay and a brown clay teapot sat nestled between six small clay teacups. There was a note attached that simply stated " Enjoy the tea.' Luk was confused. What an odd thing to send.

He walked it through to his kitchen and carefully removed each delicate piece standing it on his worktop. Then he removed the silk layer. Underneath taped to the bottom of the box was a brown A4 sized envelope and it looked full. Luk pulled the tape off securing the packet and he ripped open the top. His mouth dropped open when he saw the contents. It was stuffed with bank notes. Luk emptied the notes onto his worktop. When he was done counting he stuffed it all back into the envelope and into the box and closed the lid. He poured himself a glass of brandy and drained the glass. One hundred thousand Hong Kong dollars was the final amount that he had counted. That was the equivalent to almost three months salary to Luk. He was stunned, nervous and excited all in one.

Lam had listened to Luk for well over an hour. She learned that what had started out as small jobs began to shift into more disturbing territory. By now Luk had been 'working' for his attacker for a number of years and he had earned more than double his yearly salary. He reconciled himself that what he was doing was not so serious, he wasn't letting killers off the hook, it was mainly money laundering and bribery. He figured that if a few triads managed to slip through the net, they would slip up again and be caught eventually. So he continued without much guilt.

Things changed when Luk was given information about a rival triad group. It was a drug-related drop that was on his attackers home turf, and they needed it stopped. He told Luk that they expected that there would be in excess of eighty kilograms of cocaine, and five senior triad members present. Not wanting to cause an all-out triad war, Luk was asked to intervene. It needed to become a police matter, not a triad one. He was given everything on a plate, names, the date, time and location. At first Luk was reluctant, but then, realizing what this could also mean for his career, he decided to do it.

Telling his chief that he'd had an anonymous tip off, Luk pulled together in one week Operation Sleeping Ghost. It was one of the biggest drug-related operations that the Hong Kong Police force had ever seen. It involved forty police officers from several different units. Luk knew that if it all went wrong, then his career would be up in flames.

The drop took place exactly as indicated at a remote warehouse in Tsuen Wan, an industrial area of Kowloon. The police, as instructed, waited until everyone was in place and Luk was ready. He gave the order for the raid and within minutes six people had been rounded up. Other officers went through vehicles and clothing, and a total of sixty kilograms of cocaine was recovered. Lam remembered the case well. It gained a lot of press at the time. Headlines like major *Drug Bust Completes Gang Downfall* stole the front page of the newspapers. She remembered the street value quoted as being in excess of $100 million Hong Kong dollars.

All six people, five men and one woman, were arrested and charged with dealing dangerous drugs and drug possession. They received Hong Kong's maximum penalty of 15 years.

It was a great success for Luk and he enjoyed the positive attention. Later that same year he was promoted to Detective and eventually became one of the specialists of the Organised Crime and Triad Bureau.

Luks attacker couldn't have been happier and of course Luk was paid handsomely.

He was busy telling Lam all of this, when a sickening thought flashed across her mind. She stopped Luk mid sentence.

"Luk, I need to ask you something."

Luk sat up in his bed and paid attention, the look on Lam's face told him that she knew. It was only a matter of time before she would work it out. But she had pieced it together sooner than he thought.

"The night that Ng and Ko died. That was a set-up. No one could work out how they knew that we were investigating them. Everyone was worried that we had a leak on the inside. But that night…." She trailed off, already knowing the answer.

"It was you…." She said slowly as the true realization hit her. She glared at the man lying in the bed before her.

"You told them that we were closing the net, and they set us up. You allowed them to do it. You allowed them to murder three police officers…" her voice, now raised in anger shook as she spoke. She stood up from the side of his bed. No longer able to contain the desperate fury that threatened to escape her body.

"It was Ghost Face all along. He was the one there that night. I wasn't seeing a ghost, it wasn't my mind playing tricks on me, it was him. I always knew that one day I would see him again and then I did, earlier today. CCTV footage of the same man walking out of a dark alleyway." She was talking to herself now rather than Luk, who sat as white as a sheet on his bed watching Lam pace up and down.

"I could recognize his face anywhere. And now you…." She stopped and turned to look at Luk. He appeared small now, sitting there in his white gown, pale faced and all strapped up with tubes coming out of his arm.

"You're telling me that this is the same man that has murdered my partner Ko, Ng, and now Chow. The same man that shot Robert Black, and the same man that is responsible for raping and murdering three innocent women. You can reconcile this with yourself?"

Luk sat in silence, knowing that his life as he knew it was over.

Lam looked at Luk with pity.

"I feel sorry for you. You will have to live with what you have done. You may not have murdered these people yourself. But today you have blood on your hands, and I will never let you forget it." Lam finished pacing. Without saying another word, she grabbed her bag and coat and left the room. Outside two police officers stood guard. She turned to them.

"No-one in and no-one out without speaking to me. Do you understand?" She spoke sharply making herself very clear.

The two officers replied in unison, "Yes Ma'am" immediately straightened their postures.

Lam marched out of the hospital and as she walked towards her car she dialed the Chief. It was time that she brought him up to speed.

By the time Lam arrived at her desk, the team had set themselves up next door. She needed to find Lily. She was the one that could lead her to Ghost Face. The Chief had agreed on a deal, and he'd given her all the resources that she needed.

Chapter 36

Lily knew that she needed to make the call. She would set up the meeting in a busy tourist area, which would make it safer for Ryan. Ghost Face would be less likely to make a big scene in public. It would be too risky otherwise. She would arrange it all from the safe house. She didn't want to risk being picked up at this stage in the game. She had clearly said to Lam, 'no deal', and she meant it. Ten years in prison was not part of the plan, and she knew that her Grandmother would find a solution, even if it did mean that she would have to leave the Country and start a new life.

She dialed the familiar number and waited.

The voice that she had grown to hate answered.

"About time." Was all he said to her. Lily dismissed the sarcasm and proceeded with her plan.

"I think we can help each other." She said to the point and without any emotion in her voice.

"Really?" was his response.

"Think of it as a simple business transaction."

"Continue," he said.

"The police have Harper and by now he has told them everything that he knows. He can identify us both. He is our only witness to the Bank robbery and the kidnapping. He'll be the one that will stand up in court and bury the two of us. I'm not about to let that happen." She said as convincingly as she could.

"So what do you have in mind?" His voice was curious now, making Lily think that she had taken him by surprise.

"I've spoken to him. He's agreed to meet me in an hour at the Peninsula Hotel. I've told him that I'll consider coming in and talk to the Police if he'll meet with me first."

"So your charms are still working?" He said mocking her. She could hear him laugh a little, making her flush with anger.

"It's a chance to remove our only witness. I'm not a natural killer, but you are. You can erase this and you can do it quickly and discreetly."

"Interesting." He said with a cool voice. There was a pause. "I'll be there."

Then the phone went dead.

Satisfied, Lily slipped her phone back into her pocket and waited.

Across the City Ghost Face switched off the phone and turned to face the other man in the room. The young man was hunched over a laptop typing manically. Ghost Face moved around the room until he was standing in front of him. He could see the reflection of the light from the computer screen flicker across his face.

"Did you get it?" He asked.

The man looked up at him and gave reluctant smile.

"Yes'.

"How far?" he asked.

"It's close. A fifteen minute drive." He replied.

Sarah was still at her desk when the call came in. She'd been monitoring her emails expecting it come through that way, so she jumped slightly when her mobile started to ring.

"Lily?" she asked.

"Yes, it's me"

Immediately Lam stood and signaled to the two men in the room next door so that they could start their trace.

"He's taken the bait." Lily said with a trace of pleasure in her voice.

"I told him that Harper will be at the Peninsula Hotel in an hour to meet me. He wants Harper. He knows he's the main witness that could put him away, so he took the bait."

"What about you Lily, where will you be?" Lam asked, trying to draw out the conversation. She looked across at her team in the other room and they signaled that they needed five more seconds.

"Lily, if you're not planning to show then you need to tell me more about

Ghost Face. I don't want Harper placed at unnecessary risk, what can we expect him to do?"

This last question Lily hadn't anticipated. She wanted to get off the phone, but also agreed with Lam. Ghost Face was unpredictable and strong. He could kill Harper easily given the opportunity.

Before she could answer Lam spoke again.

"Look, we'll work it out," she said as she looked across at the thumbs up and the smiling faces through the glass. They had successfully traced her.

"Just be careful who you trust." Lam finished and clicked off the phone leaving Lily bemused on the other end.

When Lam put the phone down she ran through to the next room.

"We've got her boss," one of the officers said happily turning the screen for her to see.

She's at the Gold Coast. Twenty-Five minutes drive away from here.

"OK" Sarah said excited that this was all finally happening.

She called the Chief.

"He took the bait," she said.

"Ghost Face will be at the Peninsula in less than an hour. He thinks Harper will be there. I'm going to get a team together and Harper and head there now. We have the location of Lily too, so I think we can round up both of them. I'm sending a team across to pick her up now. We have one shot before they disappear." She tried to hide the excitement in her voice.

"Lam, be careful. Take who ever you need with you on this. Don't forget, this man is a killer. Whatever you do don't find yourself on your own with him, and don't get Harper killed. You have enough paperwork to do already." The Chief said somberly.

"I want you to call me as soon as you have them in custody."

"OK Chief. I'll keep you in the loop." Lam said.

Chapter 37

Lily paced around her apartment unease in the pit of her stomach. The last comment from Lam had started her thinking about Ryan. He didn't deserve this, she thought. Everyone was using him as bait to get to Ghost Face, and she knew that he would kill him in an instant if he managed to get within reach. She had to believe that Lam would get to him first, but something didn't feel right. She checked her watch. It was only 5.15pm, but the sky was starting to darken. It would be pitch dark by 6pm. Ghost Face would be in the shadows looking for her and Harper by then.

She went to her kitchen to make herself some tea, she pulled out her teacup and teapot and started to prepare loose leaves of jasmine and green tea that she combined to calm her. Whilst she waited for the kettle to boil, she switched on one of her TV's to get some background noise.

She poured the boiling water into her clay teapot and stood with her hands on the counter whilst she waited for the tea to settle a while. Already she could smell the aroma.

She was about to pour the tea into her cup when a green flashing light caught her eye. She crossed the kitchen and was in front of her laptop in three paces. She quickly punched in her security code and waited for a second whilst the security images flashed up onto her screen. Lily's pulse started to race. One of her camera's, the one showing her driveway, was out. It wouldn't malfunction without assistance, she considered as she typed something into her computer. *Odd*, she thought. "The motion sensor seems to still be on, just the image has gone". She said to herself.

Lily scanned the remaining twelve cameras and sensors. Everything appeared normal on the other screens. She chided herself for being on edge. There was probably a perfectly simple explanation. She allowed herself to relax a little, she'd drink her tea then go down and check it out.

Just as Lily was about to return to the kitchen, another green light flashed on her computer. She looked in horror as the image to her garage fuzzed out of focus then disappeared off the screen.

Chapter 38

Ryan was nervous as he sat in the front of Lams Porsche. They were parked on a quiet back road behind the Hotel. The cars lights and engine switched off.

Picking up on his nerves, Lam turned to Ryan.

"Don't worry. We'll get to him before he can get to you." She said with confidence as she leaned across and patted Ryan on his Kevlar bulletproof police vest. "It's knife and bullet proof." She said.

"What if he goes for my head?" Ryan said dryly.

Lam laughed and turned back to look out the window. She had changed what she was wearing and now wore black jeans and a black long sleeved jersey; she wore the Police issue black vest over the top of her clothes with POLICE printed in bright reflective silver across the back. Ryan looked at her. To the unsuspecting on-looker the bullet proof vest went un noticed underneath her clothes, but Ryan could still see the slight tell tail shape of it underneath Lam's top, making her look more bulky than she really was. She was also expecting a fight. Ryan thought.

Lam looked at her watch. It was already 5:50pm and they had been sitting in the car for over fifteen minutes. She could feel the weight of Harpers restlessness as though it was something that she could reach out and touch. She felt completely under control. She had plain clothed police officers situated in and around the Hotel, all streets leading in and out were covered, with two further Officers patrolling the underground car park dressed as parking attendants.

Lam had sent two Officers across the harbour to pick up Lily. She expected that she would hear from them shortly. They should have arrived at the location by now. She would give them a few more minutes and then she'd call for an update.

She glanced one more time at her watch. It was time. She turned and nodded to Ryan. His task was simple enough. He needed to walk into the Peninsula lobby and sit on one of the couches. He would be monitored from all angles. At the first sign of any danger, the Officers would swoop in, grab him and take him to safety. It would all happen very quickly. Lam would be holding back out of sight. She was worried that Ghost Face may recognize her and he would run before she had the chance to get to him. They climbed out of the car and Lam removed her vest. She didn't want to draw any unwanted attention before getting into position. They walked into the Hotel separately and she immediately wandered off toward the Hotel shops, leaving Ryan to make his way to the agreed waiting area.

She leaned against the cool white marble wall and pretended to look at an impressive jewellery display in the Tiffany's window. She pulled out her phone and called one of the Officers at the Gold Coast for a status update.

The phone rang out. She tried another number and let the phone ring. It also rang out. Lam called through to the station.

"I can't get hold of Tsang or Lau," she said, irritation entering her voice. She couldn't afford for this to go wrong now.

"Keep trying them and call me back." She snapped as she clicked off her phone and continued to watch the window. She checked her watch again. It was exactly six o'clock. She glanced sideways across the lobby. Ryan was sitting with his legs crossed. Still in the same trousers as before, but she had forced one of the plain clothed officers to switch shirts with Ryan before they left the station, so the bloodied shirt didn't bring unwanted attention. He looked nervous, she noted. He was fidgeting, trying to look relaxed, but she knew that his heart would be pumping as he waited for something to happen. She scanned the busy floor and one by one was able to identify each Officer in position.

Turning back to the window she waited for a few more seconds. *Something's wrong*, she thought to herself. A wave of unease washed over. She checked her watch again watching as the minute hand continued to tick past the hour.

He's not coming, she thought with a sudden flash of panic. *I've got this all wrong. He's going after Lily.*

As soon as the realization hit, Lam raced across the lobby floor toward Ryan. "We're in the wrong place", she said to him breathlessly, skidding to a halt in front of him and grabbing his shoulders. The sudden movement made Ryan jump. He stared at her for a moment until the realization sank in.

"Oh No," he said simply.

Lam pulled the radio from her belt and spoke quickly.

"Everyone else back to the station, Wong, take Harper back to Wan Chai under police protection, and he stays there until I get back", she pulled a startled Ryan up by the back of his shirt collar and still keeping the radio fixed to her ear whilst talking, she frog marched him out of the lobby and down the street. She reached the corner of the road and a man that Ryan didn't recognize stepped out of the shadows. "Ryan, you're safe now. Go with Wong." She said releasing him and picking up her walking pace to a run.

"Where are you going?" Ryan yelled after her.

Lam flung herself into her car, pleased that she hadn't opted for a slower staff car. She pulled away from the curb and worked through the gears. The traffic was always congested along the harbour front and already the lights were starting to change unfavourably. She leaned across to the passenger side and flicked open the glove compartment quickly pulling out the police siren. Winding down her window, she slammed it onto the roof. She could see the reflection of the light on the cars in front of her. The siren now doing its work as drivers started to make way for her car. It took her five minutes to work through the myriad of drivers and pedestrians before she found herself clear enough to put her foot down.

Lam estimated that she had at least a fifteen minutes drive before she would reach the Gold Coast. She called through to the station and asked again about Tsang and Lau. No one was able to locate them.

"I'm going to need back-up", she said, as she pushed her foot to the floor and opened up the throttle.

Chapter 39

Lily was blinking hard. She was trying to keep the tears from flowing down her cheeks, willing them not to come now of all times. She flared her nostrils as she tried to draw as much air into her lungs as possible whilst the duct tape across her mouth tugged at the delicate skin on her lips. She lay looking up at her bedroom ceiling; the spotlights were bright and burned her eyes forcing them shut. She could feel the heat that they generated on her eyelids. The back of her head felt sticky against the pillow and throbbed where he had hit her. Her wrists were bound by thin rope and tied to the bedpost stretching her body to its full limit. She tried rotating her wrists in an effort to relieve some of the pressure, but it didn't work. She only succeeded in making the skin even more raw and bloody.

Lily wondered when he would come back again. It had been at least five minutes she estimated. She wriggled her arms again. It was futile. She was so tightly bound that there was no way for her to escape. She turned her head from side to side scanning her bedroom, but knew that there was nothing close at hand that could help her. She closed her eyes and lay back for a moment trying to relax the muscles in her body.

She had been such a fool to think that only the Police would be concerned with tracking her location. She hadn't considered for a moment that Ghost Face was smart enough to even think about it. She had underestimated him entirely. His desire to kill her and have her removed from the Society was immense. Ryan would just be something that he would deal with later.

He had used her own technology against her. She had naively thought that she would be completely protected in her safe house. But he was clever. He had managed to not only trace her cell phone and pin point her location, but, with the help of her own loyal employee, she thought bitterly, he had managed to hack into her security systems remotely rendering her motion sensors and alarms useless. Ghost Face had simply walked into her home completely unchallenged.

The door of Lily's bedroom opened and Ghost Face calmly walked across the plush white carpet to the edge of the bed and looked down at the woman before him. He was dressed in his usual attire; black shoes and pants, white shirt and black jacket. His black tie was loosely knotted around his neck. His hair, perfectly slicked back and freshly dyed, looked even darker against his pale white skin. Lily thought that he looked almost dead as she considered him from where she lay.

His eyes devoured her body as he traced her shape through her clothes with one hand. Lily moved and wriggled, using her free legs to push his hand away, causing him to laugh dryly.

"I've been thinking about this for a long time." He said taking a step back, out of reach of her long legs.

"I have wondered what this moment would feel like." He smiled at her, an ugly dark smile.

Lily's mind was racing. She couldn't bear for him to touch her and wanted to bite him and spit, but the duct tape pulled firm against her mouth. She only had her legs free, but knew that ultimately he would be too strong for her. She watched him through narrowed eyes as he paced at the bottom of her bed, like a big cat stalking it's prey. As he paced he slowly loosened his tie and removed it over his head, throwing it onto an adjacent chair and shrugged off his jacket, letting it drop to the floor. Then he slowly undid each button of his shirt.

Lily felt the nausea rise in her throat as she realized what this was leading to. She closed her eyes tightly and tried to think of something else, wishing that she could transport herself to another place until it was all over, or until she was dead.

Ghost Face was enjoying himself. He was in no rush this time. He could take his time and savour every movement, touch and taste. He wanted to remember it all, so that later he could draw on it at his leisure.

Before Lily could react, she felt the pressure on her lower legs. She opened her eyes to see Ghost Face sitting on her pinning her down to the bed. His hands worked quickly as he fumbled with the belt on her jeans as she struggled against him, desperate to stop this.

He was stripped to the waist now. She could see his smooth upper body was as pale as his face. He tugged the clothes off her lower half dropping them onto the floor, her phone falling out of her pocket and thudding silently onto the plush carpet. Lily clamped her legs together as tightly as she could. She was screaming at him now from behind her tape, but all that he could hear were muffled cries. Nothing that he wasn't used to, he thought. Pinning her down again with his body, he lay on top of her until his face was pushed hard against hers. Lily swiftly moved her head to the side, trying to push her neck as far away from him as she could. She could feel his rancid hot breath against her cheek. The throbbing in her head increased now, and she wanted everything to black out, she wanted to faint, to sleep, to die. Anything that would take her away from here.

He whispered in her ear, and she could feel his cold lips against her face as he spoke.

"Your parents didn't suffer", he said, breathing heavily between words.

Lily tried to move her face further away from him but he lay heavily on her, restricted her movement.

"I made sure of that." He continued, ignoring her writhing.

"It was easy to kill them, he breathed. Their routine was always the same. Dinner at the Mandarin every Thursday, so predictable, that I don't know why I hadn't thought of it sooner."

"It took just seconds to steer them off the bridge. A gentle nudge in the rear, and your Father lost control. The impact probably killed them", he mused, now oblivious to Lily twisting and turning beneath him, hatred oozing from every pore in her body.

"Although I'm sure I recall a verdict of death by drowning. It's supposed to be so painful. Your chest burns as your lungs scream for air, then your brain forces you to suck in, and all you can do is breathe. The cold liquid rushes in and the pain rips through your body. It can take up to three long, long minutes before you stop breathing, before your mind releases you from the pain." He finished his monologue, bringing himself back to the moment.

He gazed sideways at Lily, enjoying the look of horror and pain on her hot wet face.

Pulling himself up onto his knees, he slowly placed both hands around her neck and applied pressure. Immediately the blood rushed to Lily's head stopping her ability to breathe. She started to gasp, her body pushing back against him as hard as she could in an attempt to free her throat from his vice grip. Slowly darkness started to engulf Lily as she fought helplessly. The more she moved, the harder his grip became. Her muscles now weak and starved of oxygen were helpless against him. Panic flushed into her mind as she realized that she would die like this. She felt her eyes bulging. Flashes of light darted in front of her as her chest burned, desperate for air. She began to fall deeper into a dark abyss dimly aware of the man above her. His white face flowing in and out of her vision, shrinking until she could no longer see him. A loud buzzing noise was all that she could hear now as she felt her body finally submit. The fight in her ebbing away.

Lam pulled up to the house and saw the lights on. She had switched off her siren and lights a few miles back, not wanting to signal her arrival. She could just make out a police car to the left of the driveway. Poorly hidden among some trees and bushes.

She quietly stepped out of the car and pulled out her gun. She scanned the area and then ran quickly to the car. The two Police Officers lay slumped on the ground. She knelt down to feel their pulses, but they were already dead. Without wasting any time, she moved around to the start of the driveway. It was dark, so she quickly maneuvered herself up the side of the wall trying to offer some protection from the security camera. She reached the front door and tried the handle. It was locked. She looked around her and saw the garage to her left. She quickly ran to it and tried the handle. This time it opened. She lifted it until it was high enough for her to roll under. She closed the door behind her and felt her way through the darkness to an internal door. Her foot connected with something hard and she knelt down to pick it up. It was a piece of wood. She stood again feeling for the handle. She slowly pressed on it relieved when it clicked open. She stepped through into a bright hallway. She looked at the wood in her hand. It was covered in blood at one end. *Not a good sign*, she thought as she pushed it against the wall. It felt eerily quiet. She strained her ears and thought she could hear faint talking. She moved toward the staircase and listened again. Yes, she could definitely hear something. She tried the first step, but her boots creaked noisily. She stepped back and worked her boots off quickly leaving her in just her socks. She padded silently and quickly up the staircase, the sound of the voice getting louder as she did so. When she reached the top she scanned the landing and located what she thought was the master bedroom. Now she could hear the voice clearly and it sent a chill down her spine.

"Although I'm sure I recall a verdict of death by drowning. It's supposed to be so painful. Your chest burns as your lungs scream for air, then your brain forces you to suck in, and all you can do is breathe. The cold liquid rushes in and the pain rips through your body. It can take up to three long, long minutes before you stop breathing, before your mind releases you from the pain." The voice said.

"Unless you want a bullet in the back of your head, I suggest that you stop right now", Lam said slowly, her hand steady, and her gun pointing at Ghost Face.

Before she could react Ghost Face had reached down for his ankle knife with his left hand and deftly threw it across the room as hard as he could toward Lam. She moved and twisted her body out of the way of the knife but it caught in her right arm, forcing her to drop her weapon as she landed hard on her feet. Seeing the gun land, with the pain searing through her arm, she bolted across the room, but Ghost Face was too quick. He was off Lily and already crouching down picking it up when she got there. His eyes gleaming and sharp, his body sweating as he stood and pointed the gun toward her.

"Interesting turn of events" he said as he watched the blood drip down Lam's arm.

"A knife is faster than a bullet." he quipped.

Lam remained silent. She glanced across at Lily's still body, fearing the worst. She was too late, she thought.

"I should have killed you when I had the chance." He said now, teasing her with the gun.

"It was foolish of me, but." he trailed off.

"At least I get the chance to kill you thoroughly this time." He finished.

Lam's arm was burning with pain. The knife was pushed in deep and she suspected that if she looked it would be protruding out the other side.

"You think you are so clever. Fooling everyone around you, all the while building your own empire based on nothing but fear, becoming your own Master." She said, trying to buy time. "But to be a Master, you need respect." She continued getting into her stride. "Respect and loyalty."

"I have respect and loyalty," Ghost Face boomed. Laughing at her pathetic parry. "You understand nothing," he said

"You are as worthless as your partners." He said cruelly, "And you will die just like them. Without honor and without…."

The loud raspy gasp took them both by surprise, as they turned to look at the bed. It was the opportunity that Lam needed. With her good left hand she ripped the knife through her upper arm ignoring the tearing pain as she did so. As hard as she could, she threw the knife toward Ghost Face. This time his reaction was too slow.

The sharp point of the knife pierced his throat just below his adams apple. He gasped as he felt the cool rush of air force itself into his windpipe. Dropping his gun he frantically tried to pull the knife out. Blood was filling his mouth now. He could taste the warm metallic liquid as it started to bubble inside him. He was on his knees, his hands slipping on the blood soaked handle, losing his grip as his head started to swim. Then he tumbled onto his side. He was weak; life was ebbing away from him second by second, unable now to remove the foreign object from his body. He watched in disbelief as the blood changed the white carpet to red until he could see no more, until his breathing finally stopped.

Lam rushed over to Lily and giving her some dignity threw her jeans across her naked lower half. She was disoriented and confused as she cut the rope with a bloody knife and removed the duct tape as gently as she could from her mouth.

"Sorry." Lam whispered as she removed the tape pulling some of Lily's skin with it.

She wrapped Lily in the quilt with her good left arm and left her propped up against the headboard.

"It's OK, he's dead." She soothed. "You're safe now."

Lily looked at Lam and nodded silently. She turned and looked at the body on the floor next to her. Looking back toward Lam she mouthed, "Thank you."

"I just need to make a call," Lam said stepping out of the room, "I'll be right back."

She slowly walked out of the room and pulled out her cell phone.

She dialed the Chiefs number, and holding her arm tightly, waited for him to pick up.

"Lam", the familiar voice warmed her.

"Chief" she said as she slid down the wall and rested her back against it. She could feel the loss of blood had made her weak.

"We're almost there", he said. In the distance Lam could hear the faint sound of sirens. She liked the sound.

"Good" she replied and closed her eyes.

Chapter 40

When Sarah Lam woke up, it was to light pouring in behind a closed white blind. The sun seeping around the edges making it too bright for her eyes. She turned on her left side with her back to the window to try and darken the room, only to be tugged back by the drip still attached to her hand. She sighed heavily remembering why she was there and absentmindedly stroked her heavily bandaged arm with her free hand. The morphine was doing its job for now, but she knew that once removed, she would be on her own. She sat up in bed as best she could, trying to work out which of the electronic buttons was the correct one to press, and waited whilst the bed slowly whirred and moved her into a sitting position. Just then her door opened the Chief walked in. He was all smiles and carried a large bunch of flowers, which he sheepishly placed on the table at the foot of the bed.

"I didn't expect to see you up and moving so soon." He said happily sitting himself down heavily on the plastic visitors chair next to her bed.

'You look better, you have a bit of colour." He stated giving her a good once over. His eyes moved to the morphine drip next to her bed.

"Looks like you've used your quota for the night." He chuckled signaling to the empty plastic bag.

"Thanks for coming Chief, you've brightened my day." She said dryly returning the banter.

"Actually I don't feel too bad. My arm's a bit stiff." She said trying to maneuver her arm and wincing. "But I'm OK".

"Well, there's no rush. You're signed off until you are fit to come back, and that's an order."

"What time is it?" Lam asked scanning her nightstand, remembering that her watch had been removed.

"It's 10am." He said. "You've been here since last night. Do you remember what happened?" He asked, his face now suddenly full of concern.

"Only up until speaking to you. After that, I have nothing. Sorry to leave you such a bloody mess." She stated.

"You did a good job, Lam, I'm just sorry that we didn't get to you sooner."

"And Lily, how's she doing? She was in a pretty poor state by the time I got there." Lam said, remembering the blood stained pillow and bruises around her neck.

The Chief shifted in his seat and cleared his throat. It was a trait of his that Lam had picked up on over the years, which normally signaled bad news.

"She vanished." He said simply.

Lam's heart sank.

"We arrived minutes after talking with you. We found the two dead Officers by the entrance, and then Ghost Face. We searched everywhere, but she managed to slip by us."

"We nearly lost you Lam. You had lost so much blood by the time we reached you. You needed two transfusions during the night, and thirty stitches, you were in surgery for two hours. You're lucky to be here." He said, and for a moment rested his hand on hers, like her Father would have done.

He moved it way quickly, and she looked at him.

"Have you been here all night?" She asked, noticing for the first time that his shirt looked wrinkled and his eyes tired and bloodshot.

"I thought you wouldn't make it." He replied, his voice now quiet and gave her a weak smile.

"Chief, I'm OK." She said to him.

"So what will happen to Lily now? She asked, moving the conversation back to the case and away from anything personal.

"It was a no deal. We'll keep looking for her, but I'm guessing that by now, she has a new identity. She'll either be abroad, or, if she's here. It will be like looking for a needle in a haystack. The money has still not been traced, so we'll continue with the search. We may have to wait until the notes begin to circulate, but we can at least satisfy the Commissioner and the Bank that we caught and killed the ring leader." He reasoned.

"And Harper, what will happen to him now?"

"Well, he co-operated well and has told us everything that he knows. He has the chance to go back to his old job, John McIntyre and the Board have been very sympathetic. We don't see Lily as a huge threat to him any longer, and with Ghost Face now gone, he should be free to carry on as before. Although he did say that he had plans to go back to England. A fresh start for him, which is understandable." He said.

"And Luk?" She asked.

"Oh we still have him." The Chief said with a wry smile. "He's willing to talk. He'll be good for us in that way. He's trying to negotiate which prison he'll serve his time in, but he's squealing like a pig, so we'll let him carry on for now, we have a few years of ground to cover."

A nurse bustled in and checked Lam's blood pressure and changed her morphine bag. She gave the Chief a stern look and tapped her watch with her finger, indicating that the Chief's visiting time was over.

Once she had finished and left the room, the Chief stood and collected his jacket from across the back of the chair.

"I'll come and see you tomorrow", he said, we have a lot to talk about.

Lam smiled, and reached across to his hand and touched it.

He turned and looked at her. As tough as he knew she was, she looked so fragile in this room.

"No more partners for a while boss." She said with a sincerity that touched him.

"No more partners," He replied as he left the room.

Lam lay back against the bed, her head nestled in the soft white pillow. She moved her hand to the tube that connected the morphine bag to her hand and pressed the self-dosage button. It beeped once, flashing a green light and she closed her eyes as she felt the cool liquid enter her vein sending her into a deep and dreamless sleep.

Chapter 41

Lily thought that she was dreaming when she felt the pressure on her body release, and again still dreaming when she heard two voices. One was a woman's voice, she thought to herself in her foggy state, and then silence again. She was still in darkness, her eyes closed and the buzzing now replaced by a ringing in her ears, broken from time to time with the same two voices. Her body now forced her to breathe. She sucked in air, filling her lungs to the limit, aware of the burning in her chest and throat. She gasped again, this time coughing and wheezing, her body needing more air. Lily tried to open her eyes. As she blinked against the harsh light, she could feel something being thrown over her legs, then the voice of a woman.

"Sorry" The woman said softly as she leaned toward Lily and tugged at the duct tape across her mouth. She hardly noticed the short stab of pain as the skin on her upper lip tore, or felt the trickle of blood in her mouth.

Her arms now free, Lily was aware that the woman was wrapping her in her quilt. She saw that she was badly injured. Blood was oozing quickly from a wound on her arm. Lily tried to help as the woman shifted her body into a sitting position on the bed.

Then the woman spoke again.

"It's OK, he's dead." She said gently to Lily, as though she was a child. "You're safe now."

Lily looked at the woman, a surge of pure gratitude welled in her chest. She couldn't speak. Her throat was too sore and felt like sandpaper when she breathed. She nodded to the woman and mouthed, "Thank you."

Lily sat, numbly aware of the body lying on her bedroom floor. She forced herself to move, her brain slowly catching up with her, forcing her to acknowledge the reality before her. She listened for a moment to the woman in her hallway and heard the tail end of a conversation. In the far distance she could hear the faint sound of sirens. Realising that she only had minutes, Lily stood, slightly shaky and scanned the room for the rest of her clothes. She saw that her mobile phone had fallen out of her pocket in the attack and reached for it, quickly slipping it back into her jeans. She finished dressing quickly. Grabbing a pair of shoes, she carefully stepped over Ghost Face's motionless body and slid open her balcony doors.

The drop was not too far, she thought as she looked down. Lily's body ached as she landed heavily on the deck below. She was alert now and could hear the siren's getting closer. Once outside she knew that the rest would be easy. She ran quickly now behind her house and into darkness, the wind whipping her hair into her face, the adrenaline kicking in. She didn't look back. She kept pushing on, running as fast as she could across the open ground and down the hill toward the lights of Hong Kong.

Chapter 42

3 months later

The China Club was full of activity as usual as the waiters busied themselves between tables serving guests, pouring water and wine and removing plates silently, without disturbing the course of conversation. The Matre'D stood at the entrance of the vast dining room scanning the tables until he located the one that he was looking for. He turned to the young woman waiting patiently at his side.

"Miss Li your table is ready." He announced with a broad smile.

She followed him, weaving between the diners and gaining admiring looks as she did so until they reached a table for two by the window.

Theatrically the Matre'D drew out her chair and bid her to sit, and then walked back to the entrance.

She sat still whilst a waiter, dressed in a formal white high collared jacket and wearing white cotton gloves, delicately draped the starched white napkin over her lap, and poured her a glass of still water with lemon. With a silent nod she was left alone to take in her surroundings and browse the menu whilst she waited.

Even though the restaurant was filled with chatter and noise she concentrated on the gentle music that played in the background. She listened again, straining her ears and then smiled. She turned in her chair and looked behind her. There, in the corner, sitting on a perch in a tall black bamboo cage that reached halfway from the floor to the ceiling, was a solitary bird. It chirped and sang to her from behind its bars, just loud enough for her to hear. She listened for a while and then turned back to her table. She took a sip of the lemon water and gazed out of the window. In it's day the building where she now sat had been the tallest in Hong Kong, the original Bank of China. It boasted seventeen stories, of which she was on the fifteenth floor. The restaurant owners had followed the original styling and re-created an old Shanghainese tea house, updating it with a long bar, a gentlemen's smoking room and private dining rooms. The sweeping staircase entrance was decadent and filled with a fine collection of Chinese modern and contemporary art. The floors, covered in hand tufted silk rugs that felt soft and plush underfoot. Inside the main restaurant the room had been sympathetically renovated, recreating a 1950's China. The dark wood paneling that reached halfway up to the high ceilings, complimented the wooden square tables inset with white marble. The chairs were high backed traditionally styled with scrolled arms and the light fittings were a mixture of bold and bright lanterns in red and lime silks with gold, knotted tassels dropping from the centre. Overhead ancient metal fans spun slowly, a perfect finishing touch.

She looked at the building opposite. It was such a contrast, she observed. From her elevated position she could still only see half way to the top of the building. It sprawled before her, a mass of modern metal and glass. The World Asia Bank had been constructed in 1985, a feat of architecture and a mere thirty-five years after the stone building where she sat.

Considering this point, she was deep in thought when her guest arrived. She quickly stood as the Matre'D followed the same routine as with her, pulling out the chair and guiding her guest carefully into the seat.

"How are you Lillian?" Her Grandmother said reaching over and placing her hand onto Lily's.

Lily could feel the warmth work it's way up her arm until it reached her face and she smiled.

"I'm good. Better now that I am seeing you", she said with genuine affection.

"I'm told that they serve very good Jasmine tea here." Her Grandmother said with a wide smile, crinkling up her old face.

"Then we have come to the right place." Lily replied.

-THE END -

W.J. Stopforth

ABOUT THE AUTHOR

W.J.Stopforth discovered her love for writing during long, quiet evenings in deepest China. She has spent the past twenty years working in retail providing her with the opportunity to explore, travel and live in some of the World's most unique and interesting places; Hong Kong, Monaco, Cape Town and Vancouver. It was her 9 years in Asia that prompted her to write her first crime fiction novel, Lights Out, set in Hong Kong.

She lives in West Vancouver, Canada with her Husband and two children.

Made in the USA
San Bernardino, CA
25 November 2015